Ann

Praise for Shirley Wells
and Carina Press

"I really enjoy reading this series,
as so far the mysteries have been so well crafted
that I'm never entirely sure what will happen next,
or where the case will take us to."
—*BookChickCity.com* on *Dead Silent*

"This book has everything
to make a good mystery.... Fans of mystery
and suspense will enjoy this read."
—*Night Owl Reviews* on *Presumed Dead*

"I'm yet to completely figure out a Dylan Scott
mystery. There are always plenty of ingenious
twists and turns that lead me down the primrose
path....Dylan ranks in my top five mystery series.
I already want to read the next one."
—*ManicReaders.com* on *Dead Calm*

D0963530

Dying Art

SHIRLEY WELLS

CARINA
PRESS™

CARINA
PRESS™

Recycling programs
for this product may
not exist in your area.

ISBN-13: 978-0-373-00220-7

DYING ART

www.CarinaPress.com

Printed in U.S.A.

Dear Reader,

This is a very special book for me because Prue's story had been bubbling around in my head for years and it was such fun to finally write it.

Like my other Dylan Scott mysteries, it's set on my doorstep. I consider myself extremely lucky to live in the east Lancashire Pennines, where the hills, breathtakingly beautiful in summer months, can look so threatening and forbidding when winter blows in.

My dogs aren't allowed in the pubs and clubs, much to their disgust, but they happily accompany me on all other research trips. They've run miles over the moors and they've trotted alongside me through the cemetery where Prue is buried. I deliberately visited the cemetery when the weather was bad. Paths were slippery, icy rain trickled down my neck and an angry wind battered floral tributes. Even the dogs were pleased to get home that day.

This is a story of greed and of the human wreckage left in its wake. It's also a reminder that there is always someone, somewhere, who won't rest until the truth is uncovered and justice is served.

I hope you enjoy reading it as much as I enjoyed writing it. I'm always delighted to hear from readers, so do pay me a visit at www.shirleywells.com.

Happy reading,

Shirley Wells

To Murphy,
with grateful thanks.

Dying Art

ONE

DYLAN WAS A lot of things but, unfortunately, in demand wasn't one of them. So when his office phone trilled out for the first time in three days, his list of possible callers was topped by *salesman*. *Client* didn't even make the top ten.

He picked it up. "Hello?"

"You've got a customer." Tracy's words were punctuated by the clack of the gum she was constantly chewing. She always looked and sounded bored out of her skull. Magazines crammed with lies about celebrities littered the reception desk on the ground floor where she worked and, occasionally, she'd flick through them. One afternoon, Dylan had seen her polishing her nails. Usually, though, she was like a corpse. "She's on her way up."

"Does she have a name?"

"I didn't ask."

"Okay. Thanks, Tracy."

"You're welcome." Another clack of gum and the phone was dead.

A client would be more than welcome, but he wasn't raising his hopes. Even if this woman was here on business, she'd probably want him to snoop on her two-timing spouse. He wasn't desperate enough to sink to surveillance work. Yet.

The click of heels on the stairs alerted him to her imminent arrival. He took a couple of files from his desk drawer to give the impression he was busy, left his desk and walked to the door.

He had it open when she reached it. There was something familiar about the short blond hair, the tall willowy figure dressed in a clinging black skirt and jacket—

"Dylan!" She lunged forward, threw her arms around his neck, nuzzled her face against his and croaked something he didn't catch.

He let go of the door and it crashed against his elbow. *Shit! That hurt.*

He leaned back to look at her, so far back that he was in danger of losing his balance. "Maddie?"

Madeleine Murphy. The girl with the crazy name and the legs that went on forever. The most stunningly beautiful woman he'd ever had the pleasure of sleeping with. The euphemism mocked him. *Sleep* was about the only thing they hadn't done together.

"I'm so glad I found you, Dylan."

"Madeleine—" He guessed the last person to call her Madeleine had been the vicar who christened her. It sounded forced. Foolish. He cleared his throat and tried to inject a brisk businesslike tone to his voice. Why he needed to sound businesslike, he had no idea. He just did. "Well, Maddie, it's good to see you."

"You too. It's been far too long." She clung even

tighter. Her perfume smelled of fruit—apple or lemon. Or maybe flowers. "I wondered if you'd remember me."

No one who'd enjoyed a relationship with Maddie would forget her in a hurry. She'd changed, but who hadn't? She'd always been reed-thin, probably too thin, but her face hadn't been this pale. There was no sign of the vibrancy he remembered.

"Of course I remember you." He pushed the memories away and tried to move out of her embrace.

"You look well," she said, holding both his hands and running her appraising gaze from the top of his head to the tips of his shoes. Before he could comment, she put a hand against his midriff. "And you've still got the six-pack."

A smile curved his lips and he was pleased he'd sucked in a breath. Even though her touch had been brief, he could still feel the warm imprint of her hand through his shirt.

He was a practising atheist but, that morning, he'd asked any superior beings who might be listening if he could, just for once, have a good day. Perhaps someone had been paying attention after all.

He eased his hands out of hers, removed his jacket and slung it over the back of his chair. He needed to put some distance between them before he spontaneously combusted. Or something similar. The office felt a good twenty degrees hotter than usual.

"So what brings you here, Maddie?" His head was a jumble of memories but he kept his voice and his smile casual.

"Prue." She spoke as if the name should mean something to him. It didn't. "You remember Prue, don't you?" Before he could answer, she said, "Perhaps you don't. You only met her a couple of times."

Prue. The name seemed familiar, but Maddie had been popular and usually surrounded by a crowd of bright, beautiful friends. *Popular* wasn't the right word perhaps. She'd been surrounded by people, yes, but many had been too in awe of her to be classed as friends.

"You must remember that Halloween party we went to," she said. "Prue was there. She spent the entire evening with some nerd who was telling her his evolution theories. Everyone else had the good sense to avoid him but she said she didn't want to be rude."

"Prue—" A memory surfaced. Another blond head, this one belonging to a younger girl. "Your sister?"

"Yes."

"She was the one dressed as a witch because you'd forgotten to tell her the fancy dress idea had been cancelled?" He could remember wondering for days if Maddie really had forgotten or if it had been her idea of a joke. It was funny how some memories stayed with you.

Maddie smiled. "Yes, that's her. She insisted on leaving with us to get away from that awful man. We had to take her home."

And they'd been desperate to get to bed. Or to the kitchen. Or anywhere they could indulge in hot sex without fear of being arrested.

Her gaze locked with his and he wondered if her thoughts had travelled the same path.

Maddie sat across the desk from him, long legs

crossed elegantly. She was a year younger than him, which put her at thirty-nine.

The knowledge that he was forty hit him with its usual force. Forty. People said that's when life began. They were wrong. But Maddie—yes, she had to be thirty-nine and, Christ, she looked nowhere near that. She'd sure as hell worn well. Prue, if memory served him correctly, was younger, probably about thirty-five.

"She's dead. Prue's dead."

"Dead? But she was only—"

"Thirty-four."

"How did she die?"

Maddie stared at her shoes for so long that Dylan didn't think she was going to answer. Perhaps she needed a few moments.

"Start at the beginning," he suggested. "How did you find me? Why are you here?"

Maddie took a breath. "Prue was living up north, in Dawson's Clough to be precise."

Dylan suppressed a sigh. The next time he conversed with superior beings, he'd remember to impress upon them that Dawson's Clough, with its old mill chimneys set against a backdrop of bleak moors, didn't figure in his idea of a good day. That bloody northern town would forever haunt him. "I know it." Too well.

"So I gather. The police called me when she was— when she was killed."

She hadn't mentioned the *killed* part.

"I went up there and had to stay in a hotel because her house was—" Maddie took a long breath. "The police were still there and her house was a crime scene. I was reading through a local newspaper at the hotel, and there was an article about a woman who'd gone missing. People thought she'd taken off and abandoned her daughter—"

"Anita Champion?"

"Yes. That's her. The article mentioned a private investigator called Dylan Scott and I wondered if it was you. It's not a very common name, is it?"

"Not particularly."

"I looked you up on the internet," she said, "and found this office. I was going to phone but I thought it would be quicker—easier—to call in."

He wished she'd phoned. That way, he could have taken out his memories, dusted them off and enjoyed them, and packed them safely away again.

"You have to help me, Dylan. I won't rest until I know what happened to Prue."

"What do you mean? What did happen?"

"Three weeks ago, on the Friday night, she phoned me. She sounded—tense, nervous. She said she needed to talk to Tim and me. I told her to stop being such a drama queen, but she refused to say anything over the phone and said she'd come down to London the next morning on the early train." Maddie brushed an imaginary speck from her skirt. "She never came. She was dead."

"How?"

"The police—" Her lips tightened. "The police say she disturbed a burglar. They claim she fell or was pushed down the stairs, and they don't know which. They do know that she hit her head on a table."

"And you think the police have messed up?"

"Yes. I told them over and over about that phone call and how she had things on her mind, but they took no notice."

"So what do *you* think happened?"

"I have no idea." She ran her thumb along a perfectly painted fingernail. "I just know that it's all—wrong. When she called me, she sounded nervous. Frightened too. I know there was something wrong, that's all. She never wants—wanted to talk. We hadn't had heart-to-hearts since I told her Santa didn't exist. I was worried about her and the next thing I knew, she was dead. Murdered."

Maddie left her seat and took the one opposite Dylan's desk. She was so close that he could smell her perfume again. "God, it's good to see you again," she said.

"You too. How are you? Well, apart from—you know."

"Oh, I'm okay." She gave him another of those smiles. "After we broke up, my modelling career really took off. I'm still doing a bit. Of course, at my age, it's nothing too exciting. I've done a couple of TV adverts recently for anti-ageing creams targeted at the fifty-plus woman."

"Really? That's great. And you—you look great." She looked a million times better than great. If asked, Dylan would have said he preferred more curves on his women but there was something about Maddie. There always had been.

"All thanks to living on a treadmill." Her smile faded and she ran her fingers through her hair as if she didn't have time for these social niceties. "What about you?"

She lifted his left hand and touched his wedding ring. "So there's a Mrs. Scott?"

"Yes. I have a wife and two kids. A boy and a girl."

"It looks as if life has treated you well."

"I can't complain." He could, but there wasn't any point. "I worked my way up to detective sergeant and found myself on an assault charge after some piece of scum claimed I used unreasonable force when I arrested him. I ended up in prison, got kicked out off the force, and now—" He gestured to his new office. "Now I'm a private investigator of sorts."

"Of sorts?"

"It's okay. I was forced into it really, but yeah, it's okay."

"It looks lucrative."

Lucrative was one way of describing it, albeit a totally inaccurate one, and *boring* was another. If he received one more call asking him to check on the fidelity or otherwise of a spouse, he'd get himself a job counting holes in the road. In comparison, it would be a thrill a minute.

There was no doubt though that his new office gave the impression that he was a high-flying, successful investigator that no one in their right mind could afford not to employ. The office had been Bev's idea. "You've got the flashy website," she'd said, "so you need the flashy office to match. I, for one, wouldn't employ someone who didn't even own a proper office. I'll have a look round…"

This one had appealed to her because of the swanky address. The fact that it had rental fees to match hadn't bothered her at all. On the contrary, she'd soon been out buying furniture. His black desk had a red leather covering. There was a chair behind his desk, one opposite and two for guests. All were red leather and chrome in a contemporary design. The carpet was a very pale smoky grey and the walls cream. The aroma of fresh gloss paint was coming from a small kitchen.

It was a good office. Convenient. All he had to do now was find enough work to pay for it.

"So what do you want me to do?" he asked, getting his head into work mode.

One thing was certain, he wasn't going to Dawson's Clough. He had nothing against the place, except that it was up north and, consequently, always bloody freezing cold and wet, but he simply didn't want to be driving that distance and living out of a suitcase.

"I want you to find out what happened to Prue."

She made it sound so simple. Now he came to think of it, she'd always suffered from a touch of hero-worship. Way back then, she'd thought there was nothing he couldn't do. Their relationship had been wonderful for his ego.

"But if she died in Dawson's Clough, you'd do better to employ someone local to the area," he said.

"You've worked up there before." She pouted and gave him a winning smile. "I want you to do it, Dylan."

"I'd love to help, but—" He should get rid of her now. It would be easy enough to claim pressure of work, too many other cases to deal with. "Tell me about Prue."

"There's not much to tell. She rented a small house in Dawson's Clough. God knows why she chose to live there. She liked the idea of living by the moors, she said."

Dylan knew those hills well, too bloody well. On the rare occasions the sun chose to shine, they could be stunningly beautiful. Most of the time they were bleak, lonely, forbidding places.

"She said properties to rent were cheaper and more plentiful." Maddie's expression called her sister all sorts of a fool. "She was always broke. She designed and made jewellery, and tried to sell it. I suppose she sold a few pieces, I don't know. And now she's dead."

That told him nothing.

He stood to gaze out the window at the street below. A few hardy customers braved the tables outside the coffee shop opposite. They huddled deep inside their coats and smoked. Other people strode along the street quickly to keep a gnawing March wind at bay. Above, the sky was clear and blue.

"Tell me from the beginning," he said. "When I met her, she was still at school, wasn't she?"

"I suppose she must have been." Maddie seemed surprised by that. "When she left, she spent a year at college studying art and design and then took off to see Europe. She was—well, I always thought she was part gypsy. She couldn't settle in one place. She thought it would be great to work her way round Spain and Italy. Perhaps it was. She always seemed happy enough. She'd pick grapes or wait on tables and spend her free time soaking up the culture. She did it for years and finally ended up in France."

"How recently are we talking?"

"She left France a couple of months ago. No, more than that. It was November, so four months. I was surprised when she came back because she seemed settled there. We visited her once—she'd got this tiny flat in Paris that you had to climb about fourteen flights of stairs to get to."

Dylan smiled inwardly. He'd forgotten Maddie's penchant for exaggeration. "Who's we?"

"Tim and me. Tim's my husband. Second husband. I'm Maddie Chandler now."

"Ah."

"We only spent two nights there," she said. "We'd been promising to visit for ages, but could never find time. You know how it is. But we went one weekend and she seemed happy enough. God knows why. Waiting on tables twenty-three hours a day isn't fun, is it? I don't know how she stood it, but she did. That was last year. September."

She stood, kicked off her shoes, which reduced her considerable height by around five inches, and paced a circle of the office. Then she walked to stand behind him and look out the window.

"I don't know what happened. All I know is that she rang me in a right state, obviously bothered about something, and then she was killed. It's all too coincidental."

Coincidental. That word rang in Dylan's ears. He hated coincidences. He'd go so far as to say they didn't exist when it came to crime. "Who found her?"

"The police." Every time she used the word *police,* her tone was scoffing. "I'd gone to meet her at the station and, when she didn't turn up, I tried to call her. I tried landline and mobile, but I couldn't get hold of her. I wasn't worried because I assumed she'd calmed down, decided she didn't need to talk as urgently as she had the night before, and would phone me to make alternative arrangements. I was bloody annoyed though. It was typical of her to make arrangements and not turn up."

"Then what happened?"

"Thankfully, I could remember her neighbour's name, Jane Cook, so I rang her. We visited Prue just before Christmas and Jane's cat was in the house. He used to wander inside Prue's house and make himself at home. Well, he would, wouldn't he? Prue used to make a fuss of him. Anyway, I found Jane's phone number and called her. She said she'd pass on my message when she saw Prue and tell her to call me back. All I wanted was to give Prue a piece of my mind. The way she makes arrangements—made arrangements," she corrected herself, "only to let someone down was bloody infuriating. It was all right for her but some of us had other demands on our time."

"Go on," he said.

"Jane started to worry so she went round to ring the doorbell and saw that the house was in a mess. Furniture had been knocked over and there were papers everywhere. She was scared so she called the police. They found Prue lying at the bottom of the stairs. She was wearing a pair of pink pyjamas." Her voice cracked on that last statement.

Still standing behind him, she put her hand on his shoulder. "You will help me, won't you, Dylan?"

He couldn't answer that. "What was stolen?" he asked instead.

"Nothing that we know of. It was a job to tell as everything was in such a mess. The TV and DVD player were still there. They're worth nothing though. She probably bought them secondhand from eBay. Her computer hadn't been touched, but again, it was old. There was a bit of cash lying on the kitchen table too."

A thief who didn't steal anything was a new one on Dylan. "Why are the police so sure it was a burglar?"

"They claim the same thing has happened at other properties. The way he broke in, I mean, and the mess he made. And because no one could give them a full inventory of Prue's possessions, they said—quite rightly, I suppose—that anything could have been stolen."

Dylan nodded at the truth of that.

She moved her hand from his shoulder, walked another circuit of the office and then sat opposite him again. She put her elbows on the desk and rested her chin on her fists. "Something's wrong. I'm convinced of it."

He could see that. He also believed that the police must have some facts of which she wasn't aware. They wouldn't pin this crime on an unfortunate burglar if they weren't sure of their facts.

Yeah, right. Just like they wouldn't throw a detective sergeant with a promising career ahead of him in a cell on the word of a piece of scum with a record as long as the M1.

"What's the situation now?" he asked. "With the police, I mean. What are they doing?"

"Nothing. Well, they're continuing their hunt for this burglar because he's wanted in connection with several other cases, and they'll let me know as soon as they find him. They've released Prue's body, finally, and we're burying her on Tuesday."

She reached for her bag, hunted inside for a tissue and, instead of blowing her nose on it, seemed content to sit and shred it so that white flecks dropped to the new carpet.

"The funeral's being held in Dawson's Clough," she said. "Of course, that's wrong. Mum and Dad were upset so it was left to me to arrange. I thought that, as she'd chosen to live in Dawson's Clough, she'd want to be buried there. Now that I've made all the arrangements, Mum's decided she wanted her brought back to London." She shrugged. "It's too late now though and at least Tim agreed with me. He said it would be easier all round. Anyway, I don't suppose it's important. She's gone, isn't she? Her spirit's gone. All we're doing is burying skin and bones." She looked at him, huge blue eyes seeking reassurance.

"It depends on which particular god you worship," he said.

She grabbed his hand. "Will you come? Will you at least come to the funeral? Have a look round her house, talk to people and see what you think?"

He hesitated. It was time to say that there was no way until hell froze over that he would drive all the way to bloody Lancashire. Her sister was dead and he was sorry, but there was no point in his getting involved.

Lancashire CID were on the case. They were perfectly capable of getting to the bottom of it.

"For me?" She squeezed his hand. "For old times' sake? Please."

TWO

KEVIN MILLS KNEW every inch of Dawson's Clough. He knew it and loathed it. He'd been born in the town and lived here all his life and, until recently, he'd thought it the dullest, most godawful place on earth.

He often took the shortcut home through the cemetery. If he stood on one of the headstones, it was possible to climb over the wall and drop down into the lane that would take him home. Usually the cemetery was deserted. Sometimes people walked their dogs there on the way to the park. Occasionally, usually at weekends, someone would put flowers on a grave. On a Monday afternoon, though, when less than an hour of daylight remained, he could guarantee the place would be deserted. Today it wasn't.

He'd grown up with a view of the cemetery from his bedroom window. Sometimes he'd see a fox keeping close to the wall as it set off for a night's hunting. Other times, he'd see two or three cubs playing in the early morning sunshine. He'd seen badgers too. At night it was sometimes possible to see a car's headlights. Why anyone would want to park in the cemetery on a dark night, he had no idea.

Today was different. Today, a couple of grave diggers were busy.

Kevin checked his watch. It was twenty to five. He should have been home from school half an hour ago, and the grave diggers should have finished their work much earlier. He supposed they couldn't leave a grave half-dug.

They'd be getting everything ready for the dead woman, Prue Murphy. Although she'd only lived a couple of streets away from Kevin, he'd never seen her. Or if he had, it hadn't registered. Now, it was impossible to move in the town for photos of her. Her picture had been on the front page of the local papers every day for weeks.

He couldn't climb onto the headstone with the workmen watching. In any case, the cemetery seemed creepy this evening. The whole town was starting to freak him out.

He turned on his heel and began walking back to the road. It would only take him ten minutes longer to get home. He'd be in trouble for being late but, as he was always in trouble for something, it didn't matter. Eventually they'd have to realise that he'd soon be an adult. He was sixteen and it was time they stopped treating him as if he were ten.

He walked on smartly. If his mum was looking out the front window, she'd be able to see him.

When he didn't want to be seen coming or going, he took the longer route. It meant going through a small wooded area, down a lane, around the back of some old houses and then along Corporation Street where Prue Murphy had lived. He didn't often go that way and, if his dad hadn't grounded him the night she was killed, he wouldn't have had to sneak out of the house. If he hadn't crept out, he wouldn't have been anywhere near her house and he wouldn't have seen that man.

When he let himself in the house, he heard the hum of voices coming from the TV.

"Kevin? Is that you?" his mum called out.

"Yes," he called back.

She appeared in the doorway, smiling. "Have you got homework, love?"

"Yes."

"Go and do it then," she urged him. "Your dad will be home soon."

"I'm going."

"Carol's staying over at Jenny's tonight so it'll just be the three of us."

He nodded, but he'd bet his life Carol was nowhere near Jenny's house. His sister was a year older, had far more freedom than he did, and was probably giving Matthew Walker a blow job at this very moment.

"Change out of your uniform, love," she called after him, "and don't forget to hang it up."

Kevin was sick of the constant nagging so he didn't bother answering. He went straight to his bedroom, tossed his briefcase on the floor and threw himself down on his bed.

He'd slept in this bedroom all his life. A single bed had replaced the cot but, other than that, he couldn't remember it looking any different. It was the smallest room in the house. His parents had the big bedroom, Carol had the one at the back, and he had this small one in the middle.

Model aircraft dangled from the ceiling above his head. He was too old for them and often thought he should throw them in the bin. He couldn't bring himself to do that though, probably because they represented a happier time. He'd been ten or eleven when he'd developed a passion for making the models. His dad had helped him and they'd spent many a happy hour at the kitchen table gluing replica engines in place. Back then, he could have named every plane that had ever taken to the skies. Now he couldn't care less. He blew hard and a couple of the planes swayed on his breath before becoming still again.

When his dad was first made redundant, life hadn't been too bad. Money had been tight so they'd had no treats, but everyone had been fairly happy. "I'll soon get another job," his dad had said, and they'd all looked forward to better times.

Six months later, his dad had had to take the only work he was offered. A part-time driving job for a local taxi firm wasn't what he wanted but he'd decided it was better than nothing. A few months later, he was on a drunk-driving charge. He lost his driving licence for a year and that was that. There was no way he'd get a decent job now.

Now, instead of looking for work, he divided his time equally between pub, betting shop and home. He believed the world was against him when, really, any idiot could see it was all his own fault. Only a complete loser would drive a taxi of all things when he'd been drinking. But his dad preferred to blame everyone and everything else. He'd grown bitter. He was moody and angry, and best avoided. A loser of the highest order.

Kevin's mum was no help. She wouldn't stand up to him. She ignored his moods, choosing to pussy-foot around him and live on her nerves. She cooked his meals and, if he didn't turn up to eat them, she'd throw them in the bin without a word of complaint. She found a job as receptionist at the town's health centre and never moaned about most of her earnings going straight over the bar at the Queen Vic.

Kevin thumped his pillow and stared up at the model aircraft. If his dad wasn't so miserable all the time, Kevin wouldn't have been grounded that night. If he hadn't been grounded, and furious about it, he wouldn't have crept out of the house. And if he hadn't crept out of the house, he wouldn't have seen that man.

Except he hadn't seen him. Not really.

He'd met up with his mates and they'd bought a few cans of lager. Coppers would get you for drinking in the street so they went to the park, out of sight of everyone.

It was almost midnight when they split up and went their separate ways. The others lived in the town cen-tre so Kevin started walking home alone. He stopped to light a last cigarette before he had to creep back into the house. It was windy that night and it took four at-tempts to get the thing lit.

Then he saw the car or, more accurate, the car's reg-istration plate. He couldn't remember the numbers but the letters spelled out KEV. He stood, smoking his ciga-rette, and tried to dream up letters and numbers for the plates he'd have one day. KEV 1N would be good, but would cost a fortune. This time next year, with any luck, he'd pass his driving test, assuming he could afford the lessons, and he was determined to buy a cheap old car to drive while he saved up for something decent. He'd look for a personalised number plate too.

He was daydreaming about a KM1 plate when the car's lights flashed twice. Kevin looked to his right and saw a figure at the front of what he now knew was Prue Murphy's house. They spotted each other at the same time, although all Kevin saw was a shadowy figure who seemed to jerk in shock at the sight of him. Kevin thought he was coming over but, after a brief hesitation, he jumped in the car and drove off.

Kevin turned around. Three men were walking toward him. One had a couple of dogs with him, big hairy Alsatians. Kevin stepped back against the wall to let them pass. They nodded an acknowledgement and carried on their way.

He was convinced that if those men hadn't been there, that man would have said something to him.

Kevin walked on in the opposite direction, mentally going through the best way to get back into the house without being caught. At one point, he thought a car was following him but perhaps he was wrong.

He managed to creep back into the house without his parents or sister being any wiser, and forgot about the man and the car until he saw the news about Prue Murphy's murder and realised he'd been standing outside her home on the night she was killed.

Police said it might have been accidental, that she might have disturbed a burglar. They'd appealed for anyone with information to contact them, and Kevin felt bad because he hadn't. What was the point though? He couldn't give them a description of the man. Thanks to the streetlight, Kevin would have been easily recognisable but the man had been in shadow.

It was nothing to do with him. The police wouldn't thank him for giving them half a registration plate and no description of the man driving the car. More important, his dad would kill him if he knew he'd left the house when he was supposed to be grounded.

Kevin jumped off his bed and yanked off his school blazer and tie. Prue Murphy was being buried in the morning and nothing he could do or say would alter that.

THREE

TWO DOZEN NECKTIES hung from the bar in Dylan's wardrobe, but the black one wasn't among them. He had a
dark blue one that would be okay, but he'd rather find
the black one.

He hated funerals, and it felt wrong to be attending one for someone he couldn't remember. All he had
was a very vague recollection of a leggy blond-haired
girl. When in Maddie's company, it had been difficult
to notice anyone else, even her sister.

His memories of time spent with Maddie were vivid
enough. Most of their time had been spent in bed and
he could even picture the room. Dark blue, with a huge
smiling sun painted on the ceiling, it had been crammed
with clothes. Dozens of scarves and pieces of jewellery
had hung from a huge pine mirror on one wall. A man-
nequin, draped in belts and more scarves, had stood
next to the bed.

They must have gone out—to the cinema, for meals
or walks—but he was damned if he could remember
doing so. She'd shared that flat with two girlfriends
who were rarely home, and at weekends, when the flat
was theirs and theirs alone, they'd made full use of it.

"You'll never guess—" Bev came into the bedroom
and stopped when she saw the pile of clothes on the

bed. "What are you doing with this lot? Packing it? Binning it?"

"I can't find my black tie. Where the hell can it be?"

She reached in the wardrobe for the tie bar. "It'll be wherever you left it."

"Things are always where I've left them. Until you come along and move them."

She looked in drawers that he'd already checked, then rummaged through the wardrobe. There, resting on a suit still hanging in the dry cleaner's protective cover, was his tie. She handed it to him with a slightly smug expression.

"Thanks." He folded it carefully and put it in his bag. "What will I never guess?"

"Your mum." She lowered her voice. "She's got a new man in her life."

"God help us. God help him too, whoever he is. How do you know?"

"I just asked her if she fancied a spot of shopping later and she told me she had other plans." She was still whispering. "She said she's meeting up with a chap she knew years ago."

"How does that translate as her having a new man in her life?"

"It just does. She's very tight-lipped about it."

He threw shirts and underwear in his bag. "Then let's hope he whisks her away to the other hemisphere. That's it. All done. I've got time for a quick coffee before I hit the road."

He carried his bags down the stairs and there, looking decidedly perky, was his mother. He and Bev had been out to dinner last night so she'd acted as chief babysitter and stayed over, but it was rare for her to be out of bed at this early hour. Dressed in scarlet and yellow, she looked like a moulting parrot. Cheap jewellery dangled from ears, neck and wrists.

"Don't you have any more colourful clothes, Mum?"

"I do actually."

As ageing, incurable dope-smoking hippies went, she was one of the best. She rarely wore makeup, and her hair was quite grey now, but he could still see signs of the attractive young woman she'd once been.

Sitting on her lap was his stunningly beautiful daughter and he bent to kiss the top of her head. "Morning, gorgeous."

Freya clapped her hands and spouted a torrent of gibberish that Bev would swear she could understand.

Bev handed him a coffee. "When do you think you'll be back?"

"I don't know." He didn't know why he was taking the job—or even if he was. Money perhaps. It certainly had nothing to do with wanting to see Maddie again. Nothing at all. "I'll do the funeral today, talk to a few people tomorrow and then—well, I don't know. I'll call you."

His mother pulled back the curtain and peered out at a sky that seemed to have forgotten what daylight was. "It looks like rain. What an awful day for a funeral."

"I've never known a good day for one," Dylan said.

"True. But rain makes everything even more miserable. I bet there'll be a lot of people there. There always are when the dead are so young."

"Usually," he said. "Prue only had a small family though and she'd been living abroad for years."

"What a wicked waste of life." She sighed. "I hope you catch the evil person responsible, Dylan."

"Of course he will," Bev said.

Dylan admired her faith. Maddie was the same, convinced he'd solve the mystery of her sister's death. He only hoped such belief was justified.

Four days had passed since he'd seen Maddie and he'd tried to remember why they'd split up all those years ago. The sex—Christ, he could remember every hungry breath—but memories of the breakup were less clear. It was as if, one minute, his limbs had been entwined around hers, and the next minute she was nothing to him. He couldn't remember either of them ending it. He'd gone on a training course, he remembered that, and then nothing. Had that been it? Had it been a case of out of sight, out of mind? The sex had been mind-numbing, Maddie's hero-worship had fed his ego—why had he let them drift apart?

Not that it mattered now, of course.

Luke, looking half-asleep, ambled into the kitchen.

"Good grief, you're up early," Dylan said. "Am I getting a royal send-off?"

"I couldn't sleep for the noise you lot are making. When will you be back, Dad?"

"I don't know, but I'll phone, okay?"

Luke nodded. "You'll be back for the match on Saturday, won't you?"

"I certainly will." He drank his coffee, put his mug on the table and picked up his bags. "Time I was out of here, folks." He kissed Freya on the top of her head. "Be good, gorgeous." He was treated to more gibberish. He ruffled Luke's already untidy hair. "Behave yourself and do your homework."

Luke pulled a face and grinned. "Yeah. Right."

He dropped a quick kiss on his mother's cheek. "Don't get arrested on a drugs charge."

She smacked him on the arm. "Get out of here."

He would have given Bev a quick kiss but she grabbed the lapels of his jacket and clung to him. "Drive carefully, won't you? Send me a text to let me know you got there safely, and then ring me tonight, okay?"

"Yes, yes and yes."

She hugged him. "Love you."

"Love you, too." He kissed her and moved out of her grasp. "I love you all, but I'm still out of here."

He had a funeral to attend.

FOUR

WIND BLEW FROM every direction, carrying with it icy rain.

Dylan stood with Maddie and her husband Tim beneath a poor excuse for an umbrella that Maddie had taken from her bag. It would have struggled to provide protection for a child, never mind three adults. Giant oak trees, dripping above them, added to the misery of the occasion.

Maddie and Prue's parents, two aunts, and an uncle—who'd had the sense to put a hipflask in his jacket pocket—stood next to them. Maddie's mother, thin and gaunt, was being supported by her husband. Dylan felt sure she would have snapped in two if it weren't for her husband's firm grip on her arm.

A small crowd had gathered but no one seemed sure what to do.

"I suppose we wait here until the hearse arrives," Maddie said.

Chandler glanced at his watch for the third time in as many minutes. "It shouldn't be long."

Tim Chandler was nothing like the man Dylan had expected Maddie to marry. He'd pictured someone disgustingly handsome whose every waking thought was filled with Maddie. She was good pedestal material yet

Chandler had barely glanced her way. He wasn't holding her hand as she waited for the arrival of her sister's coffin or assuring her that he'd help her through this ordeal. He seemed impatient, as if he longed to be away. Dylan supposed he did. They all did. Who the hell wanted to be at this church on such a grey, wet, windy and depressing day?

Maddie cut a lonely figure. She'd spurned her mother's attempts at conversation and hadn't spoken a word to her father. He'd kept his distance from her too. Perhaps she'd made it clear that she preferred to be alone with her grief.

"I bet she didn't want flowers." Maddie pointed to several arrangements that had been left by the porch. "I don't suppose she wanted a funeral like this either. Being buried at sea in one of those do-it-yourself basket affairs would be more to Prue's taste."

"We've done the best we can," Chandler said. "She hadn't made arrangements so there's nothing to be done about it."

"Of course she hadn't made arrangements. Who the hell makes arrangements for their funeral in their thirties?" Maddie rubbed her temples as if she had a migraine.

"I'm sure it will be fine." Dylan felt obliged to say something and that was the best he could come up with.

More people arrived. He wondered if Prue had known them or if her unwanted spotlight in the media had brought them here out of curiosity. The latter, he guessed, and he was almost glad the weather was so awful. It would keep a lot at home.

He cast his glance over the crowd and wondered if her killer was present.

Dylan wore black as a mark of respect but he was in a minority. The only others wearing black were Maddie, her father and her uncle. Her mother was in grey, the aunts were in navy and Chandler had opted for a grey suit with a blue-and-red tie.

Other people, all of them strangers to Maddie, wore muted colours as they talked and laughed beneath their umbrellas. Slowly, the crowd began to enter the church. One woman, an elderly woman in a dark blue coat, eyed the family with relish as she passed and Dylan supposed she was one of those oddballs who considered a funeral good entertainment.

A young boy stood on the pavement outside the church. He was probably fifteen or sixteen, and was smoking a cigarette as he watched the mourners gather. Dylan guessed he was bunking off school.

"It's here," Maddie whispered as a hearse drove up.

Covering the coffin was a large but simple display of white flowers that Dylan assumed was from the family.

The vicar, a tall, slightly bent man, had a few words with Maddie's parents before giving the pallbearers some final instructions. The coffin was carried inside with the vicar and Prue's family following.

Dylan waited outside until the last minute and, when he went in and took a seat at the back of the congregation, he was surprised to see the church so crowded. Many must have been inside before he arrived. He did a quick head count and estimated that around a hundred and fifty people had come to this small, bitterly cold church to pay their respects. None looked like killers. Not that he had the vaguest idea what a killer looked like.

When they stood to sing the first hymn, he watched Maddie and her mother, their shoulders taut with tension. Maddie's lips were moving but he guessed no sound was coming from them. She looked up at the tall, vaulted ceiling. She fixed her gaze on the pulpit. She looked everywhere but at her sister's coffin.

The service was blessedly short and they were soon braving the wind and rain to walk the five hundred yards to the cemetery. The old stone path was rich with wet slippery moss, and Dylan offered up a quick prayer for the coffin bearers. He was lucky in that he hadn't attended many funerals but he'd spent every one worrying that someone would drop the coffin. Perhaps it was a premonition of things to come. Maybe his own body would be the one unceremoniously ejected from a dropped coffin.

Only a small proportion of the congregation attended the graveside ceremony but Dylan still risked losing an eye to someone's umbrella.

His attention was caught by a bearded man watching the proceedings from a distance. Dressed in a long overcoat, the high collar turned up to protect the back of his head from the elements, he was standing beneath a tree, possibly in an attempt to stay dry. Was he watching the ceremony or was he, like Dylan, paying more attention to the crowd of mourners?

Their gazes met for a brief moment.

"Sorry. It's this damn wind." A woman standing next

to Dylan struggled with an umbrella. A strong gust had blown it inside out. "Typical funeral weather, isn't it?" she added in a whisper.

"I suppose it is." Dylan helped to push her umbrella back into place before she took his eye out.

With his companion safely protected from the rain again, Dylan turned to have another look at the bearded stranger, but he'd gone. Vanished. The cemetery only had one exit so he must have walked past Dylan. That was impossible though. It had only taken a few seconds to sort out that umbrella.

Dylan left the mourners and walked away from the cemetery, back to the church and the path to the road. There was no sign of a man with a beard.

He returned to the graveside and waited until only Prue's immediate family remained. Maddie's mother was inconsolable, and Dylan's heart ached for her and her husband. To bury one's child was unthinkable. To bury that child when the finest medical brains had done all they could was one thing, but to bury that child because someone with absolutely no right had decided it must be so—it was inconceivable.

Chandler nudged his elbow. "Everyone's going to the Carlton Hotel for a buffet of sorts," he said, "but I'm afraid I have to get off."

"Oh?" Standing next to Chandler was a man Dylan didn't recognise. He was probably the same age as Chandler, mid-forties, but he was shorter and stockier. Several pounds of excess flesh hung over his trousers.

"Sorry, I haven't introduced you. Dylan, this is Eddie

Bryson. Eddie, this is Dylan Scott, the private investigator I told you about."

The two men shook hands.

"I'm Tim's business partner," Bryson explained. "I've driven up to meet him so that we can leave for the airport in my car."

"You're going to the airport?" Dylan said.

"Yes," Chandler said. "Business calls, unfortunately. We're leaving for the Algarve."

"Business? Sorry, but I've forgotten what it is you do. I'm sure Maddie mentioned it, but I can't remember."

"Property," Bryson said. "We deal in time shares, holiday lets, property management. Let me go and offer Maddie my condolences. Won't be a minute."

"It's a damn nuisance," Chandler said, "and it couldn't have come at a worse time, but it's something I can't get out of."

"Ah." There was nothing that Dylan couldn't have got out of if his wife had needed some support. "Well, I'm sure Maddie will be okay. Her parents, aunts, uncle—I'm sure they'll take good care of her."

"Of course they will." Chandler patted Dylan on the arm. "It's been good to meet you, Dylan. A pity it was under such difficult circumstances, but perhaps we'll meet again."

"Perhaps we will."

Chandler went back to Maddie, gave her a quick peck on the cheek, hugged his mother-in-law, shook hands with his father-in-law and, with Bryson at his side, headed off with the wind blowing his tie over his shoulder.

A disapproving silence followed him, broken when
Maddie spoke. "Sorry, I didn't ask, Dylan. You will
come to the hotel, won't you? At least we'll be able to
get a sandwich and a stiff drink."

"I will, yes. Thanks."

"Thank you. I appreciate it."

"Are you okay?" he asked.

"Yes. No. Oh, God knows what I am." She gave him
a wan smile. "I'll be a lot better once I get a drink inside me."

A group of around twenty-five, maybe thirty, ended
up at the Carlton Hotel. While the others lunged for the
sandwiches, he and Maddie headed for the bar.

"There was a chap in the cemetery," he said as they
waited for double whiskies to be poured. "He had a
beard. Long overcoat. Any idea who he might have
been?"

"No. I didn't see anyone like that. Why do you ask?"

"No reason in particular. I couldn't remember seeing him in church and he was standing some distance
away from the grave. Thanks." He broke off to take
their glasses from the barman. "Here, drink this. It'll
warm you up."

"Let's go through to the conservatory," she said, slip-
ping her arm through his. "I can't face anyone yet."

The Victorian conservatory was dotted with easy
chairs and potted ferns. It was also deserted. The front
of the hotel stood watch over the town of Dawson's
Clough but here at the back of the building was an
uninterrupted view of the moors. Dylan always hated
the thought of leaving London and making the long

trip north yet, as soon as he arrived, he was amazed all over again by the area's beauty. Dawson's Clough was a typical northern town, a mix of old and new where the long-forgotten mills fell into disrepair and shiny new buildings were erected next to them. It was the Pennine Hills surrounding the town that added the touch of magic.

"It's a nice hotel," Maddie said, looking round her. "I'm staying until Friday. I could have stayed at Prue's but I didn't fancy that. My parents are driving home after this." She looked wistful.

"You can go with them, can't you?"

"No. I promised to get the house sorted out. Thankfully, Prue always boasted about being able to travel light so she didn't have many possessions. I've arranged for a man to check out her furniture tomorrow afternoon, and I'm hoping he'll agree to take it away. Otherwise, I'll have a bonfire in her back garden."

"I'll come round at some point to have a look. I'll have a word with her neighbours too. The police will have spoken to them, and if they'd seen anything, they would have told them, but it won't do any harm."

"Thanks. Her next-door neighbour, Jane, the one with the cat, is the woman with the red hair." She pointed to where people were clustered round long tables heaving with sandwiches. "I don't know anyone else. Oh, except the bloke with the ponytail. He was a friend, or so he told me, but I've already forgotten his name."

"Do you want another drink?" Dylan asked.

She seemed surprised to see the empty glass in her hand. "Please. Then I'd better go and mingle."

"Me too."

"Everyone thinks you're a friend of the family," she said. "I haven't bothered correcting them."

It was exactly what Dylan had told anyone who'd asked.

When they had their drinks, Maddie headed off toward her aunts and Dylan helped himself to food. With his plate piled high with chicken legs, sandwiches and slices of pork pie, he went to a table in the middle of the room.

"May I join you?" he asked.

"Of course," both women replied in unison.

One was Jane Cook, Prue's neighbour. The other woman was older, probably in her seventies, and Dylan had no idea who she was. They talked about the weather for long tedious minutes.

"It always seems to rain at funerals, doesn't it?" Jane said.

Dylan nodded and smiled. It didn't, although it probably always rained at funerals in Lancashire. If it wasn't raining in Lancashire, it was snowing.

"Is that old yellow car yours?" Jane asked.

"It is, yes." His car, a stunningly gorgeous 1956 Morgan in Daytona Yellow, had never been so easily dismissed. *That old yellow car.* Dylan despaired.

"There's nothing wrong with keeping an old one on the road," she said. "These days, everyone thinks they're entitled to brand new, don't they? People should learn to make do. Money doesn't grow on trees, does it?"

It was far better to despair than to try and explain that his car was a classic, a rare classic.

"Were you and Prue friends?" he asked, getting to more important matters.

"Yes," Jane said. "We can't claim to have known her well because she only moved in to the street last November. We're neighbours, you see. I live next door to her. Doreen—" she nodded at her companion "—lives across the road."

"I fell on a patch of ice and sprained my wrist just before Christmas," Doreen said, "and Prue saw me when I came back from the hospital. We'd only said hello a couple of times before that, but, seeing the state I was in, she went and got my shopping, put my bin out for me and did all sorts of things. That girl would do anything for anyone. How someone could—well, it's wicked, isn't it? Evil."

Dylan murmured his agreement.

"What about you?" Jane asked. "How did you know her?"

"Oh, I've known her for twenty years. I hadn't seen her for ages as I'm friendlier with her sister, Maddie, but yes, I've known her awhile."

"She was such a lovely girl," Doreen said. "In one way, she kept herself to herself, but she was very friendly and, like I say, she'd do anything for anyone."

"My cat knew her well," Jane said with a small smile. "If Prue's window was open, Fudge would be straight inside, making himself comfortable on her sofa. She never seemed to mind."

Both women smiled at Fudge's antics.

"Did Maddie say that one of you called the police when she wasn't answering her phone or the door?" he asked.

"That was me." Jane pushed her plate away as if the question had stolen her appetite. "Maddie phoned to say that Prue was supposed to be in London with her. I didn't think it was anything to worry about, but I promised her I'd tell Prue to phone her as soon as I saw her. Of course, when I went round the back to knock on the door, I could see into the dining room." She shook her head. "It was such a mess. I knew immediately that something was wrong so I called the police."

"As soon as they saw it," Doreen joined in, "they broke the door down."

"They didn't," Jane said, her voice tight with impatience. "The door was unlocked. The glass was broken—police said it had been cut—and the door was unlocked."

"Oh." Doreen was disappointed. "I thought they broke the door down."

"No."

"The police don't seem to be any nearer catching the person responsible," Dylan said. "Unless you've heard anything I haven't?"

"There have been a spate of burglaries in the area," Doreen said, "and yet they still can't catch him. We'd had no trouble in our street until now, but quite a few houses closer to the town centre had been burgled. They say it's the same person who did those. He's never hurt anyone before—not that I'm excusing him—and they think she might have fallen down the stairs. Of course, she might have been pushed. No one's to know, are they?"

"They think it happened after midnight but before two o'clock," Jane said.

"It's funny no one heard anything or saw anything odd," he said.

"It is," Doreen agreed. "I'm a very light sleeper and I usually hear every sound. Not that night."

"It was windy," Jane said. "All I could hear was the wind rattling the opening light in my bedroom window. I've got a chap coming out to fix it on Thursday."

"And you didn't see anyone in the street?"

"It wasn't a night for being outside," Doreen said. "I hope they hurry up and catch him. I'm assuming he'll keep well away from our road, but you never know, do you?"

"Indeed," Dylan said.

As they had nothing interesting to tell him, and as he'd probably see them again when he visited Prue's home, he left their table and sought out the man with the ponytail, the one who claimed to be a friend. He was sitting on a barstool, his leather jacket slung across the neighbouring stool. He was wearing a white shirt and black tie.

"Hi." Dylan put out his hand. "Dylan Scott. I gather you were a friend of Prue's?"

He shook Dylan's hand. "Danny Thompson. Yeah. I suppose you could say that."

"I hadn't seen her for a while. How did you meet her?"

Thompson shrugged. "I took over a wine bar in the

town centre about a year ago. I had big plans, you know? It was going to be *the* place to go in Dawson's Clough. I sometimes have a mini-rush on when people finish work for the day but, by seven o'clock, the place is usually deserted."

"Ah. And you met Prue—how?"

"She came in one night a couple of months ago. January time maybe. She was my only customer so we got talking. At least, I got talking. She got drunk. A couple of weeks later, she was back. We discussed books and films, art and music, put the world to rights—and she got drunk again. To tell the truth, we both got drunk. Still, I had no customers so it didn't matter. She wasn't a heavy drinker so I didn't make much out of her. I enjoyed her company though."

Dylan smiled. "She sounds like a heavy drinker."

"She wasn't. Three glasses of wine and she was away with the fairies. I don't think she went out much, and she told me she never drank at home. The slippery slope, she called that. As I understood it, when things got on top of her, she'd jump in a cab to my place, have a few drinks and take a cab home."

"Really? She always seemed happy-go-lucky to me. What used to get on top of her?"

"No idea," Thompson said, "but I think there was a bloke involved. I used to tell her there were plenty more fish in the sea, but she just laughed. I think her heart had been broken. She used to say that the fairy-tales she'd read as a kid never warned her that Prince Charming was married, gay or both."

Maddie hadn't mentioned any men in her sister's

life. Perhaps she hadn't known about them. Perhaps it was easier to discuss your failed love affairs with a stranger behind a bar than a happily married sister. Although Dylan was beginning to wonder about the state of Maddie's marriage. People involved in happy marriages don't jet off to the Algarve when spouses are burying their sisters.

"Did you get involved—romantically, I mean?" Dylan asked.

Thompson smirked at that. "No. I fall into the gay category."

"Oh. Right. I see."

"You'd never know, would you?" Thompson spoke with a tinge of sarcasm. "I don't do the camp stuff."

Dylan smiled and determined to move the conversation forward. "Did she want to get involved? Did she come on to you?"

"Nope. There was a man in her life, one she couldn't have, and she didn't bother looking elsewhere. At least, that's the impression I got." He tipped up his glass, swallowed the contents and put it on the counter. "Time I was off. Who knows, maybe I'll have a couple of customers tonight. Be seeing you."

"She didn't mention any problems she was having, did she?" Dylan asked.

Thompson frowned at that. "No. Why do you ask?"

"I don't know. I was just curious. By the way, what did you say the name of your bar was?" Dylan asked.

"I didn't. But it's Danny's Wine Bar. I decided to go for originality, you know?"

"Perhaps I'll call in sometime."

"It's on King Street. Watch where everyone's going and walk in the opposite direction. You can't miss it. And bring a few friends with you."

"Be seeing you, Danny."

Jane and Doreen were next to leave. They both clutched white handkerchiefs as they hugged Maddie and offered their condolences once more. Maddie stood rigid in their embrace.

Slowly but surely, the hotel emptied of mourners until only Dylan and Maddie remained.

"I'm so relieved the day's over," Maddie said. "I thought it would never end. Still, it's just you and me now. Shall we have dinner together? A few drinks perhaps?"

"Sorry, but I can't. I've arranged to meet up with an old friend, an ex-copper, and I need to go. I'll see you tomorrow morning, shall I? At Prue's house?"

"Okay." She planted a featherlight kiss on his cheek. "Thanks for coming today, Dylan. I appreciate it. We all do."

FIVE

BY THE TIME he was sitting opposite his onetime boss and friend, ex-Detective Chief Inspector Frank Willoughby, Dylan had almost managed to shake off the chill of funerals and death. It helped that he was in one of his favourite pubs, the Dog and Fox, with a pint of his favourite beer, Black Sheep.

"You can't keep away from Lancashire, can you?" Frank's greeting was a hearty slap on the shoulder. "It must be our weather."

"That's it, Frank. I thought it was time I gave the snorkel and flippers an airing."

Frank snorted with laughter.

He'd been a damn good copper before being forced to retire on health grounds, although there was a time when Dylan had hated the sight of him. Dylan and DS Pike had been keen, enthusiastic upstanding members of the police force, but Frank, or "that arrogant northern bastard," as they liked to call him, preferred to refer to them as "soft fucking southerners."

The years had changed them both though. Frank had suffered a heart attack and Dylan had been kicked off the force and marched into a cell. As ridiculous as it might once have sounded, they'd become good friends and had a great deal of respect for each other.

"Because nothing ever happens in this place, lazy journos have to resort to printing old news. If Maddie hadn't been up here reading the local rag, she wouldn't have seen my name mentioned in connection with Anita Champion's case, and I would be safely in the south—land of the civilised."

"Don't kid yourself that you're an A-list celebrity in these parts," Frank said, "because I haven't seen your name mentioned for a year or more. I certainly missed that particular article. It must have been very small, too, because I read the paper from cover to cover. When was it in?"

"I don't know. About three weeks ago. It was when Prue was killed and Maddie came up. She stayed in a hotel and read it there."

Frank shook his head. "I never saw it."

"Perhaps she saw an old edition."

"Could be. So you're definitely taking on this case?"

"I wouldn't go that far." Dylan took a long, slow swallow of beer. Nectar. "I'm still thinking about it. I'm not sure what I can do really. I don't have phone records, email records or Prue's address book. I asked Maddie, but she wasn't much help. I know your lot got phone records and checked her email account, and I know there was an address book that they returned to Maddie, but I can't get my hands on any of it. Maddie's mislaid the address book."

Frank rolled his eyes at such stupidity. "That's a big help then. I had a look at the file and saw the phone records. On the day she died, she called her sister. Three days earlier, she called her dentist. Her landline was hardly used and she hadn't made a call from her mobile for about six weeks. There were no text messages worth noting."

"What about emails, Frank?"

"Nothing worth mentioning. I may, if I ask in the right places, be able to get copies for you."

"Yeah? I'd really appreciate that. Maddie might find Prue's address book, but she never saw phone or email records."

Frank nodded. "I'll see what I can do. What's your opinion so far?"

"I expect your mob are right and Prue's death was due to a petty thief coming a cropper. On the other hand, there's something odd about it all." A niggle of doubt had been planted. "Nothing was stolen for a start, and who's heard of a burglar who didn't take anything? It's number one on his job description."

"The suspect was disturbed, or so they reckon," Frank said. "I suppose he believed the house was empty and was shocked to discover it wasn't."

"Yeah, but he'd had enough time to turn the place upside down. Furniture was upturned, papers were strewn everywhere. If he did all that quietly enough not to disturb her, he knew she was there. If he made plenty of noise, she would have been downstairs before he'd had the chance to do so much damage."

"Not necessarily." Frank took a swig of his beer. "A young woman is dropping off to sleep when she hears a noise. She believes someone's in the house so, quite naturally, she's terrified. A lot of women would stay where they were and keep quiet."

"True."

"Or they'd do a treble-nine from the safety of their bedroom. Perhaps move a set of drawers or something in front of the door. Hide in the wardrobe maybe. Did she have a phone in the bedroom?"

"I assume so," Dylan said. "Most people keep a mobile next to them, don't they?"

"I don't."

"No, but you're still celebrating the invention of the wheel."

Frank grinned good-naturedly.

"I think we have to assume he was upstairs when Prue saw him," Dylan said. "If he'd been downstairs, I believe it's unlikely she'd have fallen. Far more likely is that he was upstairs and either she fell to her death trying to run from him, or he pushed past her trying to escape."

"Possible."

"What else did you manage to find out from your friends at the nick, then? You managed to have a snoop round, didn't you?"

Frank smiled at that. "I don't need to snoop. Yes, I managed to have a word with a couple of the investigating officers."

"And?"

"Nothing exciting, I'm afraid. They've been after the suspect for over a year. He targets houses like Prue Murphy's—semi-detached or end-terrace houses with no alarms in quiet residential areas. He's never bothered about the mess he makes. Drawers will be emptied, tables upturned, chairs damaged, DVDs or CDs tossed around. As for what he's taken, it's usually stuff that's easy to sell. It's small-time. If he nicks a couple of hundred pounds' worth, he's done a good night's work. He's a petty thief, probably someone with a drug habit. He goes for small items—hi-fi, iPods, phones, cameras—stuff that's cheap and easy to shift. The houses have been empty, the owners away for a fortnight or a weekend. How he comes by his information, they don't know. They're still looking into that. They're pretty sure he believed Prue Murphy's house was empty, and got the shock of his life when she confronted him. Like you, they believe he was upstairs because she had her back to the stairs when she fell. It was the back of her head that took the full brunt. Maybe he was upstairs, she backed away from him—I don't know."

Dylan's small seed of doubt took root. The scenario was too neat and tidy.

"Okay," he said. "So this time, he cocked up because the house was occupied. He also cocked up because, as far as we know, he didn't steal so much as a tea bag. There was a small amount of cash lying on the kitchen table and he must have seen it. If he was small-time, why didn't he pocket that? It doesn't make sense."

"Give me another theory," Frank said.

Dylan expelled his breath. "Theories are a bit thin on the ground right now. Maybe someone wanted her dead and tried to make it look like a burglary."

"Why would they? She had nothing—no money, no position of power. She was just a young woman trying to eke out a living making and selling her jewellery designs."

Frank was right. Prue Murphy simply wasn't victim material.

"How did the funeral go?" Frank asked.

"The same as they always go. Bloody depressing affairs. I didn't see anything out of the ordinary, if that's what you mean. Except—"

"Yeah?"

"Nothing really. I saw a young teenager watching people gather beforehand. It was difficult to say if he was old enough to smoke so perhaps he was just having a crafty one and happened to have it by the entrance to the church. He seemed interested though. There was someone else too, a chap with a beard looking on from a distance. I didn't see him in the church, but afterwards, while we were gathered by the grave, he was watching people." Dylan tried to recall an image of him. Probably six feet tall, early sixties maybe but agile-looking, untidy grey hair and beard. "I got the impression he was paying more attention to the mourners than to the service itself."

"You didn't speak to him?"

"No. Some blasted woman nearly put my eye out with her umbrella and when I turned round, he'd vanished. I tried to find him, but there was no sign of him."

"That's interesting."

"Yeah, but other than that, zilch. At the wake afterwards, I spoke to a couple of Prue's neighbours. They said it was windy that night so neither of them would have heard anything. They weren't much help. Oh, and I spoke to a Danny Thompson, who owns a wine bar in the town centre."

"Danny Thompson. Daniel Thompson. I'm sure I know that name. Never mind, it'll come to me. Carry on."

"He knew Prue because, every now and again, she'd take a taxi into town, get drunk in his bar and take a taxi home. He had the impression she was nursing a broken heart. He talked of a man she couldn't have."

"Married?"

"Or gay. He told me she once said something about Prince Charming always being married, gay or both."

"So she'd been dumped by some bloke," Frank said, "and was feeling sorry for herself. God, we all think that, especially when we've had a few drinks."

Frank had a point. There was probably nothing more to it than that.

"Got him," Frank said, pleased with himself. "Danny Thompson was ordered to carry out some improvements to his wine bar, something to do with health and safety. Or was it hygiene laws? I don't know now. Anyway, before he could carry out these expensive improvements, there was a convenient fire at the premises."

"You're telling me he torched it and claimed on the insurance?"

"Nope. I'm telling you that *someone* torched it and he claimed on the insurance. It could have been your man Thompson or kids messing around with matches. The insurance company asked plenty of questions but nothing conclusive came to light."

"He's not making a lot of money, or so he said."

"I'm not surprised." Frank took a swig of his beer and grinned. "Wine bars are too bloody girlie for the

Clough. We like proper drinks in proper pubs. Wine bars are for you soft southerners."

Dylan laughed, but he refused to take the bait. "The police didn't find anything else at Prue's home? Like footprints or fibres?"

"Nothing. The ground was wet, but he kept to the path. He walked round the back, cut glass from a small side window, reached inside—wearing gloves—to open the back door and let himself in. If he touched the victim, he left no evidence."

"Hmm."

"What does that mean?" Frank asked.

"It means my gut instinct says something isn't right and you should always listen to your guts, Frank. They're also telling me it's time we had another drink. Same again?"

There were worse ways for Dylan to spend time than enjoying a drink with an old friend. A couple more and the chill of funerals would have gone completely.

SIX

Prue Murphy's end-terraced house came as no surprise to Dylan. There were hundreds of similar properties in Dawson's Clough, all built in stone hewn from local quarries. A black Volkswagen was parked on the road in front of the house. He assumed it was Maddie's. A stone-slabbed path led along the side of the house to the rear. That same path would provide a right of way for anyone wanting to use the back entrances to the rest of the houses in the terrace. Although there was no front garden, several tubs of pansies set on stone slabs offered visitors a burst of warm blues and yellows.

His Morgan looked out of place on the quiet street. Daytona Yellow, like those cheery little pansies, was too vibrant against such a grey, rain-leaden sky.

The street was deserted. Jane Cook might have witnessed his arrival from the warmth of her home, or Doreen might have seen him from her house opposite, but there were no signs of life.

A streetlight stood guard about twenty yards away. Even assuming it wasn't faulty, it wouldn't have been strong enough to cast any light on Prue's house. Trees, despite being almost bare of leaves, would have blocked what little light there was.

He strode up to the front door and rang the bell. Mad-

die opened it almost immediately, as if she'd been waiting behind the door for him, and clutched at the sleeve
of his jacket to pull him inside.

He followed her into a sitting room that looked as
if the contents had been dropped from a great height.
"Bloody hell."

"I know. This is how I found it. I've no idea if the
burglar or the police are responsible. They've been
through everything."

Broken pieces of porcelain lay on the carpet. A couple of posters, torn from their frames, had been tossed
on the floor. A bookcase had been overturned, its contents left to lie on the carpet.

"I didn't know where to start, so I've done nothing.
Christ, I need a cigarette." Maddie was wearing a knitted dress-cum-sweater thing that almost touched her
knees, and she reached into a pocket at the front and
took out a pack and a lighter. "Do you want one?" She
thrust the pack at him.

"I don't smoke." He often envied those who did.

Her hands shook as she lit it. Dark circles surrounded
eyes that were a little puffy. Her naturally pale skin was
a sickly grey.

"Prue was definitely wearing pyjamas when she was
killed?" he asked.

"Sorry? Well, yes, she was. Why do you ask?"

"Oh, I'm just curious. Did she enjoy music? Might
she have gone to bed and listened to an iPod or something through earphones?"

"I wouldn't think so. She wasn't really a music person. She might have read, I suppose. She was a great reader. Why do you ask?"

"Is there a phone in her bedroom?"

"No. Why?"

"What about her mobile phone? Where was that?"

"I don't know. The police returned it to me but I've no idea where they found it."

Dylan walked into the hallway and on to the kitchen. A small window beside the door, a foot square, had been boarded up. Cupboard doors were open. Contents had been knocked to the floor.

"There was sixty pounds on the table apparently," Maddie said. "I don't know where that is. I suppose the police have it, checking for fingerprints or something."

Any burglar happy to steal a couple of hundred pounds' worth of stuff would have thought his birthday had come as he'd shoved sixty pounds in his pocket.

"What's it like upstairs?" he asked.

"The same." She hunted for an ashtray, couldn't find one and flicked ash into the remains of a broken cup. "Have a look for yourself."

He walked up the stairs and into the spare bedroom first. A single bed was pushed against the wall but, other than that, it was simply a place to store things. Four brown cardboard boxes had been torn open. They contained books, mainly well-worn paperbacks. A rug was rolled up and stood upright against a window that offered a view of a small back garden.

The bathroom looked untouched. Four leggy plants sat on the windowsill gathering dust and begging for water. Inside a small cabinet with a mirrored door, he found an array of toiletries. A cupboard beneath the washbasin housed white towels.

Another small bedroom had been set up as a workshop. Small hammers, pliers and tweezers sat alongside squares of wood on a table. Boxes and jars of cheap colourful beads were lined up. It looked as if she'd been working on a bracelet—cheap beads strung on leather. There was no evidence of precious jewels or gold and silver, but that wasn't surprising. He'd looked at her internet shop and most items sold for less than a tenner. She'd specialised in cheap and quirky rather than quality jewellery.

The main bedroom, like the other rooms, was a mess. It overlooked the front of the property and he wondered if Doreen could see him standing at the window. He turned from the window and looked around the room. It was difficult to believe that this chaos had once been Prue's refuge from the world, the place she lay awake dreaming of the future or slept peacefully with no thought of tomorrow. The bed's covers, dumped in a pile on the mattress, were pale blue dotted with delicate yellow flowers. A set of fairy lights had been draped along the headboard. A paperback—*Exit Music* by Ian Rankin—was bookmarked at page 83. Sadly, Prue's own exit music had played too early for her to finish the story. A mirror, its glass cracked, leaned against the wall. T-shirts and sweaters spilled out of a couple of drawers. Dylan looked in a wardrobe that would easily have held twice as many clothes. A quick check of the labels told him she bought her clothes from a supermarket.

He walked out of the room and stood at the top of the stairs looking down at a heavy oak table. Thanks to forensic officers, it was covered in various sorts of powder and gel. He turned round so that he had his back to the stairs. It was possible the killer came out of the spare room and threatened her, causing her to take a step backwards—

No. That didn't add up. Nothing made sense.

He walked slowly down the stairs, deep in thought. Maddie was throwing broken pieces of china and assorted crap into a black plastic bag. She'd already filled one.

"Well?" she said.

"There's no TV in her room, no iPod or radio. How do we know they weren't stolen?"

"The neighbour, Jane Cook. She'd been here a few times and, once, had helped Prue hang curtains in the bedroom. According to her, there was nothing missing."

"Assuming she's right then, Prue would have heard someone down here making a racket." He looked around him. "Our man couldn't have done this quietly."

"So?"

"So it's possible that a lot of the damage was done after she was dead."

Maddie stopped, half an ashtray in one hand, plastic bag in the other. She looked at him as if he'd become fluent in Martian. "What do you mean?"

"I think our man was looking for something specific. If he'd been looking to steal something and make a few quid, he'd have pocketed the cash. I think he killed her and then had a look round for something."

She sank onto a wooden chair and delved into her pocket for another cigarette. She didn't want to believe her sister had been killed by a chance burglar but it seemed she didn't want to ponder anything more sinister either.

She lit her cigarette and inhaled deeply. "But she had nothing. Look around you, Dylan. Why would anyone think she had anything worth stealing?"

"I don't know."

Maddie was right. There was nothing in the house of any value. Everything, from the supermarket's own brand food to the cheap dining table, screamed frugal. Prue had worked her way round Europe waiting on tables. She'd returned to England, rented the cheapest house she could find and was trying to sell her own inexpensive jewellery designs. She didn't have a car, choosing instead to cycle or use public transport. It was ridiculous to think she had anything worth stealing.

"Perhaps it was a case of mistaken identity," Dylan said. "Or perhaps I'm wrong and the police are right. Maybe she died accidentally and our burglar decided he'd have a quick look round before scarpering. Maybe he didn't notice the cash. Maybe he stole things you don't know she owned."

He wasn't convinced though. A petty thief was unlikely to hang around with a corpse.

"Was her rent paid up to date?" he asked.

"Yes, although I've had to pay for another couple of months because it was a six-month lease. The landlord's a miserable sod too. He wants the place cleared—totally empty—by Friday. Apart from that, his biggest concern is that Prue's murder might put off prospective tenants."

"He sounds a real charmer. Is he local?"

"No. He lives up in the Lake District but has a couple of dozen properties in Dawson's Clough that he lets. When Prue died, he was on holiday in Monaco so I hardly think a month's rent will affect him one way or the other." She glanced at her watch. "I've got a chap coming at two o'clock to look at the furniture. It's not worth anything, obviously, but I'm hoping he'll take it away. I'd better get the wardrobe and drawers emptied."

Armed with more black plastic bags, they headed for the stairs and Prue's bedroom.

"I'll put everything in bags and take it home to sort out," Maddie said. "Mum's given me strict instructions that anything of value, no matter how small, has to go to the charity shop. She says she can only bear this if something good comes from it."

Dylan supposed it was an admirable sentiment.

They worked in silence. Maddie, Dylan guessed, was finding the task too difficult to do anything but keep her lips pressed tightly together. He simply found it sad. And wrong. So very wrong.

"Look." Maddie held out a pink cashmere sweater still in its bag. "I bought her this for Christmas. She said it was too nice to wear but I had the feeling at the time that she didn't like it. Why didn't she say so? I could have changed it."

"Perhaps she really believed it was too nice to wear. It's cashmere, Maddie. It's worth more than the entire contents of her wardrobe."

Maddie pushed it inside one of the bags. "It's a sweater, that's all. A stupid bloody sweater."

Dylan thought she was about to lose it, and he wouldn't have blamed her if she had, but she merely gritted her teeth and grabbed two full bags. "I'll go and put these in the car. It'll give us more space to move."

After the wardrobe and drawers, there was a desk in Prue's workroom to empty. It was crammed with papers. "I'll take it all home and sort through it some other time," Maddie said.

By the time John Marshall arrived at two o'clock, they'd made good progress. Marshall was in his seventies, Dylan guessed, yet he was sprightly. He wore a suit that was a little old-fashioned perhaps, but well cared for. Shoes were highly polished.

"I'm so sorry for your loss." He sounded sincere as he shook Maddie's hand.

He inspected the few items of furniture and made pencil notes in a small book as he went from room to room.

"I don't want any money for it," Maddie said. "I know it's not worth anything. I'd be grateful if you could take it away though."

"I'll give you a fair price," he said.

Maddie shook her head. "If you want to pay, I'd rather you gave the money to charity. Oxfam, Save the Children, Cancer Research—just pick one."

"Of course." He nodded his understanding. "I can do that. I'll make sure you get a receipt."

They were in Prue's bedroom when he stopped in front of a tiny item on the wall. Dylan had paid it no attention but now he saw that it was a painting. The walls had been dotted with photos and colourful prints, but most had been torn down and thrown on the carpet. Presumably the intruder hadn't noticed this one. Or he'd grown tired of tossing stuff to the floor. About three inches by three, it depicted an old-fashioned black phone and an airmail envelope. When you looked closely, you could see that the background was a fountain pen's gold nib.

Marshall took it from the wall, carried it to the window for the extra light and studied it closely.

"This is interesting," he said.

"It's yours if you want it," Maddie said.

"Oh, I couldn't take this." He studied it some more. "I'm only an amateur when it comes to modern art. My enthusiasm far outweighs my knowledge, I'm afraid. However, this—oh, my, this is very exciting."

"In what way?" Dylan asked.

"Well, unless I'm very much mistaken—" his eyes sparkled with excitement as he looked at Dylan "—I think there's a possibility that this was painted by Jack McIntyre."

The name meant nothing to Dylan.

"*The* Jack McIntyre?" Maddie asked and, when he nodded, she laughed. It was a despairing sound. "Mr. Marshall, my sister was more likely to book a ticket to the moon than she was to own anything by McIntyre."

"Perhaps I'm wrong," Marshall said.

"You are," Maddie said. "I've seen McIntyre's paintings and they're huge."

"Indeed they are." Marshall didn't look upset by her

scornful tone. "He has dabbled in miniatures though. I've seen a picture of one and it's very similar to this. Miniatures are fascinating, aren't they? Some say it's a dying art. Indeed, art historians say it's already dead, that it died when we got the camera. It's nonsense, of course. We've always had some wonderful artists who concentrate on the miniature. I find them really exciting. I know McIntyre isn't noted for miniatures, but I also know he's produced several and that collectors value them highly. I'd love to believe this is one of his."

"Who exactly is this McIntyre chap?" Dylan asked.

"Dylan," Maddie scoffed. "Which rock have you been living under? He's one of the most famous painters alive."

"Actually," Marshall said, "he's dead."

"Is he?" Maddie wasn't interested. "Take it. Really, it's yours if you want it."

"McIntyre died in a boating accident," Marshall explained, ignoring Maddie. "A great loss to the art world, of course. But this—" He inspected the miniature painting once more. "This looks to me as if it could be one of his. I've only seen that one picture, and no one seems to know how many there are in the world, but if I were you, I'd take good care of it and get it valued by an expert. If it is a McIntyre, you'd be looking at tens of thousands of pounds."

"What?" Dylan couldn't believe it. The painting was three by three. Inches. Any half-decent artist could have knocked that out in five minutes.

"Maybe more," Marshall said.

Maddie was having none of it. All she wanted was

this ordeal over. She tossed the painting in one of the bags of clothes. "I'll get it looked at, but at the moment, I'm more concerned about getting rid of this furniture. The property's rented, Mr. Marshall, so if you can help, I'll be very grateful."

"Of course." He took a small diary from his pocket and flicked through the pages. "I can send a van round to collect it on Friday morning, if that's any use to you."

Maggie's shoulders sagged in relief. "That would be perfect. Thank you so much."

Marshall made a few more notes in his book and it was another fifteen minutes before he was at the front door preparing to leave. "Make sure you take good care of the miniature. If I were you, I'd take it to Christie's or Sotheby's to have it valued."

"I will. And thank you again." Maddie closed the door after him.

They stepped over full bags to get to the kitchen.

"Thank goodness for that," Maddie said. "If I get the place cleared up, I can go home as soon as he's collected the furniture on Friday. Mr. Grumpy Landlord can have his keys and that will be that. Let's have a coffee to celebrate. I think I can manage to find a couple of mugs. Although God knows what Prue's cheap instant tastes like."

Dylan followed her to the kitchen. "What about the painting?"

"What about it?" She shook her head, smiling. "In case you haven't noticed, my sister couldn't even afford real baked beans. She bought the tasteless own brand junk. You think she's likely to have a valuable work of art in her house?"

"I think someone came here looking for something."

Her hand stilled above the kettle and she swung round to face him. "What—you think—?"

"I think a painting worth tens of thousands of pounds would be worth stealing. Some people might find it worth killing for."

"It's a nice story, but it can't have been painted by McIntyre. How the hell would Prue get such a thing?"

"I don't know," Dylan said. "Maybe she saw it at a car boot sale and, unbeknown to her, picked up a real bargain."

"In that case, how would anyone know she had it?"

Dylan had been pondering that same question. If the intruder had known she owned it, it would have been taken. Unless he was disturbed before he saw it. "You need to get it valued."

"You don't really believe it's worth anything, do you?"

Dylan looked around him. Everything was second-hand and cheap. There could be few places less likely to house a valuable painting. Assuming Marshall was right and it had been painted by McIntyre, and assuming someone knew she had it—no, it didn't make sense. Anyone looking for a valuable miniature would look at the walls first. It was bloody odd though.

"I believe she was killed for a reason. And tens of thousands of pounds is one hell of a good reason."

SEVEN

DANNY'S WINE BAR was everything Dylan hated. Dazzling white, apart from ridiculously uncomfortable barstools and chairs topped in red leather, it was more suited to dental surgery than comfortable drinking place. Contestants in a talent show were strutting their stuff on a huge screen but, thankfully, the audio was switched off. It was no wonder the place was short on customers.

Two young girls dressed in short skirts and skimpy tops were perched on those stools. Thompson was behind the bar, flirting with them.

"Hey," he greeted Dylan. "Good to see you. What are you having?"

Dylan ran his gaze slowly over the drinks on offer. No decent beers were on show. No beer at all as far as he could see, except for the non-alcoholic variety, and his brain couldn't compute that one. He couldn't understand a world that believed there was a need for alcohol-free beer, caffeine-free coffee and bloody meat-free veggie burgers.

"I'll have a Scotch, please." As he opened his wallet, he noticed that Thompson didn't rely on measures. He simply poured an extremely generous quantity into a chunky glass. It reminded Dylan of a bar he'd been to in Barcelona where the barman had done the same thing. To this day he couldn't say how he'd got from that bar to his hotel room. Or why he'd woken the next morning, fully clothed, lying on the bathroom floor.

"Thanks, Danny."

The two girls were drinking a blue concoction from bottles. It looked like antifreeze, which, given that a howling gale was blowing outside, probably wouldn't be a bad thing, but Dylan assumed it was one of the popular vodka-and-fruit drinks. Neither girl looked old enough to drink. He doubted their parents knew they were wearing next to nothing and chatting up a barman while they drank vodka.

Thompson wasn't complaining. For a bloke who claimed to be gay, he was enjoying their attention far too much. Or perhaps their custom was the attraction.

A blast on a car's horn had both girls jumping off those stools to land on six-inch heels. Amid giggles, they assured Thompson they'd see him tomorrow, and dashed outside to the waiting taxi.

"You're still in the Clough then?" Thompson turned his attention to Dylan. "It must be our great weather."

"Awful, isn't it? I've got friends in the area so I'm up here for a few more days. I thought I'd come and see the famous Danny's Wine Bar. It looks good."

"Thanks."

"Everything looks new. Great decor. It must have cost a few bob."

"It is new, but I had no choice. There was a fire not so long back. Some idiots thought it would be a good idea to soak some rags in petrol and put them through the letterbox." He nodded at the door. "God knows what fun they find in that."

Dylan tutted at people's stupidity. "Did they do much damage?"

"Enough," Thompson said. "It was tricky for a while because the insurance company wasn't keen on paying up. They never are, are they? They're quick enough to sell you insurance but not so speedy when you need to claim."

"That's true." Dylan's back was already aching from being perched on the tall stool. He stood up to admire the photos on the walls. They showed different aspects of the wine bar, and weren't bad at all. "They paid up in the end though, I take it?"

"Yeah, thankfully. Actually, it worked out well for me." He winked at Dylan. "I needed to upgrade the wiring and sort out the toilets so I got it all done on the insurance."

"Perfect timing, eh?"

"Well, yes, but it was touch and go. I had a hell of a time getting the money out of the insurance bods. They thought I was conning them. What a crazy idea. Who the hell would set fire to their own premises?"

Someone who couldn't afford the improvements he'd been ordered to make?

"It certainly looks good now," Dylan said. "I like these photos."

"Good, aren't they? All done by a local photographer. She's a student, doing media studies or some such thing in Manchester. If ever you need a photographer, let me know and I'll give you her number."

"I will. Thanks."

They chatted about the weather, about recent changes that town planners had made to obstruct the flow of traffic round the town hall, and about how Burnley Football Club's fortunes had been up and down for years. Thompson was a very talkative host.

The door flew open, letting in a blast of icy air and a woman in her fifties whose long black hair, black coat and pinched face gave her a witchlike appearance.

"It's brass monkey weather out there," she said. "Can't stop, Danny, but I've brought you the money. Fifteen quid, wasn't it?"

"I'll check." He searched under the bar and finally held up a brown envelope that had *Eileen £15* scrawled on it in red pen. "Exactly right, love. Here you go."

He handed her the envelope and she ripped it open. Inside, wrapped in pink tissue paper, were two bracelets. Dylan was no jewellery expert but if those hadn't been made by Prue Murphy he'd eat his weight in cheap beads.

"Did Prue make those?" he asked.

"Gorgeous, aren't they?" Eileen said. "There won't be any more now, though, will there? Such a bloody shame. I don't suppose they've caught the bugger who did for her?" She looked to the two men for an answer.

"Not yet," Thompson said.

"Did you know her well?" Dylan asked.

"I didn't know her at all," Eileen said.

"She thought I might be able to sell a few of her things in here," Thompson explained. "I bought half a dozen bracelets and a couple of necklaces from her and put them on show behind the bar. This is the last of them. Eileen saw them and fell in love, didn't you, sweetheart?"

"I did. They're gorgeous." She put the jewellery back in the envelope and stuffed that in her handbag. "Sorry, I can't stop. I'll have to get home and start cooking his dinner or he'll skin me alive. Be seeing you!"

Another gust of cold air nipped inside as she vanished into the night.

"Have you sold many of Prue's things?" Dylan asked.

"That's the lot. Six bracelets and a couple of necklaces. And that's taken a couple of months. Mind," he said, "in view of what's happened, I'm glad I bought them from Prue. She was happy to leave them here and see if I got any takers, but I didn't like that idea. It's the same with Gemma's photos." He waved a hand at the pictures on the walls. "I bought a couple of those to sell. They went quite quickly so I'll see her about getting some more."

It seemed odd that Prue, who allegedly only visited the wine bar half a dozen times when she didn't want to get drunk alone, should have business on her mind when she came.

His insurance company hadn't believed Thompson's claim for the fire damage was genuine, and Dylan didn't believe he'd bought those pieces of jewellery from Prue. It hardly mattered now though. Prue wasn't around to worry about a few pounds in lost sales.

"Are you having another?" Thompson pointed to Dylan's empty glass.

"Why not? Will you join me?"

Thompson hesitated for a millisecond. "I don't mind if I do. Thanks, Dylan."

While Thompson poured extremely generous measures into two glasses, Dylan gazed out at the street. It was raining heavily now and, apart from the fish and chip shop opposite, which was doing a fairly good trade, all was quiet.

"Is Prue's sister still up here?" Thompson asked. "Or is she back in London?"

"She's in London."

Thompson didn't seem surprised. "There's nothing for her here now, is there? It's not as if they got on very well."

"They didn't see much of each other, probably because Prue spent so many years living abroad, but they got on all right, didn't they?" Dylan thought of the cashmere sweater, the gift from Maddie that Prue had never worn.

"Prue said they were chalk and cheese," Thompson said. "The sister's a model, isn't she?"

"Yes."

"She's got the looks for it. Prue was pretty in a different sort of way but I think she was always a bit overshadowed by her sister. Older, isn't she?"

"Yes, by five years. What makes you think Prue felt overshadowed?"

"She was convinced she wasn't as pretty or as clever as her big sister. She mentioned something about the sister having married twice. She reckoned both husbands were too good for her."

"Really? What else did she say?"

"There was a boyfriend once." Thompson took a swig of whisky and looked set to gossip the evening away. That suited Dylan. "You have to remember that Prue was legless when she told me all this, but she said there was a bloke when she was a teenager that she really liked. I don't know whether he took one look at her sister and changed sides or whether, as Prue thought, the sister deliberately set out to steal him. I got the impression that, as soon as she'd taken him from Prue, she dumped him."

"Really? Anything is possible, I suppose. Few men could resist Maddie." Dylan knew that only too well.

"She's a looker, isn't she?"

"Yeah. What else did Prue talk about?"

"She used to make me smile when she talked about her landlord. She was always nicely spoken until she mentioned him. That bastard of a landlord, she used to call him. Mind you, I can't say I blame her. He sounds like a right money-grabbing sod. According to the contract she signed, she was supposed to have a cooker and a washing machine. Well, she had them all right, but they didn't work. She kept phoning him and he promised to get them fixed. He never did. When she took out the lease, he said he was going to get new carpets put down, but he didn't do that either. She bought cheap secondhand furniture and reckoned she spent more time moving it around to hide the stains on the carpet than she did using it."

"He sounds a joy." Dylan was meeting him tomorrow so he'd be able to make up his own mind.

"That's putting it mildly. He used to call in without

warning, too, and she didn't like that. She'd just got out of the bath one day when he arrived."

"Oh?"

"And there was a time she walked in to find him in her kitchen. She'd told him she was going away for the weekend. Well, whatever she was doing was cancelled so she came home early. She had the shock of her life when she found him in the house. She was furious."

"I'm not surprised."

"He's got a real flash place up in the Lake District, so I heard," Thompson said. "He comes down here quite often, though, because he's got dozens of houses that he lets. It's all right for some. Easy money that."

"It certainly is." Dylan was pleased to see his host switch off the big screen. Neither of them had been watching it. It had been an annoying distraction. "So when did you last see Prue?"

"She was in here a couple of weeks before it happened," Thompson said, "and I saw her a couple of days beforehand just to say a quick hello. I was nipping in to the bookies and she was heading for that new supermarket on Drake Street."

At best, gambling was a mug's game. For someone like Thompson, whose business wasn't doing too well, it was a ridiculous idea. Maybe he had debts that he had no hope of paying and was hoping a couple of fast horses or dogs would help him out.

"How did she seem?"

"Fine." Thompson shrugged. "The same as always. Why do you ask?"

"Oh, I'm just curious. I hadn't kept in touch with

her. I regret that, and I'm finding it hard to accept she's gone. I wondered if she was happy and if she had plans."

"She was fine."

"I wonder why that burglar chose to break in," Dylan said. "The police reckon he always targets empty properties. He must have thought Prue would be away somewhere. She didn't say anything to you, did she?"

"Nothing. Like I said, she was her usual self. She didn't mention anything out of the ordinary."

A taxi pulled up outside and disgorged four young men, all in their late twenties. They swept inside the wine bar and sounded as if they'd already had more to drink than was good for them.

Their arrival convinced Dylan it was time to call it a night.

EIGHT

GUILT GNAWED AT Ruth as she watched her daughter open a bottle of wine. Getting through to Maddie was beyond her and she felt bad because she knew that, over the past few years, she'd stopped trying.

Maddie and Tim's home was equally alien to her. It was cold and anonymous. Nothing hinted at the hopes and dreams of the occupants.

She'd been worried about Maddie and had felt honour-bound to come but, as always, she wished she hadn't. There was a chilly atmosphere between them, an atmosphere that had never existed between her and Prue. Oh, Prue—

"What time will Tim be home?" she asked.

Her daughter spun round to face her, frowning as if she resented the question. "Soon. I offered to meet him from the airport, but Eddie's bringing him. Tim said it would save me hanging around if the plane was late." She shrugged. "Eddie doesn't mind and it's not far out of his way."

It was the longest speech Ruth had heard from Maddie this afternoon.

"That was considerate of Tim," Ruth said. "I expect he thinks you've got more than enough on your plate without acting as chauffeur for him."

"Meeting someone from the airport is hardly acting as a chauffeur, Mother."

"No."

Ruth would never forget the sheer joy of seeing Maddie for the first time. The excitement of carrying her first child had been nothing compared to seeing that round face for the first time, the little tuft of featherlight hair and those tiny but, oh, so immaculate fingers and toes. Maddie had been perfect in every way. Of course Ruth was biased, but she'd never seen a more beautiful baby before or since.

Maddie had grown into an adorable toddler, one with a sunny smile that had lit up rooms, and one able to charm adoration from all who saw her. When Maddie had raced into her arms, Ruth hadn't imagined that, one day, she would be almost afraid to speak to her daughter.

A couple of days after Maddie's fifth birthday—Ruth could still remember the fairy-tale castle cake she'd baked for that special day—Prue had been born. Ruth's happiness had known no limits. She had two beautiful daughters who were perfect in every way and her life was complete. Prue had been a smiling, placid child with a loving, giving nature.

And Maddie had been unbearable.

Ruth and Andrew had worried about sibling rivalry and they'd taken great pains to make sure Maddie got lots of attention. The more affection they gave her, the more she pushed them away. She hadn't even been able to look at Prue.

As the two girls had grown up, Maddie had grown

spiteful toward Prue. Yet Prue had tolerated it without a word of complaint. She'd been so easygoing, so kind and generous, so bloody understanding.

The sting of tears had Ruth taking a deep breath.

"Shall I take some of Prue's things home, darling?" she asked. "It will save you having to go through it all."

"There's no point. I've almost finished it. Anything of importance is going to the solicitor and the rest is being binned."

"Right. Well, don't throw anything good away." She smiled to soften her words.

"Like what?"

"Stuff that meant a lot to Prue," Ruth said.

"Oh, no, that would never do, would it?"

Ruth flinched at such hostility. "If it's all too much for you—"

"Yes? If it's all too much for me, what should I do? Like who would care?"

"Maddie, darling, don't be so hostile. We haven't asked you to do any of this. You volunteered to sort everything out. You said you *wanted* to arrange the funeral. You employed that private investigator—"

"His name is Dylan."

"Dylan, yes."

"Don't you want to know what happened to your precious daughter?" Maddie asked.

"I know what happened, darling. And I'm sure the police will be able to tell us more soon. There was certainly no need to bring in someone else. No one can bring her back to us, can they?"

"Why do you care? You're not paying for it."

Ruth longed to make her escape but a car's headlights lit up the kitchen and she knew she'd have to stay long enough to say hello to Tim.

Maddie turned to smile as the two men walked into the kitchen. She accepted a peck on both cheeks from Eddie and a quick hug from Tim.

Ruth was also given kisses and hugs.

"Is everything okay?" Tim asked.

"Fine, thanks," Maddie said.

"Ruth?"

"Yes, of course, Tim. I just thought I'd call in and see how Maddie was coping. Did you have a good flight?"

"The good part was that it was on time," Tim said.

"How are you bearing up, Maddie?" Eddie asked.

"I'm okay, thanks." Maddie held the wine bottle aloft. "Drink?"

"Are you sure?" Eddie asked, ignoring the question and the bottle. "We felt terrible leaving you at such a time. It's just awful that you've had to cope with all this on your own."

He made it sound as if Ruth had done nothing to help. Perhaps that was true, but it was only because she hadn't been allowed to.

"I'm fine." Maddie patted his arm and smiled at him. "But thanks, Eddie."

Maddie was playing the martyr and Eddie had fallen for it and drawn a smile from her. Ruth bit back on the unkind thought but, really, Maddie wasn't on her own. Maddie had *wanted* to take control. No one had asked her to.

"Eddie? Are you having a drink or not?" Tim asked.

"Go on then. I'll have a quick one for the road. Better make it a small one though."

"What about you, Ruth?"

"I'm driving. So no, thanks." Ruth would have a stiff drink when she got home. Not that she was getting into that habit. It would be far too easy to try to numb the pain of Prue's death with alcohol but she wasn't that stupid.

Both men looked tense. Perhaps their trip hadn't been as successful as they'd hoped. Eddie was three years younger than Tim but looked a decade older. He was, according to Tim, the brains behind the partnership. She supposed Tim offered the charm, sophistication and good looks. Clothes were honoured to grace his six-foot-tall, slim frame. Shoes were of the softest leather. His dark hair was kept short. Tiny lines around slate-grey eyes gave the impression of sincerity and of someone who laughed a lot. Ruth couldn't remember the last time she'd heard a laugh tumble from his lips.

She couldn't pretend to know her son-in-law well though. Tim and Maddie were far too busy to bother with the old folk.

She wondered if the marriage was a happy one. She hoped so but she had her doubts.

Eddie didn't intend to linger, thank goodness. After a few minutes spent talking about the delights of sun-kissed countries, he drained his glass and gave Tim a hearty slap on the back. "I'll love you and leave you."

"Thanks for the lift home," Tim said.

"No worries. Let's fix something up for a night out.

It will do you good, Maddie. There's no point brooding, is there?"

"None at all," she said. "We'll arrange something soon. Good to see you, Eddie."

When Eddie had gone, Ruth had no need to stay. "It's time I was off, too," she said. "It's been good to see you, Tim. And Maddie, if you need me to take Prue's things—"

"I don't. Stop fussing, Mother. I can deal with it. Anyway, it's too late now because it's all done. I just need to get that painting—"

"Which painting, darling?"

"It's nothing. There was a painting in Prue's bedroom that the secondhand furniture dealer thought might be worth a few pounds. It won't be, but I'd better get it checked just in case."

"What sort of painting?" Tim asked.

"It's just a tatty little miniature. I'll tell you about it later."

She would tell Tim, Ruth thought, but she wasn't about to tell her own mother. Ruth didn't really care. If Maddie found something of value and wanted to sell it and keep the money, that was fine. What she resented was feeling as if the task of taking care of Prue's things had been snatched from her.

"I'll be in touch then," she said, picking up her coat.

Tim escorted her to the front door, opened it for her, gave her a quick peck on the cheek and was gone, closing the door behind him.

Ruth walked over to her car, hit the key fob to unlock the doors and then realised she'd left her scarf on the kitchen table. She considered leaving it there but it was one Prue had given her and she didn't want to be parted from it.

She walked back to the door and was just about to knock when she heard Tim's voice raised in anger. "Is it so bloody difficult to make an effort?"

"When I've endured a week like this one?" Maddie shouted. "Yes. When I've just buried my sister? Yes. When I've spent the week sorting through my dead sister's things? Yes."

Ruth shrank back against the wall. They were arguing in the hall. Would they notice that her car hadn't moved?

"Forgive me for asking," Tim said, and Ruth could hear sarcasm dripping from each syllable, "but exactly when did this sister come to mean so much to you? You saw her—what?—twice in the last three years?"

"Three times."

"Three times in three years. I suppose you've conveniently forgotten that you couldn't stand her company."

"I've forgotten nothing. I just wish everyone would leave me alone. First my mother turns up trying to be nice when we all know she wishes the other daughter had died. Then you start on about money—"

"I didn't start on about money. I simply said that I have to work to help pay for private detectives and shrinks that you insist on—"

Ruth couldn't bear to hear any more. The scarf would have to stay where it was. Perhaps Maddie would return it to her. It didn't matter. It was only a scarf, albeit one Prue had given her.

My mother turns up trying to be nice when we all know she wishes the other daughter had died. How could Maddie say such a thing? How could she even think such a thing?

Ruth climbed in her car, fired the engine and, with tears streaming down her face, drove away from the house.

NINE

Dylan had arranged to meet Toby Windsor at ten o'clock. By ten-fifteen, there was no sign of him.

Having insisted that Maddie have Prue's house empty by Friday, Windsor had then informed her he wouldn't be able to get to the property and go through the inventory until today, Tuesday. Dylan supposed they shouldn't have been surprised, as Windsor appeared to take delight in messing people around. As yet, Dylan had heard nothing good about Prue's landlord.

Dylan planned to spend the week in Dawson's Clough talking to anyone and everyone who'd known Prue so he'd offered to keep the house keys, save Maddie the journey from London, and meet Windsor himself. He was curious about the bloke.

He walked through the empty rooms as he waited. Danny Thompson was right in that the washing machine didn't work. The cooker had two rings that worked but the grill and oven refused to even get warm. He could see his breath on the chilly air, but as there had been no heating on since Prue was killed, that wasn't surprising, especially considering the low temperatures and the heavy rain that had hit the area. The place felt damp and cold, and without Prue's cheap furniture hiding stains on the carpet or peeling wallpaper, utterly depressing.

It was difficult to imagine that Jane Cook's lovely home was only on the other side of the wall. When Dylan had called on her, he'd been welcomed into a warm, cheerful house where Fudge, the cat, lazed on a windowsill that had attracted a few weak rays of sunshine. A plant-filled conservatory provided comfy seats that offered a view of a small but neat, colourful garden. It was like entering a different world.

"Prue planned to make a start on her garden this spring," Jane had said. "She would have had her work cut out because it hasn't been touched for years. I offered to give her a hand and let her have cuttings from my garden…"

Perhaps the next tenant would sort it out. They'd have a difficult task. It was a waterlogged, overgrown mess at the moment although the dilapidated wooden shed looked as if it was about to do everyone a favour by falling down of its own volition.

Dylan must have spoken to every resident on this quiet road but he'd learned nothing of interest. People were shocked that a neighbour had been killed in her own home, but no one knew anything about Prue that might help find her killer. A couple of people had installed new security alarms, and a few planned to press the local council to install CCTV, but he guessed that when the shock faded, Prue would be forgotten and life in this street would carry on as normal.

He wandered along the hall to the front of the house and was in time to see a white Mercedes glide to a halt outside. The man who eased himself out was mid-fifties, balding and overweight. His dark hair was thin but everything else about him, from his neck through his girth to his fingers, was fat. He was wearing a suit that must have reinforced seams.

Rain was lashing down now so Dylan went to the front door and held it open for him. "Toby Windsor?"

The name suited him. He looked like the Toby jugs that hung from beams in Dylan's favourite pub.

"That's me. Who are you?"

"Dylan Scott." He shook his hand and grazed his knuckle on the enormous gold ring Windsor wore. "I'm a friend of the family. Mrs. Chandler couldn't make it today so I'm here to go through the inventory and hand over the keys on her behalf."

Windsor didn't look overjoyed at this piece of news. "If any damage has been done—"

"There's no damage." The window that the intruder had broken to gain entrance had been repaired. Also, Jane Cook had been able to tell Dylan what Prue had done to the house. "Quite the opposite, in fact. Miss Murphy had the sitting-room window repaired. She preferred to pay for the repair herself, I gather, than wait for you to get around to organising it. She painted the kitchen and bathroom. She paid a plumber to repair the leaking cistern."

"I'll check everything," Windsor said.

He heaved himself upstairs and Dylan followed.

Windsor stopped in Prue's bedroom. It was bare but that didn't stop him having a good look round before checking that the light worked, the window opened and closed, and the electric sockets were securely fastened to the wall.

"You wouldn't believe what some tenants do," he said. "About six months ago, a couple stopped paying their rent. I thought, 'Here we go again.' It's a right bugger getting rid of 'em, I can tell you. They have rights whether they pay their rent or not but the landlord doesn't have a leg to stand on. The landlord can't even go and ask for the rent more than once because it's classed as harassment. I'd give 'em bloody harassment. This couple I was telling you about? The good thing was that they buggered off. I was glad about that because, like I said, it's the devil's own job getting rid of 'em. But they only took the bloody doors off. Every bloody door in the house. Gone. Bastards!"

"Really?" They probably considered it suitable recompense for putting up with a faulty washing machine and cooker.

"You wouldn't believe what some of 'em do." Windsor strode to the spare room and, again, made a fuss of checking sockets, light and window. "A landlord's lot isn't an easy one, believe me."

Windsor muttered his way from room to room with Dylan following and trying to get a word in.

"The washing machine and cooker haven't been working," he managed to say when they reached the kitchen. "But you'll know that because Prue contacted you about it. Several times."

"Yeah, I was meaning to—"

"The window's been repaired." Dylan showed him the small window where the intruder gained access.

"It looks okay." Windsor's tone was grudging.

"You were in Monaco when she was killed, I gather?"

"That's right, yeah."

"The police believe a petty thief was responsible," Dylan said.

"It doesn't surprise me at all. These days, if it's standing still, some bugger will nick it. No matter how secure you make your home, some little shit will find a way in. Bastards."

"True. It's odd though, isn't it?"

"How do you mean?"

"Everything. The way this thief is supposed to only target empty properties. The way he didn't steal anything."

"There was nothing worth taking," Windsor said.

"But there was. The police reckon he's happy to make a couple of hundred quid. Well, there was sixty pounds on the table and he ignored that. The TV and DVD player were old, but they would have fetched a few quid. It makes me think he was looking for something else."

"Like what?"

"I wish I knew."

"There was nothing worth taking," Windsor said again. "I know because I called in a couple of times. Well, you have to make sure people are treating your properties as they should. Believe me, there was nothing worth stealing."

"How can you know that? Ah, but you called quite often, didn't you?" Dylan said. "Any particular reason? Or do you visit all your properties regularly?"

"I visit new tenants a few times," he said. "Just until I've got the measure of them. And it's a two-way thing.

It gives them a chance to discuss any problems they might be having."

"Only if the tenants are at home," Dylan said. "And you still wouldn't know whether there was anything worth stealing. No one would know if *I* had anything of value unless they had a good search through my home and looked in cupboards and drawers. Oh, but I forgot. You called here when you knew Prue would be away, didn't you?"

"I never did!"

"That's what I heard. I was told you visited when you knew Prue would be away for the weekend. Her appointment was cancelled and she returned to find you in the property."

"Oh, that." He shrugged huge shoulders. "Look, I'm not calling her a liar, but if she *did* tell me she was going away that weekend, I forgot. I have several properties in the Clough, Mr. Scott, and I can't be expected to keep tabs on all my tenants, can I?"

"I suppose not."

"So, yeah. Perhaps you're right. Perhaps she did have something worth nicking. I wouldn't know, would I?"

"Not unless you had a good poke around in the cupboards," Dylan said.

"I wouldn't do that, would I? I wouldn't look at people's possessions. They'd be private and I respect that." Windsor took a notebook and pen from his pocket. "Right, we just need to read the gas and electric meters."

Dylan had already done so but he was curious to see if Windsor noted down the same figures. If there was a discrepancy, he'd bet it was in the landlord's favour.

The gas meter was in a small cupboard beneath the stairs and Windsor was out of breath when he emerged. He had his readings, however, and when Dylan checked them against the ones he'd taken earlier, he was surprised to find that they were identical.

"You need to sign here," Windsor said, pushing a sheet of paper at him, "just to say we've agreed that all is in order. I'll sign here to say you've agreed on the meter readings and handed over the keys. And that's it."

Dylan signed in the correct places and they exchanged agreements. "You'll be looking to get another tenant in then?" he asked.

"Yes. It's no use to me empty, is it?" Windsor said.

"None at all."

"Right, thanks for this. We can go now." Windsor strode to the front door, pulled it open and held it for Dylan. "After you."

"Thanks."

Windsor was soon in his car. Dylan stood, with the rain lashing down, to take one last look at Prue Murphy's home. He hoped it held no clues because they wouldn't get inside it again. He dismissed the thought. The house was empty. There was nothing to be learned from those damp, cold rooms.

He dashed to his car, jumped inside and drove off.

Red lights stopped him at the crossroads and he drummed the steering wheel as he waited for them to change. At the moment they did, he drove forward and glanced briefly along the road to his left. Standing there, watching traffic, was a tall bearded man with untidy grey hair. He was wearing a long overcoat with the collar turned up against the rain.

Dylan drove on to the next junction and took a left turn. He turned left and left again, but when he re-emerged into the street, there was no sign of anyone wearing a long overcoat.

He parked, got out of the car and strode along the street. Apart from a couple of cafés, a run-down pub, a dry cleaner's and a newsagent's, there was nowhere to hide. He checked those buildings but he didn't see his bearded quarry.

During a slow walk back to his car, he wondered if he'd been mistaken, or if he really had seen the man who'd distanced himself from the mourners at Prue's funeral.

TEN

MADDIE KNEW DAMN well that Louise didn't have a client with her but she was still made to wait until the dot of eleven before being shown into her office.

"Hello, Maddie." Louise wore the gentle smile she always wore. Pushing sixty, her hair a natural grey and her face bare of makeup, she was doing what people referred to as "growing old gracefully." What was the point? She'd look a whole lot better if she did something with her hair and painted her lips. Applying a coat of lipstick wasn't a huge chore. "And before you ask, no, you may not smoke in here."

"I wasn't going to ask."

"Then we've made progress. Sit down. Would you like the chair or the couch today?"

"Definitely the couch." Maddie put her coat and bag on the chair and stretched out on the couch. For some reason, she didn't feel quite so relaxed when sitting in the chair.

The couch was more suited to a hospital than a therapist's office. It wasn't comfortable, it was too hard and cold for that, and it certainly wasn't attractive. Everything else in the room, like the huge wooden desk and captain's chair and the floor-to-ceiling bookshelves, was antique. A huge pile of coloured paperclips clung to a pyramid-shaped magnet on Louise's desk. Two children, presumably grandchildren, with beaming smiles gazed out of silver photo frames.

The pale green carpet had been quality once, but now it was worn in places. There were two windows in the room, one overlooking a small square of grass at the back and the other a side street, and blinds were angled so that they let a little light in but kept distractions out.

"So," Louise said, when Maddie was comfortable, "how are you today?"

"I'm good."

"I'm delighted to hear that. So what shall we talk about? Prue? The funeral? Tim?"

"The new man in my life." Maddie waited for some sign of shock but, of course, there was nothing. Louise didn't so much as raise an eyebrow.

"Very well," Louise said. "Tell me about the new man in your life."

Maddie closed her eyes and relaxed. "Actually, he's not so new. We were together years ago, when I was eighteen."

"Ah. Go on."

"I've found him again."

"Was he lost?"

"To me, yes. We split up. We had a quarrel, you see, and he went away. But that's not important because I've found him again. He's still the same. Handsome. Fun. Sexy."

"Are you telling me he hasn't changed at all? After twenty years?"

"I'm telling you exactly that. He may look slightly

older, but that's all, and that doesn't matter, does it? It's what inside that makes a person, isn't it?"

"It is. So tell me about him? Does he have a name?"

"He has a name."

She'd thought Louise might be interested but she wasn't. She pretended to care, but it was all for show. As far as she was concerned, Maddie was just another client who handed over a big fat cheque.

"How do you feel about him?" Louise asked.

"The same as I did when I was eighteen," she said. "I loved him then. I love him now."

"Does Tim know about him?"

"No."

"Do you want to talk about that? Or would you prefer to tell me how you found him after all these years?"

"Yes." This was more like it. Perhaps Louise was interested after all. "When Prue first told me she was leaving France and moving to Lancashire, I looked up Dawson's Clough on the internet. Well, I'd never heard of it. You hadn't either, you said. So I was looking at the place on the internet—a right dump it is too—and I saw his name mentioned. I didn't know if it was the same man or not but I did some digging around and, sure enough, it was him."

"This was some time ago then," Louise said. "It's what, four months since your sister moved to Lancashire?"

"Yes."

"And you've only just contacted him? Why did you wait?"

Maddie propped herself up on her elbow to look at

Louise. "Because I was angry with him. It said on the internet that he was married and that took me by surprise. I didn't think he'd find anyone else, after me I mean."

"But why wouldn't he, Maddie? You've been married twice since then so why shouldn't he marry?"

Maddie might have known she'd say that. There were times when she wondered why she bothered coming. Everyone said Louise was good, the best there was, but Maddie had seen dozens of shrinks and therapists in her time and Louise was no better than any of them. Talk, talk, talk. What was the point? Yvette, a young model who snorted cocaine for breakfast, lunch and dinner, swore Louise had saved her life. In Maddie's view, a quick call to the Samaritans would have had the same result. In fact the person on the end of the line might have given a flying toss, which was more than Louise did.

"Why don't you colour your hair?" Maddie asked her.

"Because I like it the way it is. Because I decided to stop colouring it ten years ago. Because I have more important things to do with my time. Will any of those reasons do?"

"What do you find to do with your time that's so exciting?"

"Lots of things. I enjoy concerts, the theatre, reading, listening to music—my problem is that there aren't enough hours in the day to do it all. Why were you angry with this man? Is it because you felt he'd cast you aside? Did he make you remember how you felt when Prue was born?"

Here she went again. Louise believed that talking solved everything. She was wrong. She had no idea what it had been like when Prue was born. Until then, Maddie had been the adored child, the one both parents had loved more than life itself. Maddie had been a happy little girl who'd been able to do no wrong. Everything changed the moment Prue came kicking and screaming into the world. One minute Maddie had been Daddy's Little Girl and the next minute, Daddy had been reminding them with every breath that Prue was now his little girl and Maddie was his big girl. It was Prue who claimed her mother's attention in the night, Prue who gurgled when Daddy came home from work, Prue who had to be christened, Prue who must have exactly the same number of birthday and Christmas presents as Maddie. It had been Prue, Prue, Prue until Maddie wanted to—

"We've talked about this, haven't we, Maddie? You know you weren't cast aside, don't you?"

"Yes." Maddie gave her a broad smile. "And that's why I realised I was being silly about Dylan. That's his name, by the way. Dylan. I realised that the way we split up was as much my fault as his. The time simply wasn't right for us and there's no reason at all why he shouldn't have married. I don't suppose his wife means anything to him. So I forgave him, you see? And when Prue was killed, I knew I had to get in touch with him. It was an omen, wasn't it? Some power was telling me to contact him."

"Explain."

"What? Oh, I didn't mention that he's a PI, did I? He is. He was in the police force but got thrown out for something. I can't remember what. He did tell me but I was so pleased to see him, I couldn't take anything in. So yes, I thought it would be fun to get him to look into Prue's death."

"Fun?"

"You know what I mean."

Louise was nodding slowly. "Was he pleased to hear from you?"

"Of course he was. But I'm not rushing into any-thing." Maddie gave her a quick smile. "We've talked about that too, haven't we? We know I tend to act first and think later. It's nothing like that. Dylan's busy look-ing into Prue's death. First things first, eh? We need to make sure we're right for each other, don't we? We messed up last time so this time has to be perfect."

"I'm pleased you're not going to rush into anything, Maddie, because this is a very difficult time for you. It's hard to lose a sibling, no matter how difficult the relationship was, and you need to take good care of yourself. You can't go making any rash decisions. You know that's important, don't you?"

"Yes." It was always easier to agree with Louise. "We had some great times all those years ago, you know. And I'm not just talking about the sex, although that was out of this world."

"I should hope it was. When we're young and single with no marriage, mortgage or kids to think about, the sex damn well should be good." Louise glanced up at the large wall clock. "You said you were going to tell me about Prue's funeral the next time you saw me. Have you changed your mind?"

"There's not much to tell. It rained."

"It often seems to at funerals, doesn't it? Did you find it difficult?"

"No."

"Do you have any regrets? Are there things you wished you'd said to her? A lot of people have regrets and they can be hard to deal with."

"No. Nothing like that."

"You were telling me about the kitten, do you remember? That was on your mind."

"It was just a kitten, that's all. It was my kitten and she—"

"She what, Maddie?"

"Nothing."

"Your parents bought you a kitten and it decided to sleep on Prue's bed, isn't that right? Cats are like that, aren't they? It could have decided to sleep on the stairs or in a bathroom cupboard. Perhaps Prue didn't like it sleeping on her bed. Have you thought about that?"

Prue had *encouraged* it to sleep on her bed. She'd cuddled it and played with it and then called to it to make sure it would sleep on her bed. It had been Maddie's kitten for half a day then Prue had stolen it. Once she'd made a fuss of it, it had refused to go anywhere near Maddie. Still, Maddie made sure she got her own back. How Prue had cried when it died.

"It was just a kitten, that's all," she said.

"So you don't want to talk about your sister's funeral? You found it easy to deal with?"

"It was okay, yes," Maddie said.

"Were Prue's friends there?"

"Of course. Loads of them. Not that I knew them."

"She had a lot of friends, did she?"

"Quite a few, yes. She was a friends type of person." She knew exactly what Louise was about to say. "Yes, I know friends are important, and I have been keeping up with my friends, but I also like to be independent. My grandfather used to say that the only person you can trust is yourself."

"Do you agree with that?" Louise asked. "Would you have married Tim if you didn't trust him? People know they can trust you, don't they? Prue called you before she died. She was worried about something, you said, and she turned to you. She only did that because she knew she could trust you, didn't she?"

"Yeah." She always left this building convinced that Louise didn't have a clue about the real world. Why did she bother coming? Tim said it was because she didn't have real friends. Well, she didn't *want* friends. She could cope quite easily without them. Most of the time, these so-called friends only wanted to have a good moan and get some sympathy. She didn't have time for talking about silly things with friends. "I ought to go now. I've got another appointment."

"Your hour isn't up yet," Louise said.

"It doesn't matter. I'm doing okay so life's good."

"You haven't told me much about the new man in your life."

"Only because there isn't much to say. Yet." Maddie swung her legs off the couch and stood up. "Like I said, I'm not rushing into anything. I'll tell you more about him next time, okay?"

"Have you seen your parents lately? Apart from at the funeral, I mean?"

"Yes." It was a lie but Maddie was bored now. "We're fine. Really. We're all fine. I do have to go now, though, or I'll be late for my appointment."

She picked up her bag and walked out, leaving Louise staring after her with her usual pensive expression.

The blasted woman could wear whatever expression she liked. Louise would do well to remember that these visits were voluntary. Maddie might not bother going again.

ELEVEN

DYLAN HAD SWITCHED his phone to Silent for the night so he'd missed Maddie's text message, which came through at a little after seven that morning. It had been brief and to the point: *On way to DC. Meet @ your hotel @ 11.*

He'd tried calling her but her phone went straight to voice mail, presumably because she was driving. She hadn't responded to either of the messages he'd left.

She'd always been impulsive, he remembered, and it seemed that age had taught her nothing. If she'd checked with him first, he could have told her he was driving back to London today. She could have saved herself a long journey north.

He had no idea why she wanted to see him, or Dawson's Clough, but if she was expecting an update on his progress, she was in for a disappointment. There was no progress. He didn't believe that a petty thief had broken into Prue's home on the off chance, but he had no better theories.

He sat at a table in the hotel's reception area with a coffee and a copy of last night's local newspaper in front of him. The top story concerned a fundraising event to benefit the town's hospice. Nothing happened in sleepy Dawson's Clough. Apart from the odd murder, of course.

Maddie breezed through the front door at a little after eleven-thirty wearing skin-tight jeans, a soft pink sweater and sunglasses. Sunglasses. In Dawson's Clough. In March.

She spotted him, he stood up, and she rushed forward to put her hand on his neck and kiss his cheek. Every time he saw her, he was transported back to that blue bedroom with the huge smiley face on the ceiling. It was the devil's own job forgetting the past.

"I've been trying to call you," he said.

"Have you?" She took off her sunglasses and hunted through a large leather handbag. When she finally found her phone and switched it on, she gave him an apologetic smile. "So you have. Sorry. I was in a rush to get here."

"I'm heading back to London today so I could have saved you a journey."

"Oh." Her shoulders sagged. "Can't you stay? Just one more night?"

Christ, it was tempting. "I can't, Maddie. Sorry. I have things planned."

"Oh, well, I suppose it doesn't matter. I needed to get away anyway." She didn't say from what and Dylan didn't ask. She threw herself down in the chair opposite but before he could say anything, she stood up again.

"Can we go somewhere?" she asked. "Can we just walk?"

"Of course." An angry wind howled around the hotel's walls but it wasn't actually raining. Yet. "Is everything okay?"

"Fine." She looked jumpy. Nervy. He wondered if she was on drugs and the thought caught him by surprise. When he'd known her all those years ago, she hadn't even been tempted to take a quick puff on a cigarette. She certainly wouldn't have done drugs. That was then though. This was now.

"Are you sure?" he asked.

"Yes. Come on. I've been sitting in the car for hours. I need to stretch my legs."

He refused to think about her legs.

They left the hotel and walked via the car park for Dylan to get his jacket and Maddie to collect a thick red padded coat.

"Which way?" she asked, and he pointed in the direction of Moors Park.

She slipped her arm through his as they walked, and he could feel her begin to relax with each step.

"I wanted to tell you that I've had the painting valued," she said.

"And?" He'd managed to convince himself that Marshall had been mistaken about the painting, but he could tell from the tremor in her voice that he shouldn't have. "How much?"

"God, you'll never believe this. They said they'd put a reserve of sixty thousand pounds on it if they were selling it."

"Sixty grand?" Dylan couldn't believe anyone on the planet could be so bloody stupid as to hand over that sort of money for a painting that was three by three. Inches. "Bloody hell."

"I know. It quite shook me. I didn't know what to do with it so I've left it in a deposit box at the bank."

"It was definitely painted by that chap McIntyre?"

"Yes."

"So how did Prue get hold of it?" he asked.

"I don't know."

They walked through tall black iron gates and into the park. Apart from a few ducks on the pond, and an elderly woman shuffling along with an equally elderly spaniel, it was deserted.

"Prue couldn't have known she had it," Maddie said. "If she had, she would have sold it, wouldn't she? Someone must have thought it was worthless and donated it to a charity shop or something. Prue shopped at Oxfam. She got her furniture from car boot sales. There's no way she could have known what it was, is there?"

Dylan wasn't so sure. He believed that the person who broke into her home had been looking for something specific. And sixty grand's worth of painting was very specific indeed. On the other hand, if they'd been after that painting, they would have slipped it in their pocket. It had been hanging on the wall in Prue's bedroom for all the world to see.

"She couldn't afford to buy it," Maddie said, "and she wasn't the type to steal so much as an apple from a market stall. There's no way she could have known she owned something so valuable."

A gust of wind rocked them both and he felt her shiver in her coat.

"You could have phoned to tell me," he said. "There was no need to come all this way."

She gripped his arm tighter and leaned her face close to his. "I wanted to see you and this gave me the perfect excuse."

"Why?"

She smiled at that. "Because it's been too long, Dylan. I've missed you."

She was his for the taking and the realisation hit him like a kick in the stomach.

He wasn't kidding himself that she'd spared him a thought during the years since they'd had fun in that blue bedroom. She'd been married twice so she'd been too busy making out with others. But now—was her marriage so bad that she was looking elsewhere? Would anyone do? He had the feeling they would.

One thing was certain, he wasn't going to encourage her. That way led to disaster. She might not be happily married, but he most definitely was.

That thought caught him by surprise too. He and Bev had had more than their fair share of ups and downs— more downs than ups if he included the months he'd spent banished from the marital home—but now, everything was as it should be. He was happy. Happy was perhaps stretching it a bit. Wives, kids, jobs, mortgages—none of it left much room for happiness. He was certainly content with his lot though.

"Missed me indeed." He tried to laugh off her words. "I bet you haven't thought about me once."

"Of course I have." She stopped walking to gaze up at him. "Haven't you thought about me?"

"Now and then." He gave her a smile, but he refused to go down that route. "So how did Prue get hold of a valuable painting?"

Wide-eyed, laughing and looking more relaxed now, she punched him on the arm. "Stop changing the subject."

"Am I? Perhaps I am. But I'm curious. Where would anyone buy such a thing? Well, no, she couldn't have bought it. She studied art and design though, didn't she? It seems as if I'm the only person on the planet who hasn't heard of Jack McIntyre so I bet she knew exactly what it was."

"She couldn't have. She would have sold it."

Maybe. Maybe not.

They walked past the small lake and to the children's play area. Maddie pushed a swing back and forth, a wistful expression on her face. He wondered if she wanted children. Perhaps she had a couple. She hadn't mentioned any and none had attended Prue's funeral, so he'd assumed she didn't. He wasn't going to ask. He wanted to keep things as impersonal as possible.

"I put the meter readings from Prue's house in the mail to you," he said, changing the subject yet again. "The landlord signed everything to say the property was in an acceptable condition."

"Isn't he a miserable git?"

"Perhaps he has a right to be. He was telling me how some tenants up sticks and leave with rent outstanding. One couple even took all the doors with them. Perhaps it gets you like that."

"I only spoke to him on the phone and he gave me the creeps."

Dylan had to admit that Windsor wasn't the most amenable bloke he'd ever met. "It's all done and dusted so you won't have to speak to him again."

"Thanks. I mean, thank you for dealing with him."

"It was no problem and I wanted to meet him. Your sister had complained about him. You remember Danny Thompson? The chap with the ponytail who was at Prue's funeral?"

"Got him. What about him?"

"He was telling me that Prue didn't like her landlord. Apparently, he used to turn up at the house with no warning. She had to keep reminding him that things needed fixing and he never did anything about it."

Maddie shuddered. "God knows how she stood living in that hovel."

"It wasn't so bad. The house next door is lovely."

"Yes, but Prue's wasn't. It was cold, damp and dingy. The carpets were disgusting."

He couldn't argue with that. "Come on," he said, nodding up at heavy black clouds. "Let's get back before the storm hits."

"Shall we have dinner together this evening?" Her tone was pleading.

"Sorry, I can't. As I said, I'm heading back to London." As she looked set to argue, he rushed on, "I have plans that I can't get out of. Sorry. Some other time, okay?"

"Promise?"

"Promise."

Dylan would have preferred to walk more quickly to the hotel but Maddie refused to be rushed. As she was hanging on his arm, he could hardly drag her along behind him. He wanted to be alone, to make sense of his thoughts.

Uppermost at this moment was that he could easily have dinner with Maddie and end up in bed with her. That was so unbelievable that his brain refused to do anything but mull it over and over. Bev wasn't expecting him, Maddie was needy, and there was no reason why he couldn't stay in Dawson's Clough for one more night.

He pushed the thought away and tried to convince his brain to think about Prue and valuable paintings.

Prue's owning a painting by Jack McIntyre didn't make sense. It had been valued at a minimum of sixty grand. *Minimum.* If she'd sold it, she could have put down a deposit on a very nice house. She wouldn't have needed to be beholden to her scumbag landlord. Of course, if she'd had no idea of its worth—

"What about lunch then?" Maddie asked.

"Sorry, I can't." He could, but he wasn't going to. He didn't trust his reactions to her. Besides, he wanted to be alone and put his thoughts in some sort of order. "I need to check out of my hotel and get moving. If only you'd called me, Maddie, I could have told you I was heading south."

"It doesn't matter," she said. "I wanted a break so I'll book myself in at the spa and treat myself to a couple of days of luxury."

"Good idea." They were almost back at the hotel. "How well did you and Prue get along?"

"Fine. Why?"

"Oh, I'm just curious. Thompson, the chap with the ponytail, didn't think you were close. He was under the impression you didn't get along too well."

"That's ridiculous." She was irritated now whereas she had been looking more relaxed. "Just because we didn't see much of each other, people assume we weren't close. Why did she phone me, hmm? Why would she do that if we weren't close?"

She let go of his arm and ran both hands through her hair. "We were just normal sisters, okay? We had the usual love/hate relationship. We were close but we didn't live in each other's pockets. She had her life and I had mine."

Dylan nodded, surprised by her outburst. "I get the picture."

They walked up the hotel's driveway just as the first fat raindrops fell.

"Right, I'm out of here," Dylan said. "Enjoy your time at the spa and I'll call you as soon as I come up with anything."

"Okay." She slid her arms around his waist and leaned in close. "Next time, I won't let you escape so easily. You've been warned, Dylan Scott."

Next time, he might not try to escape…

TWELVE

IT WAS AFTER six o'clock when Dylan finally walked into his house. And it was manic.

"I didn't think you'd be back tonight," Bev said. "Lucy's coming round. We're having a girly night in. I've got the wine and the ice cream—everything."

"Pardon me for living here." He was tempted by the idea of a boys' night out, but he had work to do. "Why don't you have a girly night *out* then? I'll be chief babysitter."

"I can't, can I?" She looked in dismay at her jeans and tugged on her shirt. "Or perhaps I can. Yes, great idea. I've got enough time to change. Thanks, Dylan. I'll phone her."

Luke was supposed to have been enjoying a sleepover at Tom's but Tom had the flu.

"Your dad's here now," Bev said in her jolly voice, "so you can ask Jamie if he wants to stay the night. Give him a call. Tell him your dad will pick him up."

"Just hand me my chauffeur's cap," Dylan said, but no one heard him. Bev was racing around with a mascara wand in her hand and Luke was reaching for the phone to call Jamie.

Freya was sniffling and grumbling and, as everyone was having fun or about to have fun, and ignoring her, Dylan decided she was entitled to be moody. Grand plans were in place for her first birthday, but she wouldn't know that.

This summed up family life, he supposed. Everyone wanted to be part of a unit, but they also craved their own space. It was give and take, with everyone having to fit in around everyone else. Dylan knew he should be grateful that his family were well, happy and busy, but he couldn't help wishing he had a more exciting way to spend an evening than chauffeuring kids around and babysitting.

That persistent nagging inner voice reminded him again that he was forty years old. Hot sex in blue bedrooms with big smiley faces watching on was for kids, not forty-year-olds.

It was nine o'clock before he managed to pour himself a drink and switch on his computer. Freya was asleep, Luke and Jamie were upstairs making enough noise for fifty kids, and Bev was out getting drunk with Lucy. He had peace of sorts.

He forgot blue bedrooms and smiley faces, tried to forget the hot sex, and threw himself into finding out all he could about the artist Jack McIntyre. He was surprised by how much information was available.

His art was a mix of landscapes and portraits. Experimental, the experts called it. Crap, Dylan called it.

No, he was being unfair. It was *okay*. At least it was easy to see what it was supposed to be. It simply wasn't worth the money. Any of the art students at the local college could come up with something as good.

As Maddie had said, his paintings were large. Some

were vast. He only found two mentions of miniatures. One was a story about two that McIntyre had given to a friend and that had later been auctioned. Few people, including the article's author, knew much about his miniatures. The other story told how a miniature had sold at auction last month for a staggering eighty-two thousand pounds. If Dylan lived to be a hundred and forty, he would never understand how anyone could hand over so much cash for something so small and useless.

Most stories concerned McIntyre's tragic death last November at the age of sixty-two. Until then, it seemed that, having stopped painting around five years earlier, McIntyre had been living the life of a beach bum, albeit a very wealthy beach bum. Home had been a tiny cottage on the French coast.

One journalist had managed a rare interview with McIntyre and had asked why he'd stopped painting. McIntyre had claimed that his muse had abandoned him. Why did artists always have to trot out crap like that? Blame it on the muse. Everyone else had to drag themselves out of bed and do a day's work but artists, the wealthy ones at least, could pound their foreheads, sit around doing nothing all day and blame an uncooperative muse. It was complete bollocks.

On the day of the tragedy, McIntyre's agent, Jeremy Collins, paid him a visit, presumably to persuade McIntyre to pick up a brush again. A painter not painting must be any agent's worst nightmare. Whether Collins was successful on this occasion would never be known because they took McIntyre's boat out and neither lived to tell the tale.

Other stories about McIntyre centred on his art, and especially how the value of his work had increased after his death.

Most images showed a smiling, confident man. McIntyre looked relaxed and at ease as he mingled with guests at one or another of his exhibitions. In many photos, he was holding a glass of wine or champagne. He stood beside huge canvases, smiling for the camera and probably laughing all the way to his Swiss bank account. There were no pictures of miniatures.

Dylan wished he had a couple of those large paintings to sell.

McIntyre and his wife had lived apart for years, and there were rumours that they'd been seeking a divorce. Dylan would bet that Mrs. McIntyre was relieved she hadn't gone down that route as his last will and testament must have made interesting reading.

McIntyre had come from a privileged background so money had probably meant very little to him. He'd been used to it all his life. Education had been at an exclusive boarding school, so exclusive that Dylan had never heard of it, followed by a couple of years at Cambridge studying the classics. He never actually graduated because he dropped out, deciding he'd like to concentrate on his art instead. Nice if you could afford it.

Dylan's research was interrupted by the banging of the front door as it opened and closed. He glanced at his watch and was surprised to find that it was almost midnight. He was surprised, too, that Luke and Jamie had finally stopped making a racket.

He closed his laptop and went to investigate.

Bev was kneeling on the floor, gathering up the contents of her handbag.

"I dropped it," she said unnecessarily.

"So I see. Did you have a good night?" Dylan bent down and picked up three hairbrushes, two small mirrors, enough paracetamol to see an elephant through an amputation, cinema ticket stubs and loose change.

"The best. We had a lot of laughs. Although we might have had a bit too much to drink."

There was no *might* about it.

"What about you?" she asked. "Everything all right here? Are my babies okay?"

God, save me from drunken women. "Yes. Everything's fine."

Clutching her full bag, she stood, looked around her, swayed alarmingly and gave him a smile. "I think I'd better go on up to bed."

"Good idea, sweetheart. I'll be up myself in a couple of minutes." Not that she'd know anything about it.

She swayed toward him and he gave her a quick kiss.

Once she was safely up the stairs, he went to the kitchen, poured himself another drink and switched on his laptop again.

Prue Murphy had lived in France until last November. Jack McIntyre had lived in France until last November. Coincidence?

Prue couldn't have bought that miniature, she wasn't the type to steal anything, and it was highly unlikely that she'd found it on a dusty shelf in a charity shop. The only other option was that it had been a gift.

Maybe she'd had a rich lover. Prue had been a fan

of art, and a gift like that would have won her heart forever. Dylan hadn't known her, but he'd guess she'd been too sentimental to sell a gift, even such an extravagant one. It seemed unlikely that Maddie wouldn't have known of any wealthy boyfriends though. The sisters hadn't been close, at least they hadn't seen much of each other, but rich friends would surely have cropped up in conversation.

Maybe a friend of McIntyre's had given it to her? She'd lived in France, McIntyre had presumably had friends there. It was possible, Dylan supposed, but it seemed such an odd and extravagant choice of gift.

Perhaps the artist himself had given it to Prue. How could they have met though? A wealthy artist like McIntyre was unlikely to frequent the same sort of places as a girl who waited on tables. The age difference was huge, too, making a meeting between the two even more unlikely. People in their thirties simply didn't go to the same places as sixty-year-olds.

Perhaps, after all, Prue had taken a liking to the miniature at a car boot sale or an Oxfam shop.

If John Marshall hadn't arrived to take away Prue's few items of furniture, Maddie could easily have thrown that miniature in a box destined for a charity shop. Most secondhand furniture dealers wouldn't know a McIntyre from a Rembrandt. Maybe the painting's previous owner, not knowing its value, had thrown it in a box for Oxfam too. Staff at the charity shop could have slapped a sticker on it and Prue might have handed over two pounds for it. That seemed a far more likely scenario.

Yet Prue had lived in France until November. McIntyre had lived in France until November. Admittedly, McIntyre had had little choice in the matter of leaving France.

Dylan would chat to a few people who'd known the artist. His wife would be easy enough to find. There wasn't a great deal of information about McIntyre's agent—or gallerist, as he was referred to—but his son, Martin Collins, still had the business. Dylan had probably walked past his London gallery many times without knowing it.

He switched off the laptop and leaned back with his eyes closed. It was odd. Bloody odd. Prue had lived in France until November. McIntyre had lived in France until November. Was that significant?

Probably not, because McIntyre would probably still be living there now if he hadn't drowned.

THIRTEEN

DARREN NUDGED KEVIN'S arm. "Don't look now, but she's heading this way."

Kevin tugged at his school tie to loosen it. Carly Trueman had sought him out for the second time this week. It had to be him and not Darren she was after, because he'd been on his own on Monday when she'd run to catch him up.

Carly was gorgeous. Some kids teased her for being fat, but she wasn't. She was more curvy than the other girls, that was all. She had a big smile and an even bigger attitude.

He threw back his shoulders and walked taller. No way was he going to let on he'd noticed her, but he knew she was almost by his side.

Then she was there, her heavy schoolbag knocking against his hip.

"Hiya," he said, trying to look surprised.

"Hiya." She fell into step with them as they walked down the school's drive and out of the gates.

"I'm off," Darren said with a wink for Kevin. "Here's my dad and we're going straight to the football. See you tomorrow, Kev. See you, Carly."

"See you," Kevin said, feeling awkward now that he was alone with Carly.

"Are you walking home?" she asked him.

"Yeah. You?"

"Yeah. You coming my way, then?"

"Can do." It was half a mile out of his way, but it didn't matter. There was nothing worth rushing home for.

He could feel his ears burning scarlet with a mix of embarrassment and pride. He wished he could think of something to say to her, but she made him feel tongue-tied. It had been just the same on Monday afternoon.

According to school gossip, she'd just broken up with Lennon, who was by far the coolest kid in school. Lennon claimed he'd shagged her, and Kevin didn't know whether to believe that or not. She was only fifteen so he preferred to think that Lennon had lied.

"How are things at home?" she asked.

"Okay." He shrugged. "The same as ever."

"Your dad still not working?"

"Only at gambling and supping beer."

"It's a shame, isn't it?" she said. "I like your dad. When he was doing the taxiing, Mum always asked for him when we had to go to the hospital. She said he was reliable, friendly and helpful. And he was. I hated going to that place, but your dad always used to cheer me up. He was a good laugh."

Kevin couldn't remember the last time he'd heard someone say a kind word about his dad, and he felt something inside him thaw a little. Before his dad had lost his licence, and long before he decided to spend most of his life alternating between pub and bookies, he *had* been kind and helpful. He'd made Kevin laugh too.

"How is your nan anyway?" he asked.

Carly pulled a face. "She's up in Rosehill now so I don't have to see her very often. She never knows who I am when I do go. It's Alzheimer's."

"Right."

"It must be horrible getting old, mustn't it?"

"Gross," he said. "But probably better than not getting old."

"Yeah."

They walked on. Slowly.

"Do you fancy doing something tomorrow night?" Carly asked.

"Like what?" The question was casual enough but his heart was hammering fit to burst. He'd give all he had to go out with her. He had no idea if she'd shagged Lennon, but she was sure to have snogged him.

"I don't know. Just hang around."

"If you like," he said.

"Okay then." She gave him a broad smile. "Meet me outside the Raven at six, okay?"

"Okay."

They'd been walking close together but had to separate to avoid a woman striding in the opposite direction with two little dogs going every way but where they were supposed to. She tugged on their leads, but they were still intent on tripping up pedestrians.

Once they'd passed her, they walked closer together again. The smell from the fish and chip shop made Kevin's stomach rumble, and he wished he had enough money to buy some for them to share.

A dark car was parked at the back of the shop.

Carly nudged him. "What are you looking at?"

"What?" He'd been craning his neck and had to go closer for another look. "Oh, nothing. I thought that car was—no, nothing."

"You thought that car was what?"

"Nothing."

"Come on, Kev. Don't be a tease."

"I saw a bloke one night." He hadn't mentioned it to anyone but he didn't feel quite so silly telling Carly. "You know that woman Prue Murphy who was killed? It was on the telly and in all the papers."

"Of course I know. What about her?"

"Well, I was outside her house the night it happened. I'd been out with Darren and the rest of them and I stopped for a smoke on my way home. This bloke came from the side of the Murphy woman's house and got into a big blue car. Or black. I don't know. I only noticed the registration number."

"Bloody hell, Kev. You reckon you saw the burglar?"

"I don't know." The more he thought about it, the crazier it sounded. "He didn't look like a burglar. I can't really say because I didn't see him well enough. I'd recognise the car, but not him. But no, he didn't look like a burglar. There's not many of them pull up in posh cars, is there? I reckon he was wearing a suit too. Who heard of a burglar wearing a suit?"

Her eyes were wide with a mix of admiration and shock. "You should have gone to the police and told them."

"I couldn't. I'd been grounded that night. Anyway, like I said, I don't know that I'd recognise him again.

They wouldn't thank me for giving them half a registration plate and no description of the bloke, would they?"

"I don't know. I suppose not."

"Of course they wouldn't. And if Dad knew I'd gone out of the house that night, he'd go bloody spare."

She nodded in sympathy. Kevin didn't want sympathy.

"It was probably nothing," he said. "He wasn't carrying anything so he couldn't have been a burglar. He was probably just a visitor she'd had. He probably left her before the burglar got in. He looked at me a bit funny, but probably because he thought I was up to no good. I expect it was nothing. I was just wondering if that car behind the chippy was the same one, that's all."

"And was it?"

"No."

They reached Carly's house.

"See you tomorrow night then." Her smile was full of promise. "Be outside the Raven at six, okay? Don't be late."

"I won't."

Kevin walked on, his stride long and easy now. A smile lifted the corners of his mouth. He had a date with Carly. He only had a bloody date with Carly. She liked him, he knew it, and she was sure to let him snog her. *Roll on tomorrow night.*

FOURTEEN

DAVINA MCINTYRE'S HOME was everything Dylan had expected. He'd spent most of yesterday digging into the lives of McIntyre's family and friends, and had won himself an appointment with Martin Collins, son of McIntyre's agent, and with Mrs. McIntyre herself. He'd checked out estate agents on the internet and knew that houses in this area came with price tags in the region of eight to ten million pounds. The off-street parking alone would be worth a million pounds. Mrs. McIntyre's home was painted a clean white and boasted a gated front garden.

He climbed steep steps to the front door and prodded a brass bell push. The woman who answered his ring was late twenties or early thirties, too young to be Jack McIntyre's widow.

"You'll be Mr. Scott?" she guessed.

"That's right. Is Mrs. McIntyre here?"

"She isn't, I'm afraid. Sorry. She phoned to say she'd been stuck in traffic, but she shouldn't be too long. Would you like to wait for her?"

"If I could. It will save me another journey."

"Come in." She held the door open fully for him to pass and he stepped into a wide hallway.

"What a lovely home," he said.

"Isn't it?" She looked wistful. "I come to clean three mornings a week and even that's a joy. It's beautiful."

"A nice area, too, especially with the open spaces of Holland Park on the doorstep."

Smiling, she nodded. "Everything about it is perfect. I tell Davina she's got more bathrooms than I've had hot dinners. She just laughs."

"You get on well with her?"

"Oh, yes. She's very good to me and, like I say, I enjoy coming here." She stood still, seemed to have an inner debate with herself, and then said, "Come and have a look at the games room. She won't mind."

She led the way to the back of the house and into the games room. "My two boys would kill for this," she said.

It was vast and boasted a snooker table, easy chairs and card tables as well as its own shower room and kitchenette.

Dylan whistled. "How the other half live."

"I know. It's like something from another planet, isn't it?"

As far as Dylan knew, Davina McIntyre lived alone. It seemed a huge house for a single person to rattle around in. "Is she a keen snooker player?"

The cleaner laughed. "No. She has three sisters and a brother, though, and all their kids enjoy it. She had twelve people staying for Christmas, and the young ones spent all their time in here."

"I'm not surprised."

She gave him a mini-tour of the ground floor rooms—cosy sitting room, formal sitting room, huge dining room and vast kitchen—and was about to show him the garden when the front door opened and in walked Davina McIntyre.

"You'll be Mr. Scott," she said, walking forward with a slender hand outstretched. "I'm so sorry I'm late but the traffic's been a nightmare today. Has Shelley looked after you?"

He shook that slender hand. "She has. Thank you. And thank you for agreeing to see me, Mrs. McIntyre."

"Davina, please."

"Dylan."

"How could I not see you?" she said, smiling. "You have me intrigued, Dylan. Your call was very mysterious."

She was tall, slim and composed. Auburn hair framed a carefully made-up face. Long fingernails had been painted pink. According to the internet, not that anything on there could be taken as gospel, she was fifty-four. She appeared much younger until you looked more closely and saw tiny lines around her eyes and at the corners of her mouth. Everything about her and her movements was serene and calm. He couldn't imagine her ever being ruffled.

"I showed him the games room," Shelley said. "That was okay, wasn't it?"

"Of course." Davina laughed softly, explaining to Dylan, "Shelley is obsessed with my games room. I often wish I could dismantle it and carry it brick by brick to her garden."

"Like it would fit in my garden," Shelley scoffed in a good-natured way.

"Is it warm in there?" Davina asked.

"It is," Shelley said. "Shall I bring you some coffee or something through there?"

"Coffee would be perfect. What about you, Dylan? Coffee? Tea? Or would you prefer something stronger?"

Dylan had left his car at home and taken the tube to Kensington High Street, but polite circles would claim it was too early for anything stronger than coffee. "Coffee sounds good, thank you."

They walked on to the games room where she offered him a comfy armchair by a small table and took the one opposite. She was wearing a soft blue sweater and black trousers. Black shoes with tiny heels were slipped off and she curled her feet beneath her on the chair.

"So," she said, "now that your phone call has me so intrigued, you'd better tell me what I can do for you."

"Sorry, I didn't mean to sound mysterious. I'm a private investigator and I'm working for a woman whose sister was killed recently. Does the name Prue Murphy mean anything to you?"

"No. Should it?"

"It's possible, probable even, that Prue paid the price for disturbing a chance burglar. However, her sister isn't convinced. You see, Prue phoned her sister the night she died. She sounded worried. Frightened."

"I'm sorry to hear that," she said, "but what does it have to do with me?"

"When clearing her house, we found a painting, a miniature."

"One of Jack's?"

"Yes."

She unfolded her legs and stood up. "Excuse me a moment, Dylan."

She left the room, and returned a minute later with two miniatures in her hand. "Like these?"

Dylan took them from her and realised that once you'd seen one McIntyre painting, you'd recognise others. These were just like the one that had hung on Prue's wall. Hers had shown an old black phone and an air-mail envelope whereas one of these was of a train and a plane and the other showed a dinner plate and cutlery.

"It's odd," he said, "but I haven't been able to find much information about his miniatures. Few people seem to know about them."

"That's not odd at all because Jack didn't take them seriously. I don't know how many he did, but it wasn't many. They were just a bit of fun. They were like messages. This one—" she pointed to the dinner plate "—was a dinner invite. We'd had a quarrel about something, I can't remember what, and this was Jack's way of worming his way back into my good books. He wanted to have dinner with me. The other told me it was time we took a holiday." She smiled at his surprise. "Haven't you heard that a picture paints a thousand words, Dylan?"

"Yes, but I've never thought of paintings as messages. Wouldn't words get the message across more quickly?"

"Of course they would, but they wouldn't be as much fun, would they?" She took the miniatures from him and placed them on the table, then sat on the chair again with her feet tucked beneath her.

"The miniature we found in Prue Murphy's home was of an old black phone and an airmail envelope," he said. "What could that mean?"

She shrugged. "Only the person it was given to would know that."

"Something like 'Keep in touch' perhaps? Or maybe 'Don't call me, I'll call you'?"

"It could be. Who knows?"

Not Dylan.

"Prue Murphy couldn't afford one of your late husband's paintings, Davina, and she was an honest person. I was wondering if perhaps she was known to Mr. McIntyre, or to his friends. You're sure her name means nothing to you?"

"Positive."

She smiled as Shelley came into the room bearing coffee, biscuits and muffins. "Thanks, Shelley. You're a gem." She helped herself to a chocolate muffin and said for Dylan's benefit, "My biggest vice—I'm a cake fiend. Try one of Shelley's muffins. They're wonderful."

Dylan did so, and had to admit they were good.

"A friend of mine has a small shop," Davina said, "and she's going to sell them. Delicious, aren't they?"

"They are indeed."

It was a full five minutes before he was able to bring the subject back to Prue. "Is it possible your husband could have known her, do you think?" he asked.

"It's possible, I suppose. Was she young and pretty?"

"Yes."

"Then it's possible she once modelled for Jack," she said. "Or she may have been one of his fans. Young aspiring artists, especially female ones, adored him. Jack had charm, talent and money, and young people are attracted to such things. He adored them too. He appreciated beautiful things." She tucked a strand of hair behind her ear. "Jack was a wonderful man, Dylan. Everyone loved him. I fell in love with him when I was twenty-one and I never fell out of love."

She spoke slowly. Each word was thought about before being carefully delivered.

"I'm sorry," Dylan said. "His death must have been very difficult for you."

"Yes." She took a sip of her coffee and, again, flicked that strand of hair behind her ear. "I was a twenty-one-year-old art student when a friend and I decided to take a holiday in Paris. We thought we were so sophisticated and clever, and were so envious of the artists living there. We spent every minute we could with them." She was smiling as she spoke and looked years younger. "Jack had been living there for a year. He was twenty-nine then and unknown, but I knew he'd make it. I knew that, one day, people the world over would be appreciating his work."

"Love at first sight then," Dylan said with a smile.

"We married on my twenty-second birthday." She seemed to hug the memories close. "I thought I was the luckiest girl alive. I *knew* I was the happiest."

She'd probably forgotten Prue's name, but she was eager to talk about Jack McIntyre and Dylan was more than willing to listen.

"So—forgive me asking—the rumours about a forthcoming divorce are inaccurate?" Several respectable newspapers had speculated that the McIntyres were heading for the divorce courts.

"Totally. We'd been living apart for a while and, of course, journalists want a story, don't they? I had my life in London but Jack wanted to live the life of a beachcomber in France. I'm afraid I'm not the type to live in a two-room cottage."

"It would be a culture shock after this." He waved his arms to take in the room, the house and the select area of London.

"Yes. We certainly never talked about divorce though. We were happy with things as they were. Jack was making a point, that's all. He was trying to tell the world that he was starting a new life, the life *he* wanted. He was tired of painting and of being in the public eye. He had phases like that but they never lasted long. More than anything, he hated being ignored. He craved the adoration. If he'd thought people were forgetting him, he would soon have come running back to us." She sighed. "If he'd known what the future held—"

Once again, she left the room and returned with half a dozen photos and a newspaper clipping. "This is where he was living." She shook her head at such stupidity. "I mean, just look at it."

The cottage—Overlander—on the north coast of France looked idyllic. It was the sort of place for couples to enjoy a weekend away from the real world. It was too small to be classed a home but it would make the perfect weekend bolthole.

Davina lifted her cup and took a sip of coffee. "When I heard the news, I couldn't believe it. He was an expert sailor and a strong swimmer, you see, so I believed he'd turn up. I know they found the boat pretty quickly, but I felt sure he could have swum to shore. They said that the chances of the bodies being washed up were slim and, when they only found Jeremy's, I was convinced that Jack must still be alive. I expected to hear his voice every time I answered the phone. Or I thought he might be standing on the step when I opened the door."

Dylan nodded his understanding, but really, it was only in films that people survived weeks at sea by clinging to a convenient piece of driftwood, or were rescued by nuns having stumbled around a desert island with amnesia.

"I knew Jeremy was visiting him that day," she said. "I was hopeful that he'd be successful where we'd all failed. I thought a word from him might bring Jack back to the real world. I was waiting for good news. I certainly wasn't expecting the news I got. One minute I was waiting to hear that Jack had seen sense and was coming home, the next I was helping to organise a memorial service."

"A difficult task," Dylan said. "It must have been well attended. Was it held in London?"

"Of course."

"Did Jack's friends from France attend?"

She shrugged. "A few did, yes."

"Did you ever visit him in France?"

"No. I saw him when he came to England and, of course, we often spoke on the phone."

"And you're sure he never mentioned Prue Murphy?"

"Not that I recall. More coffee?"

"No. Thanks." He stood up. "It's time I was off, Davina. I've already taken up too much of your time."

"Are you sure you won't have another coffee?"

She wanted the company. She'd loved McIntyre and lost him and Dylan supposed that people willing to talk about the love of her life were few and far between. "Thanks, but I must go."

As he walked down the road to the tube station, Dylan wondered why she'd lied to him. Three times he'd asked if Prue's name meant anything to her and three times she'd denied all knowledge. She'd lied. Dylan was sure of it.

FIFTEEN

AFTER LEAVING DAVINA McIntyre, Dylan took the tube to Victoria, passed time with a coffee and a sandwich, and then went to the Blair Gallery to keep his appointment with Martin Collins.

The building was fairly nondescript from the outside. Only a stainless steel plaque by large wooden doors told people that it was in fact an art gallery.

The interior was spacious and airy with tall ceilings. Half a dozen bright canvases adorned the walls and beneath each one was a discreet Price on Application tag. Dylan supposed that if you had to ask, you couldn't afford them.

He approached a woman sitting behind a curved desk. "I have an appointment with Martin Collins."

"I'll let him know you're here. What name is it?"

"Dylan Scott. Thanks."

She picked up the phone, announced Dylan's arrival and, a couple of minutes later, a man of about Dylan's age strode across the floor. He was about five feet ten, with thinning dark hair and rimless glasses. He wore black jeans and a bright pink shirt. "Dylan Scott?"

"Yes."

"Good to meet you, Dylan. I'm Martin. And I'm up to my eyes in an installation this morning. Do you mind if I work while we talk? What is it I can do for you? The installation's this way. We can talk while we walk."

Christ. Dylan wondered if he'd ever get a word in. Martin Collins was one of those energetic types that made you long to shove a tranquilliser down his throat. Whereas Davina McIntyre had been calm and serene, this bloke was a bundle of nervous energy.

"As I explained on the phone, I'm interested in your association with Jack McIntyre," Dylan said. "I'm actually a private investigator and—"

"Really?" Collins stopped mid-stride. "And what interest would you have in Jack?"

"My client's sister was killed and—"

"Oh?" Collins carried on walking but his pace was slower.

"Yes. Now, it could be that she disturbed a burglar. However, when emptying her house, we came across one of McIntyre's miniatures."

"Really?"

"Yes, and I'm trying to find out how she came to have such a thing."

"I see." Collins pushed open a tall wooden door and they entered a space, closed to the public, that could have housed a small aircraft. "This is the new installation. As you can see, there's plenty of work to be done yet."

To Dylan, it looked like the makings of a scrap yard. Chunks of metal, mostly car innards, sat in piles. Whether they'd been arranged in those piles, he didn't know. He did know that what some people called art, he called bullshit.

"But it can wait a few minutes." Collins added a rueful, "Besides, it looks as if everyone's decided to take a coffee break. Now, you were saying?"

"The McIntyre miniature. I'm trying to find out how it came to be in my client's sister's house."

"Sorry, but I can't help. We never had any dealings with his miniatures, you see. They were Jack's idea of a joke, and they were private. He gave them to friends if and when the mood took him."

"They're very valuable jokes," Dylan said.

"They are now, but, as I said, we had nothing to do with them." He walked over to a stepladder, picked up a clipboard and ticked off a couple of items before returning his attention to Dylan. "Now, if you're wanting to sell it, I am in touch with several collectors. Describe it to me."

"It shows a phone, one of the old-fashioned black ones, and an airmail envelope, but I don't think my client is looking for a buyer just yet."

Collins shook his head. "That means nothing to me, but it wouldn't. As I said, he used to give them away as gifts. That was up to him. People are eager to get their hands on his work, any work. Since his death prices have rocketed."

"So it seems. I've spoken to Mrs. McIntyre and she says the miniatures are messages. Is that right?"

"Messages. Jokes. They're whatever Jack decided they should be."

"I see. Tell me, did you know McIntyre well?"

"Fairly well, yes. My father was his friend as well as

his agent so they spent a lot of time together. Jack was a regular visitor to our house."

"I'm sorry about your father."

"Thank you. Life goes on," Collins said.

"I believe he visited McIntyre on the day of the accident to try and persuade him to take up painting again. Is that right?"

"That's—" He broke off as three young men and a woman came into the room. "Excuse me, Dylan."

He left Dylan and went to issue instructions as to where each piece must go. This involved a lot of pointing at items on the clipboard and a lot of discussion. As he walked back to Dylan, he was shrugging his shoulders as if he was trying to banish tension from his neck muscles.

"Sorry about that," he said. "I need to fetch some plans from my office. Do you mind if we talk while we walk?"

Dylan did, but he had to be grateful for anything. "Of course not."

"My father—yes, he'd tried several times to convince Jack to paint again but, that time, he was more hopeful. He was ever the optimist. I'd wanted to go with him, but I was at an exhibition and I couldn't get out of that. I thought that if I went and explained to Jack such basic things like us all needing the income, he might come round. But there, I couldn't go and—well, it's all academic now, isn't it?"

"Yes."

They took a crowded lift to the third floor. When

that ejected them, they walked along the corridor to an office at the end.

"This is home to me," Collins said with a tight smile as he surveyed the cramped conditions. "There." He prodded a large framed photo on the wall. "That's me at the Jodi Trench exhibition." At Dylan's blank expression, he explained, "It was taken the same evening that my father and Jack took the boat out."

"Oh, I see."

But Dylan didn't see. He was trying to find out if McIntyre, or one of his friends, could have known Prue and given her a miniature. Why would Collins, who looked too busy and stressed to be bothered about anything so trivial as his father's death, take the time to show him that photo?

"I mean—if it hadn't been for that exhibition," Collins said, "I might have gone out on Jack's boat with him and my father. I could have been drowned too."

"Ah, yes."

People seemed willing to talk about McIntyre but no one seemed in the least interested in Prue Murphy. Dylan would have to make them interested.

"To get back to my client," he said. "Does the name Prue Murphy mean anything to you?"

"It doesn't, I'm afraid." Collins was busy gathering up papers.

"So could you tell me how someone might get hold of a McIntyre miniature?"

Collins stopped. He looked taken aback by the question. "I have no idea how your—what was her name?"

Give me strength. "Prue Murphy."

"Right, well, I'm afraid I have no idea how she got it. Did she know Jack?"

"That's what I'm trying to find out."

"If she did, he may have given it to her." He gave a sly smile. "I'm afraid I didn't know Jack's lady friends."

"Oh? Were there many?"

Dark eyebrows shot up. "Just a few."

"Really? The only person I've spoken to who knew Jack McIntyre is his wife. Widow."

"Davina won't tell you about them. She was able to close her mind to them. Jack, you'll learn, changed his women as often as most of us change our shirts. Your friend—Prue Murphy—was she young, pretty, artistic?"

That was almost the same question Davina had asked him.

"She was thirty-four, pretty and—yes, she studied art, and she was designing her own jewellery. She was also broke. She lived in France, and worked at anything. Waiting tables, stuff like that."

Collins nodded. "She sounds as if she'd have been exactly Jack's type."

"I wonder how they could have met though."

Collins shrugged. "Who knows? And now, if you don't mind, I need to get back to the installation."

"Of course. It's time I was off anyway."

They headed back to the lift.

"Your gallery seems to be doing well," Dylan remarked.

"It's promising," Collins said. "I'm just starting to do some work—since Dad died, I mean. He wouldn't agree with me, but he was a little stuck in his ways and the whole place needed updating. Now that it's mine, I can crack on and update it. Of course, financially it's not particularly easy. Lawyers take forever to sort out someone's estate, don't they? Still, at least they are sorting it. I suppose Davina told you about Jack's house in Cornwall?"

"No."

"She's adamant that Jack bought it for her, which is feasible because she has family down there, but of course she can't gain access to it. She's hopping mad about it but there's nothing that can be done. It'll be years before Jack's estate can be sorted out."

"Why's that?"

"French law is involved for a start," Collins said, "and, of course, without a body, he's only officially missing. Missing presumed dead."

"Is she the sole beneficiary?"

"I couldn't say. She's the *main* beneficiary, I know that." The lift deposited them on the ground floor. "Right, I must crack on. Good to meet you, Dylan, and if you decide to sell that miniature, you know where I am."

"I do. Thanks for your time, Martin. I appreciate it."

SIXTEEN

KEVIN HAD NEVER known time to drag by so slowly. Since walking home from school with Carly yesterday, it was as if each minute had lasted an hour and each day a week. He'd only seen her in school a couple of times today and hadn't managed to say anything to her other than "See you tonight."

"Don't be late," she'd said, her smile teasing.

He *would* be late if he didn't get a move on. No matter how fast he shoved sausage and chips in his mouth, his plate remained half-full. His mum ate as slowly as usual and his dad, elbows on the table, was more interested in reading the paper. He ate with one hand and turned pages with the other. It was rare for his dad to put in an appearance this early, especially on a Friday, and Kevin wished he hadn't.

"I've got to go in a minute," Kevin said.

"Go? Go where?" his dad asked.

"I told you. I've got football practice." He hadn't mentioned anything about the nonexistent football practice before, but he hoped his dad would assume he'd been too drunk to remember. "I need to be there by six."

"Up at the school?" his mum asked.

"Of course. And if I'm not there by six, I'll be in trouble."

"Well, that's good, isn't it, Ron? Good that the school want him in the team."

"So long as you don't expect me to fork out for new boots and kit every other fortnight," his dad said.

"What I've got is fine." That part at least was true. His old boots might pinch his feet but he could still squeeze into them. He swallowed the last of his chips. "Can I go now then?"

"Of course you can, love," his mum said. "We don't want you in trouble with the school, do we? What time will you be back?"

"It might be late." Kevin was getting good at thinking on his feet. "After we've finished, they want us to sort some stuff out in the gym. The practice will finish at about nine or half-past. It could be half-past ten by the time we've finished in the gym. I expect I'll be back by eleven. You said that was okay when I don't have school the next day."

"Make sure you come straight home," his dad said.

"I will."

Kevin grabbed the bag that was stuffed with his football kit and walked out the house. His shoulders sagged in relief with every step. A quick glance at his watch told him that if he cut though the cemetery, he'd easily be at the Raven by six.

The cemetery was dark and spooky. He was grateful to people who put small lanterns on the graves of their loved ones, as any small light helped dispel the creepiness. He dropped his bag behind a gravestone, made a mental note to come back this way to collect it, and ran down the bank into the town centre.

He was breathless by the time he arrived but at least he was warm. There was supposed to be snow coming any day, but Kevin would believe that when he saw it. He loved snow. He still had his sledge in the garage and he wasn't too old to enjoy racing down the hills on it. The snow that fell in March was always rubbish though. They never had enough to stick at this time of the year.

He stamped his feet as he stood outside the Raven. The pub was busy and he tried not to look the customers in the eye as they came and went. It wouldn't be good for his health if one of his dad's drinking pals spotted him hanging around outside.

Minutes ticked by and the warmth he'd generated by running deserted him. He shoved his hands in his pockets and wished he'd worn his thick coat. Another look at his watch. It was six-twenty.

Perhaps she wasn't coming. Maybe this was her idea of a joke. Why would she be interested in him? She'd been Lennon's girl and Kevin couldn't complete with Lennon in any way. Lennon was taller, better looking, good at sport and his parents were loaded.

"Hey, it's freezing. I hope you're going to keep me warm, Kevin Mills."

He swung round, glad the darkness hid the red blush that he could feel spreading across his face. "I thought you weren't coming."

"I said I would, didn't I?"

"Yeah."

She tucked her arm through his and Kevin *really* hoped his dad's drinking pals didn't see him. "What do you fancy doing?" she asked.

Kevin hadn't thought that far ahead. "I don't mind."

"We could get a couple of cans from Ali's and drink them down by the bridge."

"What? Beer?"

She hooted with laughter. "Unless you want a lemonade, Joker. Come on."

He didn't mind the buying beer part, he could just about afford a couple of cans, but going down to the bridge wasn't very appealing. Everyone went there and he'd wanted to be alone with her. Still, he wasn't going to complain. This was their first date, after all. Hopefully, there would be others.

Ali's shop was enjoying a brisk trade. It usually was because it was rarely closed and Ali made sure it stocked everything that anyone might need. It was almost impossible to find that one thing you needed, but it was sure to be there. Tall shelves were piled high.

"Shall we get a pack of six?" Carly asked. "I'll go halves and it's only fifty pence more than the four."

"Okay."

They grabbed the tins and took them to the counter where Ali's wife stood guard over the till. Kevin wondered what she looked like behind the burka she wore. Ali was a chatty man with a sense of humour but his wife never said anything other than what you owed her. Still, at least she didn't demand proof of age ID.

They left the shop and walked on down to the bridge with the cans safely tucked under Kevin's arm.

"Have you seen that bloke again?" Carly asked. "You know, the bloke who came out of that dead woman's house?"

"No. Well, I don't think so. How would I know? I told you, I wouldn't recognise him."

It started to rain, and they quickened their pace until they reached the bridge. As Kevin had guessed, there were half a dozen other kids there. There weren't many places to go in Dawson's Clough if you wanted a drink. The pubs were strict on underage drinking, and coppers kept an eye on the town centre and made sure everyone remembered it was an alcohol-free zone. People gathered under the bridge where it was dry and protected from the wind. The river was only about ten feet across and the paths on either side had big stones that made fairly comfortable seats.

Kevin knew the others. Four were in his year at school. They were drinking and smoking and generally larking around. He was glad he'd come, especially when Carly put her arms round him for warmth. He felt good showing everyone that she was his girl.

The others drifted off soon after ten o'clock.

"I'd better be going soon," Carly said when they were alone. "Let's finish this last can and then go, yeah?"

"Right." He tugged on the ring pull, took a swig from the can and handed it to her.

"Thanks."

Now that they were alone, Kevin couldn't think of a single thing to say. His mind was a blank. He made a fuss of lighting a cigarette and smoking that.

"We'd better go," Carly said when the can was empty. "I'll be in all sorts of trouble if I'm late in."

"Come on then." Secretly, he was pleased he wouldn't

be late. He didn't relish walking through the cemetery at this hour but he mustn't forget his football kit.

She tucked her arm through his as they walked through the town centre. People were coming out of the pubs and calling at the fish and chip shop or the kebab shop for their suppers. A couple of police cars crawled along looking for signs of trouble.

It seemed no time at all before they were standing, awkwardly in Kevin's case, outside Carly's house.

"That was good fun, wasn't it?" she said.

"We'll do it again sometime, shall we?" he asked.

She put her arms round his waist and lifted her face. "Tomorrow too soon for you?"

"Er, no."

"Good."

Afterwards, walking home, he tried to remember if he'd kissed her first or if she'd kissed him. He was pretty sure she'd kissed him. Either way, it had been the best thing ever. Ever.

He broke into a run with an enormous smile on his face.

He had to go back into the town centre to get home, but he didn't care. There were still quite a few people around. A lot were happy after a night in the pub. Perhaps Dawson's Clough wasn't such a bad place after all.

He was walking past the square when he saw the car. He wouldn't have recognised it if it hadn't been for the registration plate. It was dark blue. And it was empty.

Kevin crossed the road for a better look. A couple of yards away, a man was talking into his phone. Kevin had told Carly he wouldn't recognise the man who'd been outside the Murphy woman's house that night, but he did.

The chap recognised him too. He snapped his phone shut. "Well, well, well. We meet again."

Beer sloshed around in Kevin's gut making him want to throw up. He took a step back.

"Ah, so you do recognise me," the man said. "That's a pity."

"Why? I haven't told anyone. I won't tell anyone. A mate said I should go to the police, but I haven't. I won't." Realising he'd contradicted himself, he gulped in a terrified breath of cold night air. "I don't care what you were doing at her house. Truly. You can trust me."

SEVENTEEN

DYLAN FOUND IT difficult to remember that this flat had once been his home. When Bev had thrown him out, telling him he was a "drunkard and a bloody loser," she'd found this awful flat for him and he hadn't been here a week before his mother had turned up on his doorstep. He shuddered at the memory. Life had been hell and he'd hated everything about this glorified shoebox.

When he'd returned to the marital home, his mother had stayed on here. She'd been looking for somewhere to buy ever since but was no further forward. She looked settled here, and Dylan had to admit that the flat looked nothing like it had when he'd lived in it. It was full of colour for one thing. Bright pictures broke up white walls, butterfly mobiles hung from ceilings, rugs and cushions adorned floors and furniture.

It was still small though. Still cramped. Far too small for a party of six. Dylan, Bev and the kids had been invited to lunch to meet the new man in his mother's life. Boris. Who the hell looked at a newborn baby and called the poor bugger Boris?

His mother didn't look particularly excited. She was busy lighting candles and inhaling burning incense.

You needed strong lungs to survive in Vicky Scott's company for long.

Not trusting her choice of drinks, Dylan had brought along a couple of bottles of decent wine. He opened one and filled two glasses, one for him and one for Bev. His mother rarely drank alcohol. She preferred nettle tea or whatever her favourite evil-tasting concoction of the moment was.

"What time's he coming?" Bev asked her.

"Twelve-thirty," Vicky said, "and I don't want you getting any ideas. I don't want him getting any either. He's just an old friend. We had fun when we were out in Turkey but that's forty years ago. People change. They become staid."

"You haven't." Dylan would love her to become staid. Or just plain normal would do.

Vicky didn't argue with that. "I don't think I'll see him again."

Dylan had been hoping that Boris would whisk her back to Turkey or maybe make a home with her on the Isle of Man but that hope was receding. It seemed that Boris wasn't exciting enough for her. Few men were.

"How's the nut casserole coming along?" he asked and she looked at him in surprise.

"How did you know we were having nut casserole?"

"Oh, just a lucky guess."

Out of the corner of his eye, he saw Bev smiling to herself as she played around with Freya. Luke, as always, followed his grandmother around like a shadow. As odd at it was, he adored the woman.

"Does the table look all right?" Vicky asked.

"For someone who's not really interested, you're very concerned about that table," Bev said. "And yes, it looks lovely. Perfect. He'll be very impressed."

Vicky pulled a face. "I'm not out to impress him. But let's have a nice afternoon, shall we?"

"Of course we will," Bev said as if there had never been any doubt. "Our taxi's booked for three so you'll have plenty of time alone with him."

"Ha. Away with you."

Dylan would rather be at home getting ready for the morning. His first job after leaving Collins's gallery had been to phone his one-time boss, Frank.

"Tell me it's crazy to go to France," he'd said.

"I'd like to," Frank had replied, "but it's probably what I'd do. It's the unexpected things that make cases interesting, and a Jack McIntyre miniature is very unexpected."

"Do you fancy coming along for a pub crawl?"

"God, yes. Anything to get me away from the clinging vine."

The clinging vine was Frank's neighbour. Esme was an over-friendly woman determined to be the fourth Mrs. Willoughby. Frank was adamant there would be no fourth Mrs. Willoughby.

"When are you planning to go?" Frank had asked.

"The sooner the better. Tomorrow?"

"Suits me. I'm not sure what time the first train to London leaves on a Sunday but I'll be on it…"

Bev thought he was crazy to go and she was probably right.

He was dragged from his thoughts by the doorbell.

His mother ran fingers through her hair, presumably to tidy it although it had the opposite effect, before going to answer it.

Boris, a smiling man in his sixties, came into the room and introductions were made all round. Dylan was shocked to see such a normal-looking bloke. He wasn't sure what he'd been expecting—long hair and a Love and Peace T-shirt at the very least—but he hadn't expected someone so ordinary.

Bev must have been equally surprised because she was so busy staring at him that she didn't notice his outstretched hand.

He was around the five-feet-ten mark with dark hair that was sprinkled with grey. There was something familiar about him but Dylan was damned if he could think what it was.

Surprisingly, he'd brought wine and flowers. Decent wine too.

Any fool could see that this man wasn't Vicky Scott's type. He didn't look as if he knitted yoghurt for one thing. He looked too sensible and respectable to have anything in common with Dylan's dope-smoking mother.

Lunch—if you could call munching your way through a nut casserole lunch—was a strange affair. The conversation flowed as easily as the wine, but Dylan's mum was adrift with her memories and it was Bev who was watching Boris's every move and hanging on his every word. She was fascinated by the man.

Freya had eaten before they left home and slept through the whole thing. Dylan was envious.

Luke ate as he usually did. As if he hadn't been fed for six months.

Boris had his own courier business although he was looking forward to retirement so was delegating more and more. He'd been married and divorced, then married again. He was a widower now as his second wife had died eighteen months ago. He'd lived just over a mile from Dylan for the past twenty years.

"I can't tell you how good it was to bump into Vicky again after all these years," he said, smiling fondly. "We had great times together, didn't we, Vicky?"

She looked at him, smiled and nodded. "The best."

"We were young and foolish," Boris said with a laugh. "When I think back—" He shook his head as if he couldn't believe the antics of the young and foolish people they'd been. "Still, we grew up eventually. That's the main thing, isn't it?"

"Do you have children?" Bev asked him.

"No. My first wife couldn't have them. We had dogs instead," he said with a wry smile. "We never had less than two at any one time. Then, when I married again, well—it was too late for children." He talked of plans he had for his retirement. "What I'd really like to do is hire a Harley-Davidson and drive along Route 66. Imagine that."

Dylan looked at his mother, thinking she'd see this as a wonderful adventure, but she was concentrating on her food, a quiet smile on her face. He could imagine her riding pillion on a huge Harley with the wind in her hair and a joint in her hand.

After lunch, they chatted easily about the economy,

the government and the weather, and Dylan was surprised to find that he liked Boris. He said as much to Bev in the taxi on the way home.

"He's lovely, isn't he?" she said.

Dylan watched the driver to make sure he took a left turn up ahead. The cunning bastards would take a much longer route to his house if they were in the mood. This one, however, turned left so Dylan sat back and relaxed.

"Dylan?"

"Yes?"

"Did you notice anything—anything about him? About Boris?"

"Like what?"

"Like the way he looked."

"No. Well, I did think he reminded me of someone, but I couldn't think who it was."

"He reminded me of someone too," she said.

"Oh? Who?"

She was a long time answering and when she finally did speak, Dylan thought he must have misheard.

"You."

EIGHTEEN

FOR THE FIRST time ever, Sarah wished Ron would stick to his Saturday ritual and go to the pub or the bookies. He kept uttering meaningless platitudes until she could no longer bear to look at him.

"He'll be all right," he said. "He'll have stayed with one of his mates and be too scared to tell us. Knowing them, they had a few beers too many and are too hungover to even think about crawling home."

Sarah nodded, but as hard as she tried, she couldn't believe it. That wasn't the son she knew and loved. He might be a bit rebellious right now, and she knew he wasn't particularly happy, but he knew the difference between right and wrong and he wouldn't let them worry unnecessarily.

"You know what sixteen-year-olds are like," Ron said. "Look at the trouble I used to get in."

Sarah wanted to scream at him.

"Maybe he's gone further afield," Ron said.

She tried to calm down but her heart was pounding in her ears and she was a breath away from losing control.

She should have called the police last night. If it hadn't been for Ron, she would have. She'd sat up till gone midnight but had then climbed into bed because she hadn't wanted Ron to know that Kevin was still out. At best, there would have been a blazing row. Ron had been drinking for hours so it might have been even worse.

She'd woken early, before six o'clock, and had gone straight to Kevin's bedroom. His bed hadn't been slept in.

At first, she'd thought, like Ron, that he'd stayed the night at a friend's house. If he'd called to ask if he could, his dad would have said no so he wouldn't have bothered. He was sixteen and believed he should be treated like an adult whereas Ron treated him like a ten-year-old. Sometimes, Sarah thought Ron said no to everything just to make himself feel better, to kid himself that he still had some control and influence.

At eight o'clock, she'd phoned his friends' parents but no one had seen him. No one knew anything about football practice at the school last night either. Just before nine, she'd phoned the police.

Two young constables had knocked on the door less than half an hour later. They'd asked questions—what had Kevin been wearing? where did he say he was going? who was he friendly with? had anything been troubling him?

Sarah had answered their questions as best she could but each one had sent a dart of pure fear through her heart.

The policemen had spoken reassuringly. They'd smilingly told her that sixteen-year-olds never think about the consequences of staying out of the house. Every police officer in the county would be looking for Kevin, they'd said.

It was almost three o'clock now and Sarah's terror was increasing with every passing minute so that she was struggling to breathe. Panic made her dizzy, caused her throat to dry up and her heart to race.

She'd made them several cups of tea, most of which had remained untouched, but they'd had no breakfast or lunch. She couldn't face food and, when she'd offered to get Ron something, he'd said he'd have something later.

She gasped as a dark shadow passed the window seconds before the doorbell rang.

"I'll get it, love." Ron was already on his feet.

He returned to the kitchen with a young man following him.

"Hello, Mrs. Mills. Sarah, isn't it? I'm Detective Sergeant Alan Green. I don't have any real news, but I'm the officer in charge and, believe me, we're doing all we can to find your son."

Sarah nodded, but she couldn't speak for the wedge of fear in her throat.

"Shall we sit down?" the sergeant asked.

"Yes. Sorry. Come on through here," Ron said.

They trooped into the sitting room. Sarah, worried that her legs wouldn't support her, sank onto the sofa. Ron sat beside her and the sergeant stood for a moment gazing out the window. When he turned round, he gave them a confident smile and sat in the armchair.

"If Kevin was going from here to the town centre," he said, "which way would he go?"

Sarah frowned, puzzled by the question. "Well, if he was in a hurry, he'd cut through the cemetery."

Sergeant Green looked worried, she thought. And young. God, he didn't look much older than Kevin.

"That makes sense then," he said. "We've found the bag containing his football kit. It was behind one of the gravestones in the cemetery."

He gave them a moment to let that sink in. Except it didn't. Ron reached for her hand and gave it a squeeze.

"What was it doing there?" Ron asked.

"We've spoken to some of his friends, and we know that he met up with a young girl, a Carly Trueman, at six o'clock last night. If he'd told you he was meeting her, would you have allowed him to go?"

"Well—" Ron didn't have an answer to that one.

"It depends," Sarah said. A girl? He'd met a girl?

"If it was important to him, might he have invented the football practice as an excuse?" Sergeant Green asked.

"Yes." Sarah knew it was possible. "Who is this girl?"

"She's a school friend of Kevin's," he said, and he looked sad that they didn't know. But how would they know? There were eight hundred pupils at the school and they knew very few of them. "Carly said they had a few cans of beer under Cooperative Bridge and then Kevin walked her home. He left her shortly before eleven o'clock and, as far as she knows, he was intending to come straight home."

"So what did he do? Was he all right then? Did that girl say he was all right? Was he unwell? Is that it?"

"She said he was fine. He was in good spirits."

"How much had he had to drink?" Ron asked.

"Three cans of beer. Maybe four."

"Oh, God." Sarah bit her lip. The physical pain was far easier to bear than the mental anguish. "If he was drunk, anything could have happened to him. What about the hospital? We should call the hospital?"

"There's no record of anyone fitting Kevin's description being admitted to any of the medical centres last night."

The questions went on, and Sarah felt as if she was discussing a stranger. It didn't seem possible that her Kevin had lied about football practice to meet up with a girl. It didn't seem possible that he'd—vanished.

Two more police officers arrived.

"We need to look at Kevin's room," Sergeant Green said. "Also, you said you'd find a better photo for us."

While the officers searched through Kevin's bedroom for any clue as to where he might have gone, Sarah went to the kitchen, where she'd put half a dozen recent photos of Kevin. In each one, he was smiling and carefree. She hoped now that, wherever he was, he was smiling. She longed to see him walk into the house, bang the doors, throw his coat down and head straight for the bread bin or the biscuit jar.

She handed over the photos.

"Thank you." Sergeant Green gave her arm a reassuring squeeze that didn't reassure at all. "We're doing everything we can to find your son, Sarah."

NINETEEN

NOW THAT THEY were actually in France, Dylan knew Bev was right. This *was* completely insane. Prue Murphy had been murdered in Dawson's Clough and that's where he should be asking questions.

They'd spent all of yesterday in Paris talking to people who'd known Prue—residents of the building where she'd lived, staff at the café where she'd worked, local shopkeepers. Without exception, these people remembered Prue fondly and had been shocked and saddened to learn of her death. Many had received Christmas cards from her. None, however, had heard her mention Jack McIntyre. No one knew of any paintings or anything of value she'd owned.

He'd hoped someone might confirm that she'd been a friend of McIntyre's. But so what if they had? It meant nothing.

This morning, Dylan was driving along the picturesque coastal road in search of McIntyre's cottage. Frank, sitting beside him, was too busy admiring the scenery to say much. If the directions they had were correct, all they had to do was keep on this road through the village and carry on for another couple of miles.

It was easier to look for McIntyre's cottage than think about Bev's wild theories. Dylan had told her in no uncertain terms that no way on God's earth did Boris look like him. He just didn't. She must have drunk more wine than he'd thought. Dylan had spent many years wondering who his father might be, and he still had no idea, but he did know that it wasn't Boris. It was ridiculous. He pushed the notion from his mind.

The village was small but undeniably pretty with gardens a mass of cheerful colour. Sadly, a sky heavy with grey cloud didn't do it justice.

"I can't see us having much of a pub crawl tonight," Frank said.

They hadn't had much of one last night either. France, it seemed, closed on Sundays.

"No. I've spied two restaurants and one small bar so far."

"The French have always been more interested in their food than their drink."

"They're good with wine. And champagne." Dylan drove out of the village, and continued along the coast road.

"It's not what you'd call populated, is it?" Frank said.

The road, more track than road, was deserted. All Dylan could see was countryside to his right and sea to his left. The sea was the same dull colour as the sky.

"That's what McIntyre wanted," Dylan said. "He wanted to get away from the public eye. Or so everyone says. I'd never heard of him so I can't imagine he was beating off the paparazzi at every turn."

"But you're a complete numbskull when it comes to art."

Dylan grinned. "I prefer to believe that people who'll

pay upwards of sixty grand for a three-by-three painting are the numbskulls."

"There's a shed." Frank pointed. "And there's a cottage. That must be it."

"Must be. Yes, because here's the track." Dylan turned off the road and winced as his Morgan bounced off deep ruts. "Who the hell would want to live here?"

"Someone who wanted to get away from the world."

The track to the cottage didn't look as if it had been used since Adam was a lad. It meandered halfway to the beach and then stopped. If McIntyre had owned a car, he would have had a hundred yards to carry his groceries from track to cottage.

"And squatters perhaps," Frank added.

They abandoned the Morgan and crossed the pebbly foreshore to the tiny cottage. It was so small that the ground floor would have fitted comfortably in Davina McIntyre's games room.

"Do you think this is it?" Dylan asked.

Frank nodded to a wooden sign by the door. "There can't be too many cottages called Overlander near the village, can there?"

Dylan peered through a window into a small sitting room. A couple of books lay on a table, patiently waiting for their owner to return. An empty yellow jug sat in the window. An old wooden clock showed the correct time. It was as if the cottage's owner had simply stepped out to stroll along the shore.

"It's the perfect home for a painter," Frank said.

"What makes you say that? In any case, he wasn't. A painter I mean. He'd quit."

Frank was looking through another window. "Look at this room. The windows, the light—an ideal studio."

"But he wasn't painting," Dylan said again.

"Once a painter, always a painter."

This room was larger but empty except for a sofa, a couple of wooden cupboards and a square table. Apart from that and the sitting room, there was a tiny kitchen that looked out to sea. Dylan guessed there would be a bathroom and either one or two bedrooms upstairs.

Fifty yards away was the shed or, more likely, boat-house. Without speaking, they walked over to inspect it. It only had two small windows and a look through those showed them nothing of interest. Apart from a few tools, half a dozen plastic containers and several metres of coiled rope, it was empty.

They stood and gazed out to sea, where gulls circled and tried to deafen them.

"I'd like a place like this," Frank said.

"It would be a long walk to the pub."

"A mile and a half? Two miles? That would be a pleasant stroll on a summer's evening."

They walked back to the cottage and peered through the windows again. There wasn't a speck of dust to be seen so someone had to be keeping an eye on it until the French authorities allowed McIntyre's estate to be wound up.

The sound of a car's engine had Dylan looking up. "We've got company, Frank."

A battered beige Citroën parked next to the Morgan and the passenger, a round woman carrying a basket, strode toward them to deliver a torrent of abuse in French.

"I expect that translates as 'What the fuck are you doing here?'" Frank murmured.

The woman, fresh-faced and pushing sixty, might be harmless enough but her companion currently crossing the ground in long, angry strides was built along the lines of an armoured tank.

"Do you speak English?" Dylan asked him.

"Well enough to tell you you're trespassing."

He was English. Up close, he was huge. Beneath a grubby black coat with dozens of zipped pockets, he wore a checked red shirt that strained to cover his massive chest. Thankfully, of the two, the woman looked more eager for a fight.

"Yes, sorry about that," Dylan said. "We're from England and—well, it's a long story but we're looking for someone who might have known Jack McIntyre."

"Then you're in luck. You've found two of us." Even his voice was big, deep and strong.

"And you are?" Frank asked.

"We're the caretakers. And you're still trespassing."

"Then let me make introductions," Dylan said. "This is DCI Frank Willoughby—"

Dylan had no intention of mentioning that Frank was retired and had only come along for the pub crawl, but Frank went one better. He reached into his pocket and pulled out ID that was inspected.

"I'm Dylan Scott. And you're—?"

"I'm Elliott Tolman. This is my wife, Coletta. Like I said, we're caretakers. Coletta used to keep house for

Jack and I did a few odd jobs. Now, we both keep an eye on the place."

Dylan put out his hand and it was reluctantly shaken.

Tolman clearly wasn't impressed by being in the presence of a DCI. He seemed slightly happier with the situation than his wife but still looked as if he wanted to break every bone in their bodies. Twice.

Those grey clouds had turned an angry black, and a few plump raindrops landed on them.

"We spoke to Davina, Mr. McIntyre's widow, and she gave us this address," Dylan said. Davina *had* given him the address of this cottage, but only because he'd made a mental note when looking at the photos and newspaper clipping she'd shown him.

Tolman spoke to his wife in French. She looked at Dylan and Frank, then began stomping across the pebbles to the cottage. They all followed. She took a bunch of keys from her pocket and opened the door to the cottage. They trooped inside.

With four of them in the minuscule kitchen, it was difficult to breathe. Somehow, someone had crammed a cooker, a small fridge-freezer and a washing machine into the room. The walls were covered not with paintings as one might have expected but with framed black-and-white photographs of beach scenes.

"The case we're working on—" Dylan began. "Amongst a woman's possessions, we found one of Mr. McIntyre's paintings. A miniature. We're trying to find out if the woman in question knew him."

"You talk to Mrs. Davina?" Coletta asked.

"Yes," Dylan said.

"That's why we're here." Frank gave her his most reassuring smile.

Dylan took the dog-eared photo of Prue from his pocket and held it out. "We need to know if this woman knew Jack McIntyre."

Tolman took it from him and seemed to flinch. Without saying a word, he handed it to his wife.

"Prue!" Coletta squinted at Dylan. "Why you want to know about Prue?"

"You know her?" Frank asked.

"Of course." Coletta looked to her husband and clearly regretted admitting as much. He simply shrugged.

"She was a friend of Mr. McIntyre's?" Dylan asked.

Coletta looked at Tolman again and received another shrug. "Of course," she said.

"Why do you want to know?" Tolman asked.

Dylan thought about suggesting they move to another room, one where they could swing a cat if they chose to, but he wasn't going to push his luck. Tolman still looked anything but friendly.

"I'm afraid Prue is dead," Dylan said.

Coletta's English wasn't good, but she understood that. A hand flew to her mouth as if she needed to stop herself crying out.

"Dead?" Her voice was a shocked whisper. "But how? She was so young. Always so healthy."

Her English was a lot better than Dylan had realised. And certainly a lot better than his French.

"There's a possibility that she disturbed a burglar in her home," Dylan said. "She was killed, I'm afraid."

Coletta dug in the pocket of her trousers for a hand-kerchief. She dabbed at suddenly damp eyes and then blew her nose. "Wicked."

"When was this?" Tolman still looked suspicious.

"She was buried just over a week ago," Dylan said. "I'm an old friend of Prue's—and of Maddie, her sister. Although everything points to Prue disturbing a burglar, we feel we need to look into it. You see, she phoned her sister the night it happened and she sounded worried. Frightened even. She was planning to visit her sister the next day but, of course, she never turned up."

"Wicked," Coletta said again.

"You need to sit down. You've had a shock." Frank took Coletta by the arm and led her out of the kitchen. Dylan and Tolman followed them to the sitting room where, finally, they had space to breathe.

"We found one of Mr. McIntyre's paintings when we were sorting out her possessions," Dylan explained.

"She didn't speak of him?" Coletta asked.

"No." Not to her parents or her sister. Not to anyone else that Dylan knew of. Except Danny Thompson perhaps. During a drunken session at his wine bar, she'd given Thompson the impression that there had been a man she couldn't have. Married or gay. Presumably McIntyre only came under the former heading.

"Did she come here?" Frank asked.

Coletta spouted a long speech in French for Tolman. The only parts Dylan managed to catch were *both dead* and *nothing matters now*.

"Yes," she said. "She was here for about two months."

"Living here?" Dylan asked.

"Yes."

Prue Murphy, who'd rented the cheapest property she could find and who bought her clothes from charity shops and supermarkets, had lived with the renowned—and wealthy—artist Jack McIntyre? And no one had known about it?

Surely she would have told her sister. Dylan wasn't convinced that Maddie and Prue had been the best of friends, but surely Prue would have mentioned McIntyre. She may have been reluctant to tell her parents in case they disapproved of their daughter having a relationship with a married man, especially one old enough to be her father, but she must have told someone.

"They were—?"

"Lovers." Coletta dabbed at her eyes again. "They were happy here. So happy."

"You're police?" Tolman asked, distrust in every syllable.

"Lancashire CID," Frank said, and he flashed his ID again.

Tolman seemed to accept this. "Sit down."

Coletta was already sitting in an armchair. There were two other chairs and Tolman indicated that Dylan and Frank should take those. He was happy to tower over them.

"Most people round here didn't have a clue who Jack was," Tolman said, "because he didn't want journalists finding him. He'd given up painting—he'd lost the inclination. He was tired of living in the public eye."

"I see." Dylan waited for more but Mr. and Mrs.

Tolman were clearly shocked by the news and didn't know what to say.

"When did you last see Prue?" he asked them.

"The day—" Coletta took a deep breath. "The day of the accident."

"The day McIntyre died?"

"Yes."

Jesus. Dylan hoped McIntyre hadn't taken out his boat and said, "Goodbye, cruel world."

"Jack had been so happy," Coletta said. "Prue was good for him. She taught him to love life and she got him painting again, but she—"

"Wait a minute," Dylan said. "You say she got him painting again?"

"Yes."

"But no one was supposed to know," Tolman said. "Until he was ready to face the world—or the press at least—he was keeping quiet about it. Not that it matters now, I suppose."

"Who knew he was painting?" Frank asked.

"Prue, obviously, because she was modelling for him. Other than that, just us two," Coletta said. "I had to know because I cleaned for him and he worked all hours of the day and night. As far as I know, no one else knew."

Dylan had come to France on a whim. He'd harboured some vague hope that someone might recognise Prue and confirm that she'd been friendly enough with McIntyre for him to give her a miniature. The last thing he'd expected to hear was that Prue and the artist had been having an affair.

Dylan had been thinking life was over at forty yet McIntyre, at sixty-two, had been living a dream life with a thirty-four-year-old. Where the hell was Dylan going wrong?

"If they were so happy, why did Prue leave?" he asked.

"She didn't like being involved with a married man," Coletta said. "Who would? Also—" She gave Tolman a quick glance before continuing. "Also, Jack had something of a reputation as a ladies' man. Prue couldn't believe that he was serious about her. So she told him she was leaving. He tried to change her mind, but she was having none of it and, in the end, he booked her flight back to England. He wasn't too worried. He was confident she'd be back, you see."

Heavy rain lashed the windows and she paused to watch it for a moment.

"Jack wanted to drive her to the airport but she said she didn't like goodbyes. Also, Jack had Mr. Collins due to visit him the day she left. He was a friend of Jack's but he was also the man who looked after his paintings. Sold them, put them in exhibitions, that sort of thing. So she set off with just her clothes to walk to the village and that's when I saw her." Coletta chewed on her lip. "I was coming to clean and prepare food for Jack and his visitor, you see, and Prue was setting off for the village. She was upset but she was too proud to let anyone see. I could tell though. We hugged, we said goodbye, and I watched her walk up to the lane." She nodded in the direction of the track where Dylan had parked. "She met someone, a man. I think he must have

been lost because she was pointing in the direction of
the village and it looked like she was giving him directions. In the end, she walked with him. I assume they
were both walking back to the village. He said something to make her laugh and I was pleased to hear that."
She sighed. "That was the last time I ever saw her."

Dylan had a dozen questions but he was too surprised to ask any. Frank had no such problems.

"This man she met? What was he like? Can you describe him?"

Coletta looked at him as if he were crazy. "He was
young—perhaps thirty or forty. Maybe even fifty. He
was wearing a black padded jacket and a hat. It was
a lovely November day—cold, so he needed that hat,
but there wasn't a cloud in the sky, I remember. And
he had a backpack."

"Wasn't it odd to see a stranger so far from the village?" Frank asked.

"No. Not at all. In the summer, we get many people
coming here. They like to walk. Sometimes they have
picnics on the beach."

"And this was the same day that Mr. McIntyre
drowned?" Dylan asked.

"Yes." Coletta sniffed. "After lunch, I put dinner
ready for Jack and his friend. It was only a salad. A
few cold meats. I told Jack I'd be here for breakfast
and he told me not to worry about being early as he and
his friend would probably take the boat out and enjoy
a couple of glasses of wine. I told you, it was a lovely
sunny day," she said again.

Tolman seemed calmer and less suspicious now

and, still standing, he gave his wife's hand a reassuring squeeze. "No one knows what happened. The weather was fine, the sea calm. No one can give me a satisfactory explanation as to why the accident happened."

"Too much wine perhaps?" Frank asked.

"It could be, I suppose." Tolman clearly wasn't happy with that idea. "Jack had taken that boat out dozens of times before though and he'd never drunk so much he was incapable of bringing her home."

"It was a horrid time," Coletta said. "I didn't have an address for Prue so I couldn't let her know. She would have found out soon enough because the news spread quickly, of course, but that's not a nice way to hear, is it? It was terrible."

"Who raised the alarm?" Dylan asked.

"Me." Tolman perched on the edge of the window-sill. "Coletta came here to prepare their breakfast but there was no sign of them. Jack used to moor his boat in the village, there's a small marina there, so Coletta sent me to check that it was there. It was nowhere to be seen so we called the police."

"The boat was moored in the village?" Dylan said. "I assumed it was kept here, in the boathouse."

"Don't be daft." Tolman rolled his eyes. "We're not talking about a rowing boat. Jack's was a powerful cruiser. With the accommodation on offer, they could have stayed on it quite comfortably, but I knew Jack wouldn't do that without letting us know. So the police put out a search party and found the boat, very badly damaged, the following day. The same evening they found—what was his name? Jeremy? They found

Jeremy's body. If it hadn't been for a brief storm we had that day, they reckoned his body would never have been found."

"Jack was such a strong swimmer too," Coletta said.

There were many strong swimmers in the world but few who could drink a lot of wine and swim several miles to shore in the cold and the darkness.

"The painting we found," Dylan said, "was a miniature. Presumably Jack gave it to her? Would you know about that?"

"Who else would have given it to her?" Coletta looked at Dylan as if he were an idiot.

"What happened to his other work?" Dylan asked. "You said he was painting Prue. Who has those paintings now?"

Tolman looked at his wife and shrugged.

"Jack took them somewhere for safekeeping when he knew his agent was visiting," Coletta said. "He didn't say where they were and I didn't ask. I've always assumed that the lawyers winding up his estate have them. Or perhaps they've already been handed over to Davina. I couldn't say where they are."

"What were they like?" Dylan asked. "Large? Small? All portraits?"

"They were large," Coletta said. "I think there were about half a dozen, all of Prue. They weren't finished."

They talked for another hour but the Tolmans had little to say other than what wonderful people their employer and his lover had been.

At least the sun was shining when they walked back to the Morgan.

"There's a law against that, you know," Dylan said.

"Against what?"

"Impersonating a police officer."

Frank snorted with laughter. "Once a police officer, always a police officer. There has to be some perk to retirement and I reckoned Tolman was the type to respect authority. So what do we do now?"

"We celebrate our good fortune by going on a pub crawl."

"Okay, the first pint of the gnat's piss they call beer in these parts is on you." Frank rubbed his hands together.

"Or perhaps we'll stick to brandy. The French are better with brandy than they are with beer."

"True, but they only serve it in thimble-sized glasses…"

TWENTY

RUTH TOOK A deep breath, prodded the doorbell and listened to the chimes ring out inside the house. Nerves made her heart race and that was ridiculous.

The door opened and Maddie frowned at her. "What are you doing here?"

"May I come in?"

"Of course." Maddie strode off in the direction of the dining room, leaving Ruth to close the door behind her.

"If you've come to collect your scarf," Maddie said, "you're too late. I put it in the mail. And yes, I do know how precious it is to you, so I made sure it was recorded and registered."

"Thank you, but that's not why I'm here."

"So why are you here?"

"I've come to help you sort out Prue's things." Somewhere, buried deep in a dark place that Ruth refused to visit, was the memory of the moment their relationship had broken down. That was years ago though. Maddie had been a child then. They should be able to move on. "I know you want to do everything yourself, Maddie, but it will be easier with two of us."

Ruth wasn't taking no for an answer. She'd lost Prue but she refused to lose Maddie as well.

Maddie's cold exterior told her it was already too

late, that all hope had been lost when Maddie, just ten years old, had run to Ruth. Ruth had slapped her. Shaken her. She hadn't known what else to do.

"It's here." Maddie nodded at a tall pile of clothes on the dining table. "Most of it's stuff no one would be caught dead in."

Ruth flinched at both the expression and the hard tone of voice. "Don't fight me, Maddie. Let's do this together."

Maddie shrugged. "Would you like a coffee?"

"I'd love one, darling. Thank you."

Maddie's shoes tapped on the wooden floor in the hall as she walked to the kitchen.

Ruth lifted a coat from the pile of clothing. She held it to her face, but could find no trace of Prue. It was in good condition so she checked the pockets, all empty, and put it aside to go to the charity shop. She picked up another coat, one in a soft pink that she'd seen Prue wearing. Again, it was in good condition. Ruth checked the pockets and pulled out a crumpled receipt and a penny coin. *See a penny, pick it up, and all that day you'll have good luck.* She unfolded the receipt. It was for a cappuccino bought from Manchester Art Gallery, and it was dated the same day that Prue died. Ruth put the receipt on the table and the coat on the pile for the charity shop.

The next item was a sweater that looked to be at least twenty years old. Threads dangled from the cuffs and elbows and it was dotted with white paint. She could imagine Prue decorating her home in it, could see her curled up in front of the TV in it on cold winter nights.

She was tempted to take it home and keep it forever. She resisted and started a new pile for clothes to be thrown out.

She felt her heart start to race and had to take several slow, deep breaths. The void that Prue had left behind would never be filled, she knew that, but one day she hoped the raw, raw pain would subside just a little. It would have to, otherwise she wouldn't be able to cope. And cope she must, for all their sakes.

Maddie carried two coffees into the room and put them on the table, but before either of them could speak, the doorbell rang.

"Now what?" Maddie muttered before striding along that wooden floor to answer it.

"Hello, Eddie," Ruth heard her say. "Tim's not here."

"I know. I've been in Birmingham and, as I was more or less passing your door, I thought I'd call in and see how you're doing." There was a brief pause before he added, "We're worried about you, Maddie. You've got a lot on your plate right now."

"I'm fine," she said, "but thanks. Do you want a coffee? I've just made one. My mother's here."

"I'd love one. The traffic's been stop-start for hours and I thought I'd never get here."

Ruth had pinned a smile to her face before Eddie reached the dining room. Smiling, and looking as uncomfortable as most people do when dealing with the bereaved, he came forward and gave her a quick peck on the cheek. "Hello, Ruth. How are you coping?"

"I'm okay, Eddie. Thanks. How are you? Did I hear you say you'd been in Birmingham?"

"Yes." He looked relieved to be on easier territory. "A conference. Exhausting but hopefully worthwhile."

Maddie went to the kitchen, leaving them to chat awkwardly about the weather until she returned. Given that Maddie suffered with her nerves, Ruth had expected her daughter to cut down the amount of caffeine and alcohol she drank. Maddie was far too thin and she was constantly fidgeting. Ruth hoped she wasn't sinking into one of her depressions.

"Thanks." Eddie took his coffee from her. "So how are you, Maddie?"

"I'm okay. Have a seat."

"Thanks, but I'd rather stand. I've been sitting in that car for hours." He leaned back against the table. "I've said it before and I'll say it again. If there's anything I can do, anything at all, just say the word. I know what you're going through. People don't realise how much needs to be done at a time like this, do they? I remember having to sort out everything when my aunt died. It took months."

Maddie nodded. "That's exactly it, people *don't* realise. What with the funeral, putting notices in the paper, sorting out the house and contents, getting stuff together for the solicitor—it's a damn pain."

Ruth felt a bubble of anger rise. Why had Maddie insisted on doing everything? So she could play the martyr? Ruth didn't like the unkind thought but she could think of no other explanation.

"It's much worse in this case, isn't it?" Eddie said. "With the police involved, I mean."

"Yes."

He looked at her for long moments. "We've been so worried about you, but I have to say that, despite everything, you're looking as lovely as ever."

"Thank you. And who's 'we'?"

"Me. Tim."

She rolled her eyes at that. "Oh yes, I've noticed that Tim's really worried."

"Aw, come on, Maddie. Of course he's worried. We're just run off our feet at the moment, that's all."

Maybe Maddie was feeling neglected by Tim.

"I don't suppose the police have found out anything new?" he asked.

"I haven't heard a word from them," Maddie said. "Not a word since I spoke to them at Prue's funeral. They don't seem to care. I suppose they'd claim that they're busy too."

"I'm sure they're doing all they can." He took a sip of coffee. "What about your private investigator? Has he learned anything?"

"I don't know. He's calling here later today. He's been in France."

"France? What, on holiday you mean?"

"No. Didn't Tim tell you about the painting?"

"What painting?"

Maddie gave Ruth a sharp glance, almost as if she'd forgotten she was there. "I found a painting in Prue's house," she said. "Only a very tiny one—a miniature, you know? It turns out it's one of Jack McIntyre's."

"What?" Ruth had heard a painting mentioned but she'd had no idea it was a McIntyre.

"Who did you say it was painted by?" Eddie asked.

"Jack McIntyre. Haven't you heard of him?"

"No."

"He's famous. Except he's dead now. He was drowned, I think. But he lived in France, you see, so Dylan's been there to see if he can find out how one of his paintings came to be in Prue's house. Prue lived in France, remember? Dylan thinks there might be a connection."

"Wow."

"It's not worth that much," Maddie said, giving Ruth another quick, almost sly, glance, "but it's quite a surprise."

Ruth didn't care how much the painting was worth, but the fact that Maddie didn't want her to know about it hurt. All Ruth wanted was her daughter back, and no amount of money could ease the pain or the deep, hollow sense of loss.

Eddie finished his coffee and put the empty cup on the table. "It's time I was off. We have that appointment with the bank at two."

He spoke as if Maddie was supposed to know what he was talking about, but she clearly didn't. "What appointment?"

"We're trying to extend a loan. Tim told you about it yesterday when he phoned you."

She shook her head. "He hasn't mentioned it. He didn't phone me yesterday."

"He did, Maddie. I heard him. I was in his office."

"Nope. It wasn't me."

"Oh. My mistake then," Eddie said. "It's nothing to worry about, not really. We need a loan extension, that's all. Tim's been working on updating our business plan for ages. I'm sure the bank will play ball."

Ruth wondered who Tim *had* told about the meeting with the bank. Not Maddie, because he'd know she had no interest in finance or business plans, but perhaps he had someone else to talk to, someone who cared…

"Don't forget," Eddie said as he was leaving, "if there's anything I can do, anything at all, just give me a shout. Okay?"

Maddie gave him a quick hug. "Thanks."

"Good to see you again, Eddie," Ruth said.

"You, too, Ruth. Take good care of yourself, won't you?" Smiling, he gave her a peck on the cheek before he took his car keys from his pocket and left them alone.

"Eddie's not too bad, you know," Maddie said. "I never used to like him, but he's been quite thoughtful lately. Tim's too wrapped up in the business to care, and my agent's only worried about the next shoot, so it's been good to see that at least someone cares about me."

"We all care about you, Maddie. You know that."

"Yeah. Right. Let's get on with this stuff then. This skirt isn't too bad, I suppose."

The skirt was put on the charity shop pile and Maddie grabbed a leather handbag and emptied the contents onto the table.

"Look at this," Maddie said, surprise evident. "It's practically empty. Name me a woman who doesn't carry makeup, spare stockings, hairbrush, mirror, water bottle and a hundred other things. Prue's is almost empty."

Prue's bag held a wallet containing loyalty cards for two supermarkets and her debit card, a mini umbrella, a pair of gloves and a small pack of tissues. And that was it. Even Ruth had to admit it looked sad and forlorn.

Maddie decided the handbag was good enough for the charity shop and threw the contents in the rubbish bag.

"I almost forgot." Ruth handed over the receipt she'd found in Prue's coat pocket. "Prue was in Manchester on the day she died." She preferred to say "died" rather than "was killed" or "was murdered." "Died" was less brutal.

"So?"

"I thought your detective, Dylan Scott, might be interested," Ruth said.

"Oh, yes." Maddie's sudden smile seemed genuine. "He's calling in later so I'll give it to him."

Next was a box that contained assorted rubbish. Ruth could give someone a similar box if she emptied the top drawer in her kitchen. Prue's box contained cigarette lighters (Prue had never smoked), two tape measures, an old camera that didn't work, a box of matches, a menu from her local Chinese takeaway, buttons—

Maddie gasped. She turned one of the buttons over in her hand then held it tight in her closed fist.

"What's wrong?" Ruth asked, sensing a dramatic change in her daughter's mood.

"This button. This bloody button!"

Maddie threw down the button and strode off. Ruth heard her take the stairs two at a time. Doors upstairs were slammed. A couple of minutes later, she returned clutching a blue blazer.

"See?"

Ruth saw a navy double-breasted blazer, presumably Tim's. It had eight brass-coloured buttons on the front and three smaller buttons, identical to the one Maddie was holding, on the cuff of each sleeve. At least, it should have had three on each sleeve. The left sleeve only had two. The missing one, Ruth assumed, was in Maddie's hand.

"A couple of months ago, Tim returned from a trip to Portugal annoyed that he'd lost a button." Maddie was breathless from her angry dash up the stairs. "I promised to find a replacement but I couldn't, and Tim hasn't worn this blazer since."

"So he must have lost it at Prue's."

"Tim and Eddie went to Portugal for three days," Maddie said. "I met them from the airport. That evening, Tim unpacked and noticed he'd lost the button."

Maddie strode out of the room and came back with a lit cigarette in her hand. She took a long, deep pull.

"So either," she said, "my dear sister went to Portugal with Tim—"

"Or he lost it when you visited Prue and hadn't noticed until he went to Portugal. Darling, you're letting your imagination run away with you. Of course Prue didn't go to Portugal with Tim." Ruth was appalled by the way her daughter's mind worked.

"I should have guessed. When we went to France for that weekend, Tim sat up all night with her. At least, they both claimed they sat up all night—just talking."

"If that's what—"

"Bastard!" Maddie threw the jacket on the table. The button was clenched tight in her fist. "Total bastard!"

TWENTY-ONE

TORRENTIAL RAIN HAD the Morgan's windscreen wipers struggling to cope. Dylan had been driving round Manchester for the past half hour looking for somewhere to park, and the only option seemed to be the ridiculously expensive multi-storey which would earn him a soaking.

He'd had two golfing umbrellas in the car until Bev's impromptu cleaning session. Why she insisted on cleaning his car, he had no idea, but he wished she wouldn't. She didn't wash it, but she often took it upon herself to clean the inside and she always, without fail, removed things he needed. He'd bet his umbrellas were sitting in the garage where they were neither use nor sodding ornament.

Still, at least he had a purpose, which was more than he'd had when he called at Maddie's yesterday. He'd been able to tell her that Prue and McIntyre had been lovers, but he hadn't a clue what to do next. Being given the receipt from the art gallery was a godsend. He'd thought he might talk to Martin Collins again, but Collins would only repeat what he'd already told him. Dylan had also toyed with the idea of having another chat with Davina McIntyre, but she would simply insist that she'd loved McIntyre and had never heard of

Prue. Both options would be a waste of time. He'd tried to speak to the lawyer dealing with McIntyre's estate, but he was on holiday.

On seeing that receipt, Dylan had been able to pack his bags, get a good night's sleep, jump in the Morgan and make for Manchester.

"There's an exhibition of McIntyre's paintings there," Maddie had said as she'd handed over the receipt. "I checked on the internet."

"Really? That's interesting."

Maddie had shrugged at that and he'd had the feeling she was angry about something. She wasn't angry with him, but something hadn't been right in her world.

Dylan had always considered himself a good judge of character. He could read people. He could tell from a gesture whether they were lying, nervous, confident, shy, worried or whatever. Yet Maddie was a mystery to him. He couldn't fathom her at all. Given that they'd once been so close, that surprised him. He supposed they'd been a hell of a lot closer physically than mentally but, even so, he should be able to read her more easily.

"Are you sure she didn't say anything about a man in her life?" he'd asked her. "She'd been living with McIntyre. She must have said something to you."

"Nothing. And I find it hard to believe, Dylan. What would a man like McIntyre see in my sister? I mean, come on. It's laughable."

"Not really. Prue was young, pretty and knowledge-able about art. McIntyre was sixty-two and I should imagine he was flattered by Prue."

"Huh."

Dylan had come to realise that Maddie and Prue really hadn't known each other at all. They'd been born and raised in the same house to the same parents, and yet they'd lived their adult lives like strangers.

"I'll go up there and check it out," Dylan said.

"Fine. But first," she said, her smile sunny again, "let's have a glass of wine and you can tell me what my little sister got up to in France."

She was already taking a bottle of red from the rack. "Do you remember how red wine used to give you a headache?"

"It still does." He was surprised she remembered. "The first bottle's okay, and the second isn't too bad, but the third—you can bet your life I'll have a headache."

Laughing, she poured wine into large glasses and handed him one. "Do you remember that camera I had—the Polaroid?"

"No."

"You must. I took lots of pictures of you—some in Regent's Park and some—" she licked her lips "—some in bed."

Frowning, he shook his head. "I don't remember that."

"Dylan, you must. You took some of me in various states of undress. Don't you remember?"

"No." All he could remember was that confounded bedroom. In those days, though, like most red-blooded males, his dick had ruled his life.

"Do you remember—?" Whatever she'd been about to say was left unsaid because Chandler arrived.

After going through the social niceties, Dylan had

left. He'd spent the night at home, trying not to think of Polaroid images, and travelled to Manchester this morning.

Sod it. He indicated and turned onto the ramp for the multi-storey car park.

By the time he'd driven a spiral to the sixth floor and taken the lift back to ground level, the rain had eased a little. It was good to know someone was smiling down on him.

He went straight to the gallery and the McIntyre display. Six paintings had been given one wall in a vast room displaying paintings by several other artists. McIntyre's were no better and no worse than the others. They certainly weren't worth the stupid money people were prepared to pay for them.

A long bench seat was provided and Dylan sat to give the paintings a more leisurely inspection. Nope, they simply weren't worth the money. They were a varied mix. Two were beach scenes, the colours pale except, on one, a bright red diamond kite and, on the other, two red-and-white striped deckchairs. Another showed a hefty lady, her skirt swirling around chubby knees, eating an ice-cream. His favourite was of a herd of sheep gathered round a red tractor. They were okay, but they weren't anything special.

He wondered if Prue had sat on this very bench to admire her lover's work. He'd give a lot to know what she'd been thinking as she'd looked at them. He'd give a lot more to know why she'd called her sister that same day. Had something happened here at the gallery? Something to frighten her?

He had no idea and staring at a bunch of paintings wouldn't solve the mystery.

He wandered round the rest of the gallery then sat with a coffee in the café. Prue presumably caught the train to Manchester, walked to the gallery, checked out McIntyre's paintings, sat here with a cappuccino before taking the train back to Dawson's Clough. The station, the gallery—she must have been captured on CCTV a dozen times or more.

He finished his coffee and went to the main desk. Several people were leaving or arriving but the desk was quiet.

"Can I help?" a young woman asked.

Dylan gave her his best smile. "I hope so. I'm a private investigator looking into the murder of a young woman."

The woman's shocked expression increased with each word.

"We know she came here on the day she was killed," Dylan said, "and it would be an enormous help if I could check your CCTV images for the day in question."

"Sorry—we can't let you. We're not allowed because of the Data Protection Act. You have to apply to—"

"I know, and I will. But this is a matter of some urgency."

"Sorry." She folded her arms across her considerable chest as if preparing to do battle.

"No problem." He took the photo of Prue from his pocket. He'd meant to have it enlarged, but hadn't got round to it. "I wonder, would you remember seeing this woman?"

She took the photo from him and studied it closely, so closely that a small ray of hope flared but she soon dashed it. "Sorry. I don't recognise her. I'll ask my colleague."

Half an hour later, several people had seen the photo of Prue but no one had recognised her. Dylan wasn't too surprised.

He wandered around the gallery, showing the photo to more people, but the result was always the same— a regretful shaking of the head. Prue hadn't been the type to kick up a fuss in the café by claiming her coffee was cold so no one would have cause to remember her.

He left the gallery and stood by the main entrance to call Frank. He explained that Prue had visited the gallery the day she died. "I need CCTV images, Frank. For the gallery and the train stations. Something made her call Maddie that day. The sisters weren't close so I think something really bad must have happened either at the gallery, in the city or on the train home."

"Like what?"

"God knows, but something must have happened. It would be interesting to see if she's on camera and if she's with anyone who—" Not ten yards from him was a familiar character. "Got to go." Dylan snapped his phone shut. The bearded man turned, spotted him and set off at a run.

Dylan followed. "Shit!" Traffic hindered him, pedestrians got in his way, and a yappy terrier almost tripped him. He was gaining on his quarry though.

A car pulled out in front of the bearded bloke, forcing him to stop or risk getting mown down. Those extra seconds helped and Dylan was soon grabbing him by the arm, dragging him across the pavement and slamming him against a wall.

"Right, Sunshine, talk." He could barely say the words as his out-of-condition lungs struggled to pull in air. "What were you doing at Prue Murphy's funeral? What are you doing here? What do you know about her murder?"

The chap gazed back at him. He was as breathless as Dylan, but he was totally unfazed.

"Come on, out with it." Dylan gave him an encouraging shake.

He was tall, about sixty, bearded, blue-grey eyes—

"Bloody hell!" It couldn't be. Could it? As God was his witness, it bloody well was. He'd seen photos of this man. In those, he'd been clean-shaven and usually wearing a dinner jacket. He'd been smiling for cameras and raising a glass of champagne.

"You're Jack Bloody McIntyre!"

TWENTY-TWO

CARLTON AMESBURY ATTACHED the bait to the hook, put his rod in the water and waited for a fish to bite. This was his first day off work in eight and he was determined to enjoy it.

It had rained heavily all morning but, just to prove it really was spring, the sun had decided to put in an appearance this afternoon. He'd gathered rods, boxes and chair, and set off for this small lake on the edge of town.

He had it to himself because few people could be bothered with it, but it was close to home and he couldn't afford to waste petrol going further afield.

Wendy often said he should quit moaning about the job, that he should be grateful to have it, and perhaps she was right. Uncle Jim, a traffic cop, had bought him a policeman's helmet for his sixth birthday and Carlton had decided there and then that, one day, he'd wear the uniform himself. When he should have been studying at school, Carlton had mentally plotted his rise in the force. Promotion would follow promotion—

Twenty-four years later, he was sick of the damn uniform. There were more crooks wearing the blue than there were behind bars. What a bloody fool he'd been. He hadn't realised that promotion depended not on *what* you knew but on *who* you knew. Nor had he realised that if you'd been born black you could forget it. There were the odd few black coppers who climbed high, but they were most likely the ones who could—and would—dish the dirt. Blackmail.

Yeah, blackmail was the only way to get on. If you had the proof and threatened to expose them for the crooks they were, you might progress. There would be hearty slaps on the back, and those at the top would make a big song and dance about your promotion. They'd happily show the world that a black man *could* succeed in the British police force. Of course, they wouldn't actually utter the word *black*.

Carlton had a piece of ammunition but he very much doubted it would work. Frank Willoughby had been— still was—a legend at the station. Everyone thought he was the most honest, trustworthy copper who ever lived. He'd had to retire for health reasons but that didn't stop him being treated like a hero on his many visits. He was helping a friend out, some ex-copper turned private investigator, and he'd called at the station to get up-to-date information. To Carlton's mind, that was wrong. Police information shouldn't leave police walls. It didn't matter that Willoughby had been the best detective chief inspector to walk the earth. Only the facts mattered, and the facts were that Willoughby had taken a file pertaining to Prue Murphy's murder from the station.

If he could prove it, and if he kicked up a fuss and threatened to expose those who'd let Willoughby walk out with that file, no one would give a damn if Carlton's skin was black, white or fucking pink with yellow spots. He *couldn't* prove it though. They'd all take Willoughby's side. They'd stand united.

He put down his rod and lit a cigarette. He'd cut down to less than ten a day because he couldn't really afford the habit. Who could? It meant that he enjoyed every single one.

Out of the corner of his eye, he saw a flash of electric blue. A kingfisher. He used to come here as a kid and he'd been fascinated by the speed and colour of the bird. The sight still thrilled him.

It was a peaceful spot. There was no one in sight. His car sat alone on the small gravelled area. It was just him and the birds. And, hopefully, the fish.

Perhaps Wendy was right and he should be grateful he had a job. Maybe it wasn't all bad. Maybe, just maybe, something would happen without him having to expose Willoughby.

He stubbed out his cigarette and put fresh bait on his hook. With luck, he'd catch something big today.

He made a good cast and waited for a fish to bite. He tried to reel in but he'd caught something, all right. He'd bet folk had been dumping rubbish. God knows what was at the bottom—old prams, shopping trolleys, who knew? There was no way he was getting his line free. He'd have to cut it.

He was reaching for his cutters when it moved. It was far too heavy for a fish—

It was no use, he'd have to cut the line. No, it was

near the surface. It felt lighter now, so perhaps he could reel it in after all.

"Sweet fucking Jesus!"

He staggered back as an arm broke the surface of the water.

TWENTY-THREE

DYLAN DIDN'T BELIEVE this. He really didn't believe that he was sitting in a Manchester pub with the not-so-late McIntyre.

He'd had him pinned against that wall for what had seemed an age and they'd both been breathing heavily. "You are Jack Bloody McIntyre, aren't you?"

"Guilty," McIntyre had replied. "And you're Dylan Scott. I've admired your car. Very nice indeed."

If he thought he was getting in Dylan's good books by complimenting his pride and joy, he had another think coming.

"So what have you been doing at the gallery?" Dylan asked. "Admiring your paintings?"

"No."

"What have you done? Faked your own death? Killed your old girlfriend?"

"Nothing like that." He was well spoken and he seemed quite calm. Far calmer than Dylan at any rate.

Dylan didn't release his grip. No way was he risking losing McIntyre again. "So what's your story?"

"It's a long one." McIntyre pointed to a narrow side street. "There's a pub down there. It'll be packed with the scum of the earth who wouldn't recognise a dead artist or a live private investigator."

"How do you know who I am?"

"I've been watching you and I asked a few questions. I'll buy you a drink, Dylan. I can just about afford it."

"Too right you can. I know how much your paintings are worth."

"They're worth nothing to me. It's the devil's own job getting hold of your money when you're dead."

Dylan didn't want to argue in the street, he needed a drink, several drinks, and the short walk would give him time to get his thoughts in order. The fact that McIntyre might be alive hadn't crossed his mind and he felt like he'd been conned. He should have considered the possibility, damn it. "Come on then. Let's have that drink. It'll give you time to invent a good story."

"I don't need to invent anything…"

They'd crossed the road and walked down a narrow, busy street and here they were, in the darkest pub Dylan had ever seen. It was dingy but surprisingly busy.

They'd brought their drinks to this corner where it was unlikely anyone would be able to hear them over the hum of the TV at the other end of the bar. It was also so dark that no one would recognise them.

"So what's it like being dead?" Dylan asked.

"Damned inconvenient." McIntyre had bought himself whisky and he took a small sip. "It's also necessary—for the time being, at least."

"Why? Is this stunt supposed to increase the value of your paintings?"

"No." McIntyre smiled at the notion. "Although I gather I'm commanding a high price."

"Yes, well, they say fools and their money are soon

parted." Dylan had a pint of beer in front of him. He took a big swallow. It tasted flat. "Let's hear it then."

"Where shall I start?"

"Try the beginning, why don't you? From the moment you met Prue Murphy."

"Right." McIntyre thought for long moments as if he couldn't decide where the beginning was. "I met her in France last August when I was attending a friend's daughter's wedding. Caterers had been employed and Prue was working for them. There are probably worse waitresses in the world but I've never met one." He smiled as he spoke. "I struck up a conversation with her and we met up the next day. She was fun to be with, we got on well, very well, and she moved in with me in September."

That was probably a lie. Maddie and Tim had visited Prue in September. Visited her at her flat. "Go on."

"We were happy. We were in love." Dylan rolled his eyes, but McIntyre merely smiled. "Did you know Prue?"

"Yes. Sort of. Okay, no, not really. I knew her sister, Maddie. She's the one who's asked me to look into Prue's murder."

"Ah. And how's Mad Maddie?"

"Do you know her?"

"Hell, no." McIntyre grimaced. "I've seen photos of her so I know she's God's personal gift to the male population, but I never had the pleasure. She was in rehab when I was with Prue."

"Rehab?" Dylan tried to keep the surprise from his

voice, but he was struggling to keep track with the events of the last hour.

"After her nervous breakdown—or whatever it was." McIntyre looked as puzzled as Dylan felt. "Didn't you know about that?"

"She hasn't mentioned it, no."

"According to Prue—and she always referred to her sister as Mad Maddie—family members could spot the signs. Maddie would be fine, although a bit up and down emotionally, and then she'd start going downhill. It's happened several times in the past and I gather this time was no different. Maddie took to her bed for three days—didn't eat, drink or talk—and ended up in some place I can't remember the name of. It's a private clinic for the, how shall we put it, mentally fragile?"

Dylan didn't know what to make of that. That the sisters hadn't got along was becoming clear to him, and he wouldn't be too surprised to learn that Maddie suffered from depression. Anyway, it wasn't important. McIntyre's relationship with Prue was what mattered.

"So why, if you were so in love, didn't Prue stay with you?" he asked.

"Because she had morals, I suppose. We came from different backgrounds, and Prue—God, she insisted on paying her way in life. If I took her to dinner one night, she had to pay the next time. You would not believe the awful places I've eaten in. She also didn't like being involved with a married man. Nor did she like the fact that I had a reputation for being a bit of a womaniser. On top of that lot, she believed that, one day, I'd return to the spotlight and spend my life at exhibitions and parties. It wasn't the sort of life she wanted. I had no intention of ever returning to that life, but I couldn't convince her of that. She decided she needed to make a fresh start for herself, far away from me. She said it was time she grew up. She was heading back to England, she said, and nothing I could say would change her mind. So I let her go. I was fairly confident she'd come back to me…" His words trailed away.

"Okay," Dylan said, prepared to accept that for now. "So she walked out that day and met a man—who was he?"

"How do you mean, she met a man?" McIntyre's eyes narrowed to small slits. "Where? When?"

"The day she left you." Dylan couldn't decide what to make of McIntyre. He didn't trust him, but he didn't trust a lot of people. "According to Coletta—"

"You've spoken to Coletta?"

"Of course. I wanted to know how Prue came to have one of your miniatures hanging on her bedroom wall. I thought it possible that she'd known you so I went and checked out your old home. I spoke to Coletta and her husband. Coletta says she saw Prue the morning she left you. Prue was supposed to be walking back to the village but she met someone. Coletta thought he might have been a tourist because Prue looked as if she was giving him directions before they walked toward the village together."

"Perhaps he *was* a tourist although they're thin on the ground in November." McIntyre's brows were drawn together as he took another sip of whisky. "I didn't see

Prue after she walked out of the cottage. Within the hour, Jeremy had arrived. He's—was my agent."

"I know."

"You've been very thorough."

"Not thorough enough, it seems. Carry on."

"We were friends, Jeremy and me, but I knew why he was coming. When people start making money from your work, they want you painting every minute of every day. They want a machine."

"So you're just a commodity." Dylan's heart bled for him.

"More or less, yes. The world thought I'd quit and I was happy to let them believe that, but I'd started painting again. Painting Prue. To say she was beautiful was an understatement. She had such an expressive face. So I was painting what I thought of as the Chaste Collection. I'd sketched her coy, happy, angry, sexy, timid and excited." He emphasised each word so that Dylan understood why he'd chosen to call the paintings the Chaste Collection. "They were nowhere close to being completed and I wasn't ready to announce their existence to the world, so I hid the paintings from Jeremy. I had a boathouse—well, you've probably seen it."

Dylan nodded.

"I hid the paintings there," McIntyre said. "Jeremy turned up and we had lunch. He tried to show me the error of my ways—told me that prices would drop, people would lose interest in my work, the usual stuff. It didn't take too long for him to realise that I wasn't going to even talk about painting. Once that was out of the way, we settled down to the enjoy the day. It was a lovely one too. Unseasonably warm. We wrapped up well that evening and took the boat out."

"In the dark?"

McIntyre laughed at that. "It's the best time. You can't beat sailing beneath the stars."

Yeah, yeah. "And then what happened?"

"We'd been out for about an hour, maybe even less than that, and I'd gone below to get more wine. When I returned to the deck—" He paused briefly. "It happened so quickly. A man raised a fire extinguisher and whacked Jeremy in the face, knocking him overboard. And no, I can't say what he looked like. The deck was lit up like Oxford Street at Christmas, but he had some sort of black mask over his head. Even if I'd had time to look, I wouldn't have come up with a description, but I didn't have time because he came at me with the fire extinguisher. How the hell he got on the boat or managed to stay hidden for so long, I have no idea. He meant business though. He wasn't planning on giving me a warning tap. I managed to duck so, instead of slamming the extinguisher into my head, he only caught my shoulder. That was painful enough, believe me. It also had the desired effect of knocking me off balance and into the water. I stayed under for as long as I could, but it wasn't many seconds before my boat was speeding off to the shore."

Dylan was no longer sure what to believe, but McIntyre's story was intriguing. "Go on."

"My shoulder was killing me—almost literally. It was dislocated so I couldn't move properly in the water. I swam around as best I could looking for Jeremy but there was no sign of him. I guessed he was dead. I swam for what seemed like hours until I reached the shore. I could see lights from the village so I aimed for those. I crawled ashore and crept back to my cottage. I don't know what I expected to find but there was no sign of anyone. My paintings were still there—I'd hidden them well—so I grabbed those, and took some cash from the cottage. I walked and I hitched lifts. When I reached Rouen, I checked in to the hospital under a false name and got my shoulder fixed. Then I went into hiding. I was determined to find out who wanted me—and Jeremy—dead."

His story told, McIntyre leaned back in his seat and took a large swallow of whisky.

It was some story, one Dylan didn't know whether to believe or not. He was still reeling from the shock of realising McIntyre was alive and he was likely to believe anything right now.

"So assuming you're telling the truth—" *never assume,* an inner voice mocked Dylan "—why did you go into hiding? Surely, if you'd told the police what had happened, they would have stood more chance of finding the killer?"

"You think so? Then you have more faith than I have." McIntyre emptied his glass. "Another?"

"It's my round, I believe." Dylan stood up and went to the bar for refills. The pub was still crowded. Most of the customers looked young and healthy enough to put in a full day's work. Perhaps Dylan was being too harsh. Given the state of the country, getting work wasn't easy. A dozen or so young men gathered round a TV screen to watch the racing from Chepstow. Their benefit cheques were probably resting on the backs of those nags.

He could see McIntyre thanks to a large mirror above the bar. Dylan kept watching him. He didn't want to have to chase him twice in one day. McIntyre, however, looked suddenly weary and drained.

Dylan wasn't necessarily falling for his story. He'd think about it long and hard and he'd remember his ABC. Accept nothing. Believe nothing. Check everything. If he'd paid more attention to that, the possibility of McIntyre being alive might have crossed his mind.

He returned to their table, set their drinks down and sat opposite McIntyre.

"Thanks." McIntyre chinked his glass against Dylan's. "Cheers. May the wind be on your back."

Dylan wasn't in the mood for pleasantries. All he could do was try to process the fact that McIntyre was alive. He didn't know what that meant, but he did know that it changed everything. "After you grabbed your paintings and left your home, what did you do? Where have you been all this time?"

"I've been in Paris mostly. I sold my watch for food, and earned enough money painting pictures for the tourists to get by." He smiled at that. "There are some valuable caricatures in Paris, all unsigned of course. I've been mingling among the lowest of the low, trying to find out what the word is on the street. My work tripled in value the moment I hit the water, and I want to know who stands to benefit most from that."

"How far have you got?"

"I've drawn a blank. Suspects, but no proof. My chief

suspect lived in London," McIntyre went on, "so I came over here. I was watching TV when I saw the news that Prue had been killed. I came north to Dawson's Clough and, when I saw you were involved, I knew that the police had lied about a burglar. I guessed that her death was connected to me in some way."

Which was a damn sight more than Dylan had known. "Who's your chief suspect?"

"Martin Collins."

"What? You think he murdered his own father?"

"I think he's capable of it. However, on the night in question—"

"He can prove that he was many miles away. Yes. He showed me a photo taken that night." Dylan had thought it odd that Collins had shown him that photo. "But why would he?"

"Money. Why else?"

"How would he gain though?"

"In several ways. If he knew I was painting again, and got his hands on my work, he'd make a killing. If he merely *suspected* I was painting, and thought he'd have a good look round my home for sketches, he'd make a killing. The gallery had a couple of paintings of mine, and with the high prices caused by my death, he'd make a killing. People would be selling my paintings so he'd probably make a killing there too. Whichever way you care to look at it—"

"He'd make a killing. Yes, I get the point."

"Jeremy was a true gentleman. He loved art, loved helping up-and-coming artists, and was highly respected in his field. His son, however, is one of those who knows the price of everything and the value of nothing."

"Who's your number two suspect?" he asked.

McIntyre shrugged. "I did wonder about my wife. I'm worth a lot more to her dead than alive."

"She claims she's never stopped loving you."

"She told me the same thing when I brought up the subject of divorce," McIntyre said.

"She claims divorce was never mentioned." She'd claimed a lot of things though and Dylan hadn't been convinced at the time. "Did you ever mention Prue to her?"

"Yes. I said I wanted a divorce so that I could be with Prue."

Deep down, Dylan had known she'd been lying when she'd denied all knowledge of Prue. She wouldn't be the first jealous wife to kill her husband and his lover. Davina McIntyre had just been promoted to the top of Dylan's extremely short list of suspects.

"But in the eyes of the law, you're only officially missing," he said. "Without a body—and killing someone on a boat always means it's likely that the body won't turn up—she can't get her hands on your cash, can she?"

"Perhaps she didn't realise that." McIntyre drummed a tuneless tattoo on the table.

Or perhaps money wasn't the issue. Perhaps Davina McIntyre had decided that if she couldn't have her husband, no one else would.

"What exactly happened to Prue?" McIntyre asked.

"According to the media, she disturbed a burglar. You don't think so though, do you?"

"No, I don't. I could be wrong, but it seems to me that whoever killed her was looking for something specific and the only thing she had of value, as far as we know, was that miniature. But of course, that was hanging on her bedroom wall for all to see. Anyone after that would have pocketed it. The miniature was a gift from you, right?"

"Yes."

"Did you give her more gifts? Did she own any other paintings? Do you know of anything else she owned that was of value?"

"I painted the miniature when I knew she was intent on leaving. It was just a reminder for her that she should phone or write to me." McIntyre shook his head. "She had nothing else. No paintings. Nothing of value. She wasn't a possessions sort of girl."

"So it seems. She wasn't a talkative sort of girl either. No one I've spoken to knew she had that miniature. Her sister got a chap who deals in secondhand furniture to take Prue's stuff away and it was him who recognised it as one of yours. If he hadn't, it would have gone to the nearest charity shop."

McIntyre leaned back in his chair. "So what the hell is going on?"

"I haven't the remotest idea." Wasn't that the truth. "Do you want another drink?"

"Why not? My round, I think." He gave Dylan a smile. "Don't concern yourself too much with my finances. I have one good friend—one wealthy good friend—who will keep me from starvation."

So someone other than Dylan knew the artist was alive. How many others knew?

Dylan watched McIntyre at the bar. He stood tall and erect and, beneath the straggly hair and beard, was a good-looking man. He was slim and looked to be fit. Whether he was a killer or a liar was impossible to say.

If McIntyre's tale was true—Dylan ran his fingers through his hair. True or false, he didn't have a bloody clue what to do next.

McIntyre returned with their drinks, put them on the table and sat down.

"Thanks." Dylan took a swallow of beer. He shouldn't be drinking at this time of day—especially as he would be driving to God knew where after this. Three beers wouldn't kill him though. He'd have a couple of coffees before he drove out of Manchester. "So what are you doing now?"

"I was at the gallery today to see if I saw anyone interesting about. And no, I didn't. I've also been in Dawson's Clough watching you and trying to find out how Prue is connected to all this. I've learned nothing from the lowlife in Paris so I'm working on those in London. If there are any suspicious movements of paintings, they'll know. First, however, I have to win their trust and that's taking some doing."

Dylan supposed that made sense.

"What about you?" McIntyre asked. "What are you doing now?"

"Me? Well, I've been working on the assumption

that you met your end in a boating accident so I've been concentrating on Dawson's Clough. Prue was friendly with a local wine bar owner, or so he claims, and I have my doubts about him. Also, her landlord is a dodgy character. But now that you're alive—now I know that someone tried to kill you—"

"I've put a spanner in the works, haven't I?"

He damn well had. "Yes."

"What about Clare? Have you spoken to her? Did Prue say anything to her?"

"Wait a minute. Who's Clare?"

"Clare Finch—Prue's best friend."

"I've never even heard of her. She wasn't at Prue's funeral, was she?"

"I don't know. I never met her, although I know Prue used to speak to her most weeks. She lives in Ipswich or some such place. If in trouble, I think Prue would have turned to her."

"You don't have an address or phone number for her, do you?"

"Sorry."

Dylan would have to go through the phone book and hope there weren't too many Finches in Ipswich.

"Are you going to tell the world I'm alive?" McIntyre asked.

"Who else knows? Your wealthy friend and who else?"

"No one. I told Simon because we've been friends forever and I know I can trust him. I also knew he had a flat in London going begging. When someone wants you dead, there are very few people you feel you can trust, but Simon's one. So, are you going to tell the world?"

"What would happen to the price of your paintings if people knew you were alive?"

McIntyre laughed at that. "If you have one to sell, Dylan, I'd do it now. Prices will plummet as soon as news of my resurrection breaks."

That fact alone meant that McIntyre was worth more dead than alive to a lot of people. It didn't explain Prue's murder though.

Dylan didn't know what to do about McIntyre. Nothing, he supposed. What could he do? McIntyre might be a killer, but there was damn all Dylan could do about it.

"No," he said. "I'm not going to tell the world. Give me your phone number. I take it you do possess a phone?"

"I do." McIntyre grabbed a beer mat, took a pen from his pocket and wrote down his phone number. "There you go. If you can't get hold of me, leave a message."

Dylan took the beer mat and gazed at the flowery numbers. "How much is this worth?"

"Not a lot. Although, as you say, a fool and his money are soon parted."

"So what are you planning to do now?" Dylan asked.

"I'm heading back to London tonight although I'm no longer sure the answer's there. Hell, Dylan, I don't know where the answer is."

"Me neither."

"But it's out there somewhere," McIntyre said. "Someone knows who killed Prue. And somewhere is the man who tried to send me to my watery grave."

He was right. "I'll let you know if I learn anything new." Dylan took another beer mat and wrote down his own phone number. "Will you do the same?"

"I will. You might have a chat with my lovely wife," McIntyre said. "And perhaps with Martin Collins."

"I'll do that."

"And now I have a train to catch." McIntyre drained his glass and got to his feet. "Keep in touch, Dylan."

"I will."

As McIntyre walked out of the pub, Dylan wondered if he'd ever see him again. He also wondered if he'd just had a drink with Prue Murphy's killer.

TWENTY-FOUR

"I NEED A word," Maddie said. "If you can spare the time."

Tim gave her a look, one that said he wished he was a million miles from this house, from her, from everything. "I can spare the time."

His phone rang. He looked at the display, then looked at her. "I need to take this."

"Naturally."

She could tell it was Eddie and she soon realised that Tim was furious with him. He didn't say as much, not in so many words, but his answers were clipped, his knuckles white as he gripped the phone, and his jaw set in a hard line. He didn't say a lot, he was too busy listening.

"That's your problem, Eddie. You caused the problem, you solve it. It has nothing to do with me. Nothing whatsoever." He ended the call with a vicious prod at the button.

It was funny but just as she'd started to warm to Eddie, Tim was being distinctly cool to his business partner and friend.

"Right, Maddie. What can I do for you?"

They hadn't cleared away the dinner plates yet. An empty bottle of wine still sat on the table. Ignoring it,

Tim went to the rack and chose another bottle. He removed the cork and filled his glass to the brim before holding the bottle out to Maddie. She'd already had a couple of glasses too many but she nodded, and he filled her glass.

"It's about this." She held a small brass button in her hand.

Tim frowned at it. "Am I supposed to guess the significance of that?"

"Yes." She turned it over in her hand. "This is the button you lost, remember? You came back from Portugal and said you'd lost a button from your blazer. I spent weeks trying to find a replacement."

"Ah. Got it. So you've found it?"

"So it would appear." She put the button on the table.

"That's good then." He sat opposite her and took a slug of wine.

"Indeed. And where do you think I found it? You'd assume I'd been to Portugal perhaps. Or on the same plane that carried you to that particular country. But no. I found this button when I was sorting through Prue's things."

"And?"

She wanted to throw her wine in his face, glass and all. There were times when she hated him. Really hated him with a passion that made her blood pound. Everyone thought he was the perfect husband. Charming, handsome, intelligent, witty—she hated him.

"And I'd like to know how my sister got hold of a button from my husband's jacket," she said. "I'd like to know when you saw Prue. I'd like to know exactly what was going on between the two of you."

"For God's sake." Tim rubbed his eyes as if he were too tired to keep them open. He sighed. "Do you ever wonder why you can't enjoy a normal relationship with anyone, Maddie? Do you ever stop to ask yourself why you end up seeing one shrink after another?"

"No. I'm too busy wondering what my husband was doing with my sister."

The curtains had been drawn to shut out the darkness for hours. The room felt claustrophobic. Maddie no longer liked this house. She'd like to live abroad, somewhere that was treated to sunshine and blue skies almost every day. She'd like a house with a pool.

"Nothing has been going on," Tim said. "If I lost the button at Prue's, I will have lost it at Christmas when we called in with her present. Remember?"

His calm voice of reason dissolved some of her anger. She remembered the day, of course, but not whether Tim had been wearing that blazer. She'd wanted to visit Prue out of nosiness. They always went through the routine of exchanging presents so it had been the perfect excuse. They'd driven up to Dawson's Clough, spent an hour with Prue, stayed the night in a hotel near Clitheroe and driven home the next day. She would have expected Tim to have worn a sweater, not a blazer. She tried to picture him in that awful house of Prue's, but she couldn't. She could hear his voice, full of charm and seasonal jollity, but she couldn't see his clothes.

Damn it. If they'd been part of a normal family, she or Prue would have taken photos of themselves standing in front of the Christmas tree. They weren't part of a normal family, though, so there were no photos.

"What about that night in France?" she asked.

"Which night?"

He was playing for time. "You know which night I'm talking about. The night you spent with my sister last September."

"Oh, that night. I've told you about that a dozen times but, hey, let's go through it all again, shall we? You went to bed. Your sister carried on drinking and I had another couple to keep her company. Prue was very drunk. We sat up talking—at least, she talked and I listened—and then, when she passed out, I put her to bed. She was fully clothed and too drunk to know anything about it."

"What did you talk about?"

"Life, the universe and every other damn thing."

Maddie had asked a dozen times, but she'd never got to the bottom of what happened that night.

They'd finally paid Prue a visit in France, mainly because Maddie couldn't conjure up yet more excuses to avoid it, and stayed with her for two nights. On the second night, they'd had a bit of a party. Several of Prue's friends had come along bearing bottles of wine and plates of food. It had been Prue's—and Tim's— idea of fun. Maddie had hated every second. When the guests started leaving, she'd claimed a headache and gone to bed. Tim had promised to follow her just as soon as he'd finished his drink and helped Prue tidy the kitchen. Prue had laughed and said there was no need for him to help.

The next thing Maddie knew, she'd woken up to find

Tim's side of the bed empty. She was convinced he hadn't slept in that bed all night.

Tim claimed he'd slept in their bed beside her for a couple of hours, but Maddie hadn't believed him. Prue had been suffering with the hangover from hell and she'd claimed to have been embarrassed about sitting up for hours "boring Tim stupid."

"What did I talk about, Tim? Was it all doom, gloom and failed relationships?" Prue had asked him.

"No." He'd smiled at her. "You talked of nothing you wouldn't mention when sober. Don't worry about it, Prue."

"I am *so* embarrassed."

"Don't be. There's no need." Tim had given her a brotherly kiss and a hug, and they'd left Prue to her embarrassment and caught the plane home to England.

And Maddie had wondered about that night ever since...

"Did you have an affair with Prue?" she asked. "Did it start that night in France? Is that why your button was in her home?"

"No, no and no. Get real, Maddie." He drained his glass and stood up. "I don't have time for this. I'm not being unfaithful. I have never been unfaithful. If I was going to be unfaithful, my own sister-in-law would be out of bounds. Right, end of conversation. I'm going to bed."

He did that a lot. To avoid any sort of conflict, he'd walk away. He'd go to bed or invent some excuse that took him away from the house.

Maddie didn't believe him. She'd never believed him. Or Prue. Or her parents. The only person she trusted was herself. It was easier that way.

TWENTY-FIVE

IT WAS GOOD to sit down in the Dog and Fox with Frank. Dylan felt at ease with his old boss. You knew where you stood with Frank, and you knew you could take every word he said as gospel.

"So then," Frank said. "Update me. And tell me about McIntyre."

They'd spoken briefly on the phone and had soon decided that this conversation warranted a few pints of beer.

Dylan, slowly and carefully, told Frank about his trip to the art gallery yesterday, how he'd spotted the bearded chap who'd been hanging around at Prue's funeral, and how he realised that bearded chap was none other than Jack McIntyre.

"So he's claiming attempted murder?" Frank asked, licking beer froth from his top lip. "And you believe him?"

"Without evidence to back it up—and there's none of that in this case—I don't believe anything."

"Very wise." Frank nodded his approval.

"He did, however, give me Clare Finch's name. She was Prue's best friend and she's been in Australia, working on a farm as part of some research thing, for the past few months. She only arrived back in the country yesterday. Her parents had told her about Prue and she's coming up here on Friday. She wants to see Prue's grave for some reason. Still, that suits me. It will be better to meet her face-to-face than have this discussion over the phone. And I sure as hell didn't fancy driving to Ipswich. It's a pig of a place to get to."

Not that Dylan was expecting to get anything from the conversation. In this instance, Prue hadn't turned to her best friend to share her woes because Clare had been on the other side of the world. Instead, she'd turned to Maddie.

"I asked Maddie about Clare Finch," he said, "but she'd never heard of her."

"That's no surprise, is it? Those sisters were strangers to each other." Before Dylan could comment on that, Frank went on, "Perhaps the two aren't linked. Maybe the person who wanted McIntyre killed—if indeed there is such a person—isn't the same person who wanted Prue Murphy in her box."

"You believe that?"

Frank thought for a moment, then shook his head. "Not really, no. There must be a link."

Dylan thought so but— "Prue only lived with McIntyre for a couple of months. They don't have the same circle of friends or the same lifestyle."

"Did his wife find out about it?" Frank asked. "Is she the jealous type?"

"She claims she's never heard of Prue and that divorce was never mentioned. McIntyre claims he asked for a divorce so that he could be with Prue. And there's the money side of it all. Even McIntyre pointed out that he was worth more dead than alive to her. I think I need another chat with Davina McIntyre."

"And the agent's son," Frank said. "Tell me about him."

"He's another on my list. In fact, McIntyre named him as chief suspect. According to him, Martin Collins loves money and would stop at nothing—including murdering his own father—to get it. But before that, I need to see the CCTV images from the art gallery. How long's it likely to take, Frank? I did ask at the gallery but you know what they're like."

"Law-abiding?" Frank suggested, and Dylan grinned at him.

"Yes. This sodding Data Protection Act puts the fear of God into people. Anyway, if you can swing it quickly, I'd be obliged. I want to see if anyone was hanging around when Prue was there. She rang Maddie that evening and she was frightened. It's just possible that something happened at the gallery. Or on the train."

"I'll see what I can do," Frank said.

"Thanks. I appreciate it." Dylan stood up. "My round, I think."

He carried their glasses to the bar and was waiting to be served when he caught sight of the newspaper on the corner of the bar. There, smiling up at him from the front page, was the young lad who'd been hanging around the church's entrance on the day of Prue's funeral.

"There are some evil buggers about," the barman said, nodding at the news item. "I'd like to get my hands on them. Hanging's too bloody good for 'em, and what will the bastard who did that get? A few years in a bloody holiday camp, that's what. The bloody country's gone mad."

There was no point getting into a discussion on the merits or otherwise of the penal system or capital punishment. "Can I borrow this?"

"Help yourself." The barman refilled their glasses and Dylan carried drinks and newspaper back to the table.

"What about this?" he said when he was sitting beside Frank.

Frank looked across. "Oh, yes. A young constable found his body yesterday. The poor bugger was beaten to death and his body was thrown in Bailey's Lake. Poor bugger," he said again.

"It's the lad I told you about," Dylan said. "You know, the one who was hanging around outside the church on the day of Prue's funeral? The one who was having a smoke and who looked as if he'd bunked off school? This is him."

"Are you sure?"

"One hundred percent."

Dylan read the news item. Sixteen-year-old Kevin Mills, it claimed, had told his parents he was off to football practice at his school, but there had been no football practice. Instead, he'd met up with friends, unnamed for legal reasons, and they'd gone for a few drinks in town. His football kit had been abandoned in the cemetery. It was assumed that he'd intended to collect it on his way home, but he'd never made it.

"Are there any suspects?" he asked Frank.

"None that I know of."

"What the fuck's going on? Someone tries to kill a well-known artist. Next, someone kills well-known artist's lover. Then, someone kills a young lad interested enough in Prue's funeral to hang around and watch the mourners arrive."

"There might not be any connection at all. You said yourself that Kevin Mills looked as if he was bunking off school. It was raining on the day of the funeral. Perhaps he'd just stopped to shelter and smoke his cigarette."

"Ooh, look, a pink farmyard animal just flew past. Bacon on the wing." There was a connection, all right. Dylan was damn sure of it. "Kevin Mills's death is in some way connected to Prue Murphy's."

All Dylan had to do was prove it.

TWENTY-SIX

CLARE FINCH WAS nothing like Dylan had imagined and nothing like she'd sounded on the phone. He'd expected someone like Prue, he supposed. Artistic. Pretty. Clare looked more serious and geeky but that was perhaps due to the large glasses she wore, the lack of makeup and the way she'd tied her dark hair back with an elastic band.

"It's good to meet you, Clare. Would you like a coffee or a cup of tea before we go to the church?"

She tucked a stray strand of hair behind her ear. "I'd like that, thanks. Coffee, please."

Dylan had suggested they meet at his hotel rather than the church, which had been her first idea. Churches and graves didn't strike him as the best meeting places. Besides, the hotel was near the station and, therefore, easier for her to get to. He could drive them to the church later.

She'd had a long train journey and he guessed the big bag she carried would be stuffed with books, notepads, pens, apples and probably sandwiches for the journey. She looked the sensible type, probably a Girl Guide in her youth, who would be prepared for anything.

He ushered her to a table in the hotel's warm reception area, one that offered a view of the hills, and she removed her coat and put that, a bouquet of white flowers and her bag on a chair before sitting down.

"You've been in Australia then, Clare?" he said.

"Yes, for six months. I got back last week." She tucked that strand of hair behind her ear again and it immediately fell back across her face. "I heard about Prue, of course. Mum told me. I couldn't believe it." She shuddered and hugged herself.

"You were close friends?"

"Oh, yes. We met at school. My parents moved around a lot because of Dad's job so I should have been used to changing schools every five minutes. I wasn't though. I hated it. Maybe our teacher understood that because she sat me next to Prue in class and gave Prue strict instructions to show me around and look after me." She smiled at the memories. "By the end of that first day, we'd become friends for life." Her expression clouded. In Prue's case, life had been short. "Will you tell me what happened?"

The waitress brought coffees to their table and Clare was profuse with her gratitude and her smiles. Dylan liked her.

"I can tell you all I know," he said. Well, most of it. "The police believe Prue disturbed a burglar and either fell or was pushed to her death. However, only hours before she died, she'd phoned Maddie. You know Maddie?"

"I met her once," Clare said. "It was years ago though. She and Prue didn't get along, did they? Prue used to say they lived on different planets."

Prue was right.

"Well, she phoned Maddie that day and she sounded frightened, worried about something. She arranged to travel down to London to talk to Maddie the following day. Except, of course, she was killed before morning."

Clare was listening and frowning. "I'm surprised. If she was worried about something, I would have thought Maddie was the last person she'd want to speak to. She used to describe phone calls to Maddie as duty calls. She'd say, 'She's my sister so I have to make an effort.' I'm surprised she didn't go to someone else."

"Like who?"

"I don't know. Anyone."

"She probably thought it too late or too early to call you."

Clare nodded. "Probably, but even so—why Maddie?"

Only Prue knew the answer to that particular conundrum. "Did you speak often on the phone while you were in Australia?"

"No. It was too expensive for one thing. Also, we were waiting until I got home. We'd promised ourselves that we'd have a week's holiday together—somewhere cheap and cheerful—and catch up on each other's news."

"What about when she lived in France?" Dylan asked. "Did you speak on the phone then?"

"Quite often, yes, but only because I was working for a large pharmaceutical company that had offices in France." She blushed. "The company didn't mind us making personal calls so long as they weren't too long. Prue didn't have a computer then so we couldn't email."

"Ah."

"We emailed each other a few times when I was in Australia," she said, "but we didn't say a lot. We neither of us bothered much with emails. We didn't really exchange news. Like I said, we thought we'd have a good catching-up session when I came home."

"Okay," Dylan said. "So, as I was saying, she called Maddie sounding worried. Maddie was convinced that Prue's death was due to something more sinister than a burglar so she employed me."

"What do you mean by more sinister?"

"We don't really know. Tell me, did she ever talk about Jack McIntyre?"

Clare shook her head, puzzled. "You mean *the* Jack McIntyre?"

"I do." Dylan really was the only person on the planet not to have heard of the bloke. "Did she ever mention him at all?"

"No. Never. Why do you ask?"

"She met him, apparently, when she was living in France."

"Really?" Clare looked suddenly excited for her friend. "And she didn't tell me? I can't believe that. Wow, I bet she loved that."

Dylan smiled. "I expect she did. You're sure she never mentioned him?"

"Positive. I would have remembered something like that."

Dylan's spirits sank. Prue had been far too private a person to help him with this puzzle. Her sister hadn't known about McIntyre, her best friend hadn't known—but someone had, he was sure of it.

"So," he said, "she was still living in France when you went to Australia, yes?"

"Yes, and she seemed so settled there. Really, she loved it, and I couldn't believe she was leaving. As for coming up here to live, it seemed such an odd place to choose. She liked it though and she said she'd never met such lovely friendly people." She smiled suddenly. "She stayed with her mum and dad for a couple of weeks while she got herself sorted, and I imagine she was pleased to live anywhere after that. She loved them both, but they fussed a bit. Parents do, don't they?"

"I only have one parent but, yes, she can fuss enough for six."

"Oh, I'm sorry." She sounded genuinely sympathetic.

"Don't be." Dylan was happy enough with one parent. Two meant twice the trouble. He'd always been mildly curious about his father but ever since Bev's ludicrous comment that Boris looked like him, he didn't want to know. Boris was not his father. The idea was—well, it was ludicrous.

Their coffees were finished and she looked eager to get moving.

"Shall we visit the church?" he asked. Using the word *church* was better than *grave*.

She nodded. "Thanks. It's really kind of you to offer to drive me. I appreciate it. And the company. It's not a pleasant task but it's something I feel I have to do. Can you understand that?"

"Of course." He suspected it was the only way she'd be able to convince herself that Prue was really dead.

She put on her coat, grabbed her bag and the flowers, and they walked out of the hotel and into the car park. At least the rain was holding off. The sky was a threatening grey though.

"Aw, is this your car? Isn't it sweet?"

Dylan despaired of women. He always had and he always would. One had once described his car as "pretty" and now Clare called it "sweet." What the hell was wrong with them? It wasn't sweet. It was a mean and powerful 1956 Morgan in Daytona Yellow. It was a much-coveted classic, the ultimate example of British design and engineering.

"Thanks." There was no point trying to put her straight.

She sat beside him with the flowers and her bag clutched tightly on her lap. Her fingers looked as if rigor mortis had set in.

"There isn't much to see," he said as he drove out of the car park. "There's no headstone yet—" He broke off before mentioning that the ground had to be allowed to settle before one could be erected.

She nodded and braced herself more tightly for the ordeal ahead.

As soon as they were walking along that slippery path to the graves, Dylan had a moment's panic that he wouldn't be able to find Prue's grave. There were so many. Then he remembered that tree where the man he now knew to be McIntyre had been standing.

"Here it is," he said.

There was nothing to look at, just a mound of earth, a few dead flowers, two fresh arrangements and a rain-soaked card that read *A loving father and grandfather. We'll always miss you, Fred* that must have blown across from another grave. Dylan looked at the two fresh arrangements of flowers. One was from Doreen, Prue's neighbour, the other, red roses, had a small card attached that was simply signed with a *J.* Presumably *J* for Jack.

Clare's bottom lip wobbled alarmingly but then she went into action. She gathered up the dead flowers and carried them across the grass to throw them in a bin. The card to Fred went with them. She grabbed a stray piece of cellophane that had been strewn across the neighbouring grave, used it to wiped out a plastic vase and began to arrange her white flowers.

"She loved white ones." She stepped back to check that the flowers were shown off to their best possible advantage.

"They're very nice."

"Okay, that's fine," she said. "I only wanted to see where they'd put her. We can go now."

Just as Dylan was congratulating them both on getting it over so quickly, he saw her shoulders began to shake. They were halfway between grave and car when she put her hands to her face and howled.

Dylan gave her shoulder a sympathetic squeeze and she turned her face into his chest and cried all the harder.

"She was such a lovely person." She choked out each

word. "Who could do this to her? It's not fair. She was
my best friend and I'm going to miss her so much."

He had more questions for Clare and he wished now
that he'd had the good sense to ask them before they
saw the grave. As it was, he led her, crying all the way,
to his car. He opened the door, pushed her gently into
the passenger seat and walked round to sit behind the
steering steel. And still she cried.

Dylan hunted round for the pack of tissues he knew
had been in the car a week or so back. Just as he was
mentally cursing Bev for throwing those out too, he
found them. He opened the pack, pulled one out and
handed it to Clare.

"Thank you." She took it from him, blew her nose
and reached for another. Six tissues later, she seemed
to have pulled herself together. "Sorry, Dylan."

"Don't be. She was worth a few tears."

"She certainly was. She was the best friend anyone
could have. I miss her so much."

Dylan decided he might as well ask his questions.
"Did she ever mention a chap called Danny Thompson to you?" At her blank expression, he added, "He
runs a wine bar in the town. She used to visit it now
and again."

"No. Sorry, but the name means nothing to me."

"According to him, she used to go there, get drunk
and take a cab home. Not often, just every few weeks
or so. Does that sound like something Prue would do?"

She smiled and her eyes filled with fresh tears. "God,
yes. We were always telling each other we needed to
grow up. She never will though, will she? Yes, that

sounds like something she'd do. You know when life gets a bit much? You go and get drunk and, the next morning, you're too concerned about your hangover to care about anything else."

Dylan smiled at that. "She didn't mention the wine bar to you?"

"No."

Prue Murphy had been the most tight-lipped person ever.

"Danny Thompson," Dylan said, "the owner, said she'd mentioned something to him about all the decent men being married, gay or both. Is that something she would have said?"

"Yes." A genuine smile curved her lips. "Sometimes, usually when we'd had a drink or two, we'd sit and man-watch as we called it. We'd rate them—God, that sounds bad, doesn't it? It was only a harmless bit of fun though. We'd watch men and say 'Married,' 'Gay,' 'Desperate,' 'Boring' and, if a miracle happened, 'Drop-dead gorgeous and available.' It was just harmless fun."

"Do you think she might have been involved with anyone?"

"No one I knew about."

"Might she have been involved with a married man? Was that something she would have told you?"

"She wouldn't have told me because it wouldn't have happened. No way would Prue have had anything to do with someone else's husband. We both knew the odds of that working out—zero. No, there would be too much pain involved for all concerned."

The thing about most people, Dylan thought, was

that they knew things about their friends they didn't realise they knew. Everyone did. He'd bet she knew a lot about Prue if only she'd take the time to think back and read between the lines.

"You okay?" he asked, and she nodded.

"Yes. Thanks."

He fired the engine and pulled away from the church in the direction of the town centre. She'd said she'd have a walk round before catching the train home. It had been a long journey to put those flowers on that sodden ground.

"So, Clare, if you had to describe Prue to me in half a dozen words, what would you say?"

She thought for a moment. "I'd say she was kind, generous, funny and smart. She loved art, loved great designs. She loved dogs and cats and was terrified of cows. She could cook but rarely bothered. She was loyal. She loved her parents. She hated pretentiousness. She was no one's fool. She never forgot my birthday, not once, and was always surprised when I remembered hers. She thought of others before herself." She sighed. "I can't think of a bad thing to say about her."

He'd gathered that. Perhaps Prue really had been as wonderful as people said.

"What about her sister, Maddie?" he asked. "I know you've only met her once, but Prue must have spoken about her. What sort of person does she strike you as?"

"Jealous."

Surprised, Dylan gave her a sideways glance.

"Prue dismissed that as nonsense," she said, "but nothing will ever convince me that Maddie isn't—

wasn't—jealous of Prue. Everyone loved Prue whereas people found Maddie difficult. Jealous, bitter, cruel, selfish—" She shrugged. "I don't know her, Dylan, so I'm not qualified to comment, but from things Prue used to say, that's how I'd describe Maddie. Prue, on the other hand, would defend her sister to her last breath. Once, and this made me so mad, Maddie fixed Prue up with a lad who was—well, let's say he had special needs. Prue was about sixteen at the time so Maddie would have been twenty-one. Maddie had been saying for weeks that she had this friend who was dying to meet Prue. So she arranged this date and Prue went along. Prue would do anything for a quiet life. And there was this young boy, about fifteen. Maddie thought this hysterically funny and Prue spent hours trying to explain to her sister that, actually, it wasn't funny to play jokes that involved a kid with special needs. In the end, of course, Maddie was the one left fuming because Prue had a great time with—Adrian, his name was. She took him to the funfair the following day, I remember, and they stayed friends. But that's Maddie. Cruel. And jealous."

Dylan didn't know what to make of that. If he thought of Maddie, he thought of that blasted blue bedroom. He couldn't remember ever thinking her cruel, jealous or selfish. She'd been fun. She wasn't a bundle of laughs these days, but why would she be? Her sister had died, her parents were in bits, she had funerals to arrange, police to deal with—no one would be fun under those circumstances.

God, there was now't so queer as folk, as people were fond of saying.

They'd arrived at the bus station and Dylan stopped the car. "If you walk through that alley, you'll find yourself in the shopping centre. Then, if you come back here, you can get the free bus to the station for your train."

"That's great. Thanks so much, Dylan."

"Are you sure you're okay?"

"Yes." She didn't look it. "Yes, I'm fine. Thanks."

"You have my number?"

"Of course. And if I think of anything else, I'll give you a call. And you, if you find out anything, will you let me know?"

"I will."

Dylan watched her walk in the direction of the alley where a sign read To the Shops. She stopped as she reached it, lifted her bag higher onto her shoulder, seemed to take a deep breath, and strode off. He watched until she was out of sight.

TWENTY-SEVEN

DYLAN WAS LYING on his back, staring up at the ceiling and trying to picture himself on a boat with a friend. He was imagining enjoying a bottle of wine with Frank beneath the stars on a boat that was rocking gently on a calm sea. He went below to fetch more wine, came back and was in time to see Frank attacked and knocked overboard. Someone came at him with a fire extinguisher, smashed it into his shoulder and sent him into the water. What would he do? With his boat heading back to shore, he'd do his damnedest to find Frank and, when that proved fruitless, he'd concentrate on swimming to dry land. So far so good. Then what would he do?

Easy. He'd call 999 and say "Some bastard just tried to kill me."

Why hadn't Jack McIntyre done that?

He didn't know. He did know that Clare Finch had given him something to think about. She'd been far more helpful than she could have known and had sent his mind in a completely new direction.

"Your mum's acting strange," Bev said.

"What?" Damn it, he'd lost his train of thought now. "Oh, well, that's good. It would worry me if she was acting normal."

"I'm being serious."

"So am I." Dylan had been under the impression that they'd come to bed to get some sleep but Bev sat up and switched on the lamp.

"Think about it," she said. "Boris is planning to ride a Harley along Route 66. That's Vicky's dream holiday and her dream man. Just imagine all the weirdos she'd meet. Hell, she might even meet Bob Dylan."

"Bob's probably getting a bit old to ride a Harley."

"Just think if she met him, though. I mean really met him as opposed to seeing him at a concert. She'd die a happy woman."

Knowing he'd get no sleep for a while, Dylan sat up. "But she wouldn't meet him."

"I know. Yes, I know. But she'd be sure to meet lots of like-minded people on a trip like that. It's her ideal holiday, right?"

"Probably," he said.

"And Boris has to be her ideal man, right?"

"I don't know. He might be, he might not. How would I know?"

"He is." She wasn't going to argue the point. "So, tell me this. If he's so perfect for her, why isn't she seeing him again? And she isn't. I asked her and she was adamant."

"How would I know? Maybe he squeezes toothpaste from the top. Perhaps he likes to dress up in women's clothes. How would I know, Bev? If he does nothing for her, that's it. There's nothing we can do about it."

"I have my own theory."

"Really?" He was definitely getting no sleep till this was sorted. "Do tell."

"I think she's figured out that he's your father and I think she's putting an end to it before anyone else realises. It would get too complicated for her, wouldn't it? You know what she's like."

He knew what she was like all right. As mad as a box of blasted frogs. He couldn't imagine for one moment that Boris was his father though. There were no similarities at all as far as he could see. They were about the same height and had the same colour hair, although Boris's was showing a lot of grey mixed in with the dark, and that was all. That could apply to half the male population.

"It's the eyes," Bev said.

"What?"

"You and Boris. You have the same eyes."

"Rubbish."

"Have it your way." She switched off the lamp and settled down again. "Night."

Goddamn it. He was wide-awake now.

He thumped his pillow into submission and lay on his back staring up at the darkness again. Boris was about the same height as he was, he had the same thick dark hair, and Bev thought they had the same eyes. That meant nothing. Bev swore that Freya looked like his mother whereas Dylan couldn't see the slightest resemblance. There were millions of men walking the planet who were as tall and dark-haired as Dylan. Millions. Okay, so Boris had been in Turkey at the same time as

Dylan's mother, at the same time that Dylan had been conceived, but so what?

None of it mattered anyway. Boris had been given the brush-off, and it was unlikely any of them would see him again. He'd be forgotten. Dylan had survived forty years without knowing his father's identity and he could easily survive another forty.

Bev was right, though. It was strange that his mother wasn't out buying a crash helmet and hoping to get her kicks on Route 66.

Dylan knew where Boris lived. He could pay him a visit, maybe have a chat. Not that it was an easy subject to bring up. "By the way, Boris, did you shag my mother forty years ago?"

He pushed the extremely distasteful image from his mind and concentrated on more important matters, like why Jack McIntyre hadn't gone to the police.

A small element of doubt surfaced. Perhaps, in the same situation, Dylan *would* have gone it alone. It had to be far easier to find a killer if that person believed you were dead. Also, as soon as the police told the world you were alive, who's to say the killer wouldn't try again—and succeed this time?

Who had wanted McIntyre dead? Assuming someone had, of course. Who had broken into Prue Murphy's home and killed her? And who had ended sixteen-year-old Kevin Mills's life in such a brutal fashion?

He needed to start with Kevin Mills's murder and work backwards. He'd return to Dawson's Clough and start asking questions. Detectives would be doing the same thing, of course, but they had rulebooks to follow. Dylan didn't.

TWENTY-EIGHT

DYLAN STOPPED THE Morgan outside Maddie's home in time to see her in a very tight embrace with Eddie Bryson. They were in the lounge, standing by the window and on show to anyone who happened to look inside. Maddie spotted him first and stepped back from Bryson.

Dylan got out of the car, strode up the front door and was about to ring the bell when it swung open.

"You're early, Dylan."

They'd arranged to meet this evening, but Dylan was heading back to Dawson's Clough and had decided to call here on his way. She didn't look pleased about the change of plan.

"Hi, Maddie. Yes, sorry about that. I'm driving north so I thought I'd call in here on the off chance you were in." He looked past her to Bryson. "Hello, Eddie."

"Dylan, how are you?" Bryson strode forward, his hand outstretched.

"I'm good, thanks." Dylan shook his hand and wondered just how close Bryson and Maddie were. He didn't seem her type. Neither did Tim Chandler though. All the same, that embrace had seemed extremely intimate for a Monday morning.

They all walked into the kitchen. Maddie looked tense and upset.

"How are you getting on?" Bryson asked. "Have you any idea who might have done such a thing to Maddie's poor sister?"

"I have a few leads." God, he was sounding like a copper now. A lying copper.

"That's good. It will be a relief to all concerned if you can find out what really happened."

"Time will tell," Dylan said.

"You may as well hear this, Dylan." Maddie stood with her back to them both, staring out the window. She spun round to face them. "I think Tim was having an affair with Prue."

Dylan was too surprised to speak and silence stretched between them until Bryson spoke. "And I think you're imagining it, Maddie."

So was that it? Eddie had been consoling Maddie? It was all perfectly innocent?

"What makes you think that?" Dylan asked.

"This." She opened a fist that had been tightly clenched to reveal a brass button. "Tim claims to have lost this when he went to Portugal. If that was true, how did I find it among Prue's possessions?"

Interesting. "What does Tim say?"

"He denies everything. Well, he would, wouldn't he?" Maddie paced the length of the kitchen with the button held before her like a trophy.

"How can you be sure it's the same button?" Dylan asked.

"I just know."

"It seems unlikely," Dylan said, "that Prue would have an affair with her own sister's husband."

"That proves how much you know about her."

Jealous was how Clare Finch had described Maddie. Had Maddie been so jealous of Prue that she'd imagine Prue capable of stealing her husband?

Prue hadn't been happy having an affair with a married man, Dylan was fairly sure of that. Clare Finch had confirmed it. Danny Thompson had said she'd visited his wine bar and complained that all the decent men were married or gay. Dylan had assumed she'd been referring to McIntyre. Perhaps Tim Chandler had been on her mind. Perhaps Prue *had* been involved with Chandler.

"He claims," Maddie said, "that he must have lost it when we visited Prue before Christmas, but I don't think he was wearing his blazer then."

"You don't sound too sure," Dylan said.

"How the hell can I be expected to remember what he was wearing three months ago?"

"I have to go." Bryson gave Dylan a regretful smile. "Nothing personal, Dylan. I have an appointment and I'm running late as it is. It's been good to see you though." He put a hand to Maddie's face. "You're imagining things, sweetheart. Tim loves you, I know that. Now, stop worrying. I expect it's the stress you're under right now. You're getting worked up over nothing."

She nodded and gave him a weak smile.

Bryson gave her a quick peck on the cheek, took car keys from his pocket and was gone.

The phone rang out and a frown crossed Maddie's

face. Then, in an instant, the frown was replaced by a smile. "I'll ignore it. Sorry, Dylan, I sound a right old misery, don't I? It's just that nothing seems to be going to plan at the moment."

"Life rarely does."

The phone stopped ringing.

"I know." She slipped her arm through his. "So what do you have to tell me?"

Dylan wondered if this was what middle age was all about. Twenty years ago, he would have been in Maddie's bed and to hell with the consequences. His older and possibly wiser self was busy trying to make sense of her. Her moods changed in a split second and he realised he didn't know her at all. Perhaps he never had.

What about the mental image he had of Prue? Was that even close to accurate? Everyone he'd spoken to adored her but he'd only spoken to her friends. None of those friends had a bad word for Prue. Or a good one for Maddie.

"You asked me to come," Dylan reminded her. "I don't really have anything to tell you. I'm heading back to Dawson's Clough though."

"Why?"

"A teenager, Kevin Mills, has been murdered and I think his death is connected to Prue's in some way. He was at the church when we buried Prue. I don't know why or how, but I'm sure there's a connection."

"Because you saw him at the church on the day of Prue's funeral?" Her tone was mildly scoffing.

"Yes. And because two murders in Dawson's Clough is stretching the realms of coincidence too far."

She tapped her foot on the floor. Tap, tap, tap. "When will you be back?"

"I don't know yet, but I'll let you know."

She really was angry.

"I've been wondering if there's any point to this," she said.

"To what?"

"To you wasting so much time on it. Perhaps the police are right, after all."

He leaned back against the counter. "You're thinking of pulling me off the case?"

"I don't know." She gave him a smile. "Just look at you. You'd think I'd just taken your favourite toy away. I'll have a think and we'll talk about it when you come back. Who knows, you might have found out something interesting by then. We'll have dinner and discuss it then, yes?"

Dylan nodded. "Okay."

"Wonderful. I'll look forward to it." She threw her arms round his waist and squeezed. "As for the rest, take no notice of me. I expect I'm overreacting just because every damn thing I touch at the moment seems to fall apart."

She made no effort to let him go so he held her hands and put them in front of her. "I'll call you, Maddie."

"Yes, do, and I'll book us a table somewhere special."

When he was sitting in his car, he let out his breath. *Somewhere special.* He didn't like the sound of that. He was forty years old, though, and could take care of himself. In a way, he was flattered that she enjoyed flirting with him. She probably wouldn't do anything more than flirt. Although if she believed Chandler had been having an affair with her sister, she might fancy the taste of revenge.

Prue and Chandler. It was feasible, Dylan supposed. A damn sight more feasible than Prue and McIntyre in fact.

Sex had a lot to answer for when you stopped to think about it, and he'd been thinking about it a lot lately. If he hadn't slept with Maddie, she would have employed some other investigator to look into her sister's death and he wouldn't have been plagued by memories of that blue bedroom. If Prue hadn't embarked on an affair with Jack McIntyre, she might still be alive. If Dylan's mother hadn't—

He stopped before that particular thought took root. He didn't know what his mother had done or not done.

He'd been looking forward to a decent lunch in Dawson's Clough, but now he felt compelled to take a quick detour.

For once, his sat nav took him to the correct address and he sat in the car for a moment to look at a house that was very similar to his own. This one was much bigger and had a huge, well-tended garden, but the design was the same.

Before he could change his mind, he walked up the drive, looked in vain for a doorbell and then tapped a brass knocker against the wooden door. Suddenly realising that this was the most stupid idea he'd had to date, he was about to make a run for it. But the door opened and there was Boris. He looked smaller today, and slightly scruffier, thanks to a pair of well-worn jeans, ill-fitting sweater, and the fact that he hadn't shaved this morning.

There was no way this man could be his father. Bev was putting two and two together and coming up with forty-two.

"What a nice surprise, Dylan. Come in. Is everything all right? The family well?"

"Yes, fine, thanks. I was out this way and thought I'd stop and say hello. I'm on my way north, so it will have to be a very quick hello."

They passed a spacious kitchen and ended up in what was obviously Boris's study. Apart from a desk and two chairs that looked to be antique, everything was modern. His computer screen was huge and paper thin. Classical music was coming from an iPod attached to Bang & Olufsen speakers.

"Have a seat." Boris gestured to a captain's chair. "Let me get you a coffee. I was about to have one myself."

"Well—thanks. As I said, I can't stop long, but a quick coffee would be good."

"Back in two ticks."

No way was Dylan descended from a man who said "two ticks." What the hell was Bev thinking?

Wooden framed photos of a woman—Boris's late wife, Dylan assumed—sat on the desk. On one wall was a huge photo of a gleaming Harley-Davidson. A small TV hung from a wall bracket.

"Here we go." Boris put two chunky pottery mugs on the desk. "Sorry, do you take sugar?"

Before Dylan could say that he did, the phone trilled out.

"Help yourself," Boris said, gesturing in the direction of the kitchen they'd passed at the same time as he reached for the phone.

Dylan took his mug into the kitchen and soon found the sugar. He pulled open four drawers before he found a spoon. As he stirred in a couple of spoonfuls, he looked around. It was all oak and granite—very nice—and hanging from hooks on a set of shelves were eight identical mugs to the one he'd been given.

On hearing Boris finish his call, he returned to the study.

"You have a nice house." Dylan had never coped well with small talk. "And it must be good to be able to work from home."

"It's okay," Boris said, "but you need plenty of self-discipline. It's far too easy to work long into the night. You never leave the office, you see."

"A lot of us are guilty of that. The invention of computers gave us a portable office."

"True. Well, it's really good to see you, Dylan. I was hoping I'd see a bit more of Vicky but—" his eyes twinkled "—she's shying away from me. She's said she doesn't want to get involved. I've told her that I don't either. I've had two wives—that's enough, isn't it? I was only asking her out to dinner. I wasn't expecting her to marry me."

"Women are funny creatures."

Boris smiled. "I'll give her a call in a couple of months."

"Good idea." Dylan was mentally forming a dozen questions, but asking a man about his sex life didn't come easy. "I bet you had some good times out in Turkey."

"Yes—there was a whole gang of us. We thought we were immortal and could do drink and drugs until we dropped."

"Sounds great." It sounded hell.

"We all moved around a lot. We thought nothing of travelling the world. We had no money, all we had were a few dreams and our sleeping bags, but it didn't seem to matter back then."

It was no use. Dylan couldn't ask if his mother had shared that sleeping bag. He'd indulge in some inane chat for a few minutes and then leave.

"So you're travelling north again?" Boris said. "That car of yours gets through some miles."

"I know." It was a worry and he touched the wooden desk for luck. "She hasn't let me down yet."

They talked cars. At least, Boris talked cars. Dylan had always thought he could talk cars as well as the next man, but long before they'd finished discussing Boris's first company car—a beige Ford with matching upholstery—Dylan had lost the will to live. He could see why his mother was so reluctant to ride Route 66 with him.

He was taking his last swallow of coffee when the phone rang again.

"Could I get another coffee?" he asked on an impulse.

"Help yourself." Boris reached for the phone. "Do you want one?"

Boris shook his head and greeted his caller.

Dylan picked up both mugs and took them to the kitchen. Boris's was still half full. He emptied the contents into an identical mug and wrapped Boris's mug in a couple of sheets of white kitchen towel. He rammed it in his jacket pocket, tried to hide the bulge, failed, and made himself a fresh coffee.

When he returned to the study, Boris was just finishing his call.

"Sorry," Dylan said. "I took your mug. I didn't realise you hadn't finished. Here."

"Thanks."

Boris took a sip of coffee that had to be cold by now. "I'm surprised Vicky never married, you know. She was always the type to have people around her."

"She still is," Dylan said. "But I suppose having a baby changed her. Even she had to lean toward responsibility."

He smiled at that. "True. Of course, none of us knew she was expecting you. She just upped and left one day."

"What? No one knew?"

"Not a soul."

It was the perfect time to talk possible fathers, but Dylan couldn't do it. Instead, he finished his coffee and rose, somewhat awkwardly given that he had a fair-sized mug in his pocket, to his feet.

"Thanks so much for the coffee, Boris, but I must get off or I'll be late. It's been good to see you."

"You, too, Dylan. Keep in touch, won't you?"

"I will. And you." He knew he wouldn't. At least, he hoped he wouldn't.

He walked, crablike, to his car, waving at Boris all the way.

Once inside, he fired the engine and drove off in totally the wrong direction. He couldn't believe he'd actually stolen one of Boris's mugs. It was complete and utter madness.

Now that he had it though, he needed to find a lab. If they could lift DNA from the mug and compare it to a swab taken from him, he'd be able to quash all notions of Boris being his father.

TWENTY-NINE

TRYING TO TALK to teenagers while staying off CID radar wasn't easy. It had taken Dylan three days to get to this position.

His first job on arriving in Dawson's Clough had been to meet up with Frank and see what he'd managed to find out from his chums on the force. Not a lot, was the answer. They seemed to know little more than had already been reported in the local press. Kevin Mills had met up with a girl and a few other friends and had never made it home. No one knew any more than that.

Kevin's parents had believed he was at a football practice session arranged by the school that night. There had been no activities at the school though. Kevin had dumped his football kit in the cemetery close to his home, intending to collect it at the end of the evening, and met up with his girlfriend.

Dylan had spoken to several of Kevin's school friends, but none had known anything that hadn't been reported in the local press. When he'd asked if Kevin could have known Prue, they'd all looked at him as if he'd bungee-jumped from the moon. Now, finally, he was walking through the shopping centre with Carly Trueman.

"We've told the police all we know," she said. "They

were at the school for days. We've had them asking us questions, we've had to sit through services for Kevin, we've had some woman talking about counselling—we've had the lot."

She looked pale and frightened, and her eyes darted left and right as if she expected to see a killer or Kevin's ghost.

"The police have been to my house, too," she said. "They think I was the last person to see him."

Kevin's killer was the last person to see him.

"The police are okay," he said. "They're just trying to find out what happened. His parents will feel better when they know that." At least, he hoped they found some sort of closure.

"Yeah." She gave him a long distrustful look. "So why are you here asking questions? Why don't you just ask the police?"

"I used to be a policeman, Carly, but these days, I work independently. They get busy and I have more time to get to the bottom of things." That sounded official, as if the force would welcome his input. He didn't attempt to make it clearer.

They passed a small café and he saw her gaze linger on a plate of cakes.

"Would you like a drink or something to eat?" he asked.

"I wouldn't mind."

The warmth hit them as soon as they stepped inside. There was only one customer, a woman sitting at a table who had a coffee in one hand and a sniffling toddler in the other. Hopefully, she'd be too preoccupied to wonder what this nervous-looking fifteen-year-old girl was doing with a forty-year-old man.

"What would you like, Carly?"

"A lemonade, please." She looked at the display of cakes. "And a slice of chocolate cake?"

He ordered two slices of cake, a lemonade and a pot of tea.

While they waited, he talked about the weather, and about Bev and the kids—anything to get her to relax. It didn't work. The poor kid was too shaken.

"You said a woman talked to you about counselling," he said when their food and drinks were finally in front of them and they were sitting in a warm corner. "That's not as bad as it sounds, you know. All it means really is having a chat with someone who understands how awful it is when a friend dies."

"Yeah, I know. She was all right, too. The woman who came to the school, I mean. She didn't talk to us as if we were kids. I might go." She bit into her cake. "I'll think about it."

"Good idea. It's hard to lose a friend. Talking about it often helps."

She bit her lip and nodded.

"Were you good friends, you and Kevin?" he asked.

"Yeah."

"How was he when he left you that night? Was he okay? Was there anything bothering him?"

"He was great—the same as he always was. The police kept asking me that. There's nothing I could tell them and there's nothing I can tell you. Kevin was the same as he always was."

Dylan nodded and smiled, but there was probably a lot she could tell him if he fed her the right prompts. "You'd been under the bridge, hadn't you? I hear you met up for a couple of drinks?"

"That was my idea." She picked at her cake. "There were a few of us there. We had a couple of drinks and a laugh. That was all."

"And then Kevin walked you home?"

"Yes."

"And he was happy enough?" Dylan asked.

"Of course he was." She sounded confident about that. "We were going to meet up the next night."

"He didn't discuss any problems he was having?"

"No." She shook her head slowly. "He didn't have any problems. I know his dad was drinking a lot, ever since he lost his job, but that didn't worry Kevin. He didn't like it, but as he said, there was nothing any of them could do about it."

Thanks to a chat with Frank and a scan of the local paper, Dylan knew about Kevin's father and he could sympathise. Ron Mills had been drinking and gambling in equal measures since losing his job and his driving licence. Dylan could still remember the dark days after he'd been thrown out of the police force and, as he'd seen it then, onto the scrap heap. He'd hit the drink, too. But now, Mills had lost his son. Dylan hoped the poor bugger was getting support from somewhere.

"Did you know he'd told his parents he had football practice that night?" Dylan asked.

"No, he didn't mention it. But I told my mum and dad I was going round to a girlfriend's house to do homework, and I didn't tell Kev that. It never crossed my mind." She gulped down half a glass of lemonade. "I've told the police all this."

"I know, Carly, and I'm sorry to make you go over it all again, but you might know more than you think."

"I don't know anything."

Only a few crumbs, and an empty glass remained in front of her.

"Did you know Prue Murphy?" he asked her and her head flew up.

"Why do you ask that?"

"I'm curious."

She traced something on the table. All the while her foot was tapping on the floor. "No. I didn't know her."

"Did Kevin?"

"No." Her answer was too quick and she knew it.

"I think he did, Carly. I was at her funeral and I saw Kevin hanging around the church. How did he know her?"

"He didn't know her so I don't know why you're asking about her. Kev said—" She broke off. "It was nothing though. Even he didn't know what he'd seen."

"What do you mean, Carly?"

"First off, I didn't know Prue Murphy. Second off, Kev didn't know her either."

Dylan waited but she was still tracing lines on the table. "But?" he asked.

"He saw something."

"What did he see?"

"Well—it's hard to say. You know the night she was killed? He'd been grounded that night. He'd crept out of the house, though, and he stopped near her house to have a smoke before he went home. While he was standing there, a man came out of that woman's house. He wondered if it could have been the burglar they're looking for but, like I told him, it couldn't have been. Kev said he was wearing a suit. Who heard of a burglar wearing a suit?"

So that was it. Kevin Mills had seen Prue's killer and it had cost him his life.

"Not me," he said. "What did this man look like?"

Carly shook her head and shrugged. "I told Kev he should have gone to the police but, like he said, what was the point? He couldn't have given them a description of the bloke. He thought he was wearing a suit, but that was all." She thought of something else. "It was the car he noticed. The day before—before Kev was killed—he saw a car and he thought it might have been the one outside that woman's house that night."

"Oh?"

"It was a different one though."

"What was different about it, Carly?"

"I don't know. Sorry."

"The car he saw when you were with him. What was it like? Was it a sports car? A big car? An old car?"

"Sorry," she said. "I didn't see it."

"How did he know it wasn't the same car that was parked outside Prue Murphy's house?"

"I don't know." She stopped for a moment to replay everything Kevin had said. "I don't know, but it might have had something to do with the registration plate. When I said he should have gone to the police, he said there was no point because they wouldn't thank him for giving him no description of the bloke and only half a registration plate. He couldn't have gone anyway because he didn't want his dad knowing he'd sneaked out of the house when he was supposed to be grounded."

Dylan tried everything he could to refresh her memory, but she was adamant that Kevin hadn't said more about the car and she hadn't seen the one that had been similar.

"Who else might he have spoken to about it?" he asked.

"Probably no one. He only told me because I was with him when he saw that other one."

"Who are his friends? Who's his best friend, Carly?"

"Darren's his best mate. They're always together. Then there's Jason and Ethan Rodgers." She shrugged. "He got on well with everyone though."

Dylan had spoken to Darren, and to the Rodgers brothers. They'd looked blank when he'd asked about Prue. All the same, he'd have another chat with them and find out if Kevin had mentioned cars to them.

"It's time I was going," Carly said. "Parents are panicking if we stay out later than we should."

"Of course. Do you want me to give you a lift home?"

"Thanks, but no." She smiled a little wistfully. "I like being on my own at the moment."

"Okay." He handed her his card. "If there's anything you need, if there's anything at all I can do, or if you remember anything—"

"Okay." She put his card in her pocket and gave him a smile. "Thanks. I'll call you. Be seeing you."

He watched her leave the café and stride along the pavement with her head down and her shoulders hunched. She was young and the young were blessed with resilience in abundance. She would bounce back. At least, he hoped she would.

So—Kevin, it seemed, had seen Prue Murphy's killer. That man wore a suit on the night in question and drove a car that had claimed a sixteen-year-old's attention. Because it was sporty? Because it was expensive? Because it had a personalised number plate?

Dylan took out his phone and hit Luke's number.

"Hey, Dad, you should hear my new ringtone. It's wicked. I copied it from Tom's."

"I'm fine, Luke. Thanks so much for asking. How are you?"

Luke snorted with laughter. "I'm pretty good, too. I'm hanging out at Tom's. It really is a wicked ringtone though."

"Good." Luke didn't have a care in the world, which was as it should be. "Luke, what's your dream car?"

"What? Well, a Subaru. Obviously. Why?"

"A black one? Red?"

"Don't talk daft. No, it would have to be blue with the yellow trim. Why do you want to know? Are you going to buy me one, ready for when I'm old enough to drive?"

"Nope. What's your second favourite?"

"If I couldn't have a Subaru, I'd settle for a Mini Cooper S—black and white. Or a Beetle, maybe, like that one we saw. The one that was painted to look like a motorbike, remember?"

Dylan remembered it well. Subaru, Mini or Beetle—

so long as they were painted the correct way. The paint-work attracted Luke, not the price or the technology. Luke was younger, but perhaps Kevin had also been a fan of colourful paintwork too.

"Got to go, Dad. Tom's dad's taking us to that new bowling place."

"Okay. Have fun and I'll see you at the weekend."

Phone calls to Luke were always short. Luke was too busy enjoying life to stop and chat. It didn't matter though. Dylan's main reason for calling had been to hear the sound of his son's voice, to know that he was safe and happy. Luke's car preferences had been secondary.

Kevin's choice of vehicle might have been very different. Dylan didn't know. He did know that spotting that car—and the driver—had cost Kevin his life. He also knew that, come hell or high water, he'd find the bastard who'd killed Kevin and wrecked that family.

THIRTY

DANNY THOMPSON WAS surprised to see Dylan Scott walk through the door. There was something odd about the way he was still hanging around the Clough and the way he asked so many questions.

"Hi, Dylan. It's good to see you again. What are you having? Whisky, is it?"

"Please, Danny." Scott looked at the empty bar. "Trade's a bit slow tonight."

"It's a bit slow every night." Danny had been thinking about laying on entertainment but that didn't come cheap. A couple of his mates were in a band and they'd said they might play for a couple of nights. They needed the publicity and Danny needed the trade. It could help them both. "You must be getting to like the Clough. I thought you'd be long gone by now."

"I can't keep away, Danny." Smiling, Scott perched on a stool. "It all happens up here, doesn't it? Did you know Kevin Mills?"

Danny had to stop and think for a moment. "Oh, that kid they found in the lake. Bloody hell, that was terrible, wasn't it? I don't know what I'd do if I found a body. I wouldn't sleep well at night, that's for sure."

"A copper found Kevin, though, so I expect he will have been more used to it—bodies and all."

"Yeah, I suppose so." Danny fainted at the sight of blood so God knows what he'd do if he found a stiff. He couldn't bear to think about it.

"Did you know him?" Scott asked again.

"Me? No. Did you?"

"No. I'd never seen the name until it was splashed all over the papers."

"Dreadful. When he was missing, I saw his mum on the telly. She was asking anyone who knew anything to contact the police—Christ, she was in a right state. Her husband was sitting next to her but he was no help. He just stared into space like a bloody zombie."

Danny had recognised the young lad's dad, but he had no idea where he knew him from. People said he'd worked as a taxi driver in the town for a few months so that was probably how. Danny didn't use taxis very often but there was always one pulling up outside here.

"His parents must be out of their minds," Scott said. "First Prue, then young Kevin—it makes you wonder who's next, doesn't it?"

"Hopefully, that's it." The heating was turned up full in the wine bar but Danny still shivered.

"Do you know Jack McIntyre?" Scott asked.

"*The* Jack McIntyre?"

Scott seemed to sigh before he answered. "Yes."

"Hell, no. I can't imagine him slumming it in Dawson's Clough, can you?" Danny laughed at the idea. "It's a pity. He did a mural somewhere, didn't he? One of those would look great in here. That might bring in the customers."

Scott simply smiled at the idea.

"He's dead anyway," Danny said. "Died a few months back. He drowned."

"Yes, so I heard."

"What makes you ask about him?"

"Prue knew him so I wondered if he'd ever been seen around here." Scott shrugged. "I'm just curious."

"Prue knew him? Wow." It was the first Danny had heard about it. "Are you sure? Who says so?"

"Oh, I think it's common knowledge. They met when she was living in France."

"Well, I never. She didn't mention it to me. God, I wish I had one of his paintings. They're selling for a fortune now. I wish I had half a dozen, come to that. I could retire."

"I'm surprised she didn't mention it," Scott said. "You did know she'd lived in France, didn't you?"

"Of course. God knows why she left. All that sunshine and good wine. I wouldn't come back to the Clough, would you?"

"Probably not." Scott lifted his glass and took a couple of appreciative sips.

"She didn't talk about it much," Danny said, "but she must have missed it. I remember her telling me about that sister of hers visiting. Her sister and brother-in-law visited, that's it. Prue said she got really drunk. She reckoned it was the stress of putting up with her sister for the whole weekend. She reckoned she'd never get over the embarrassment of that. Said she'd made a right prat of herself. I gather she'd said things she wished she hadn't when she was drunk."

"Like what?"

"She didn't say. I told her, they were probably just as drunk and couldn't remember what she'd said anyway."

"That's what we like to tell ourselves, isn't it?" Scott emptied his glass. "Time for another, Danny. Will you join me?"

Danny was about to refuse. For some reason, he felt he needed a clear head when talking to Scott. There were too many questions for Danny's liking. It had been the same the last time he'd been here. Danny had worried then that he might have been sent by the insurance company. To hell with it. Even if he had, no one could prove anything. The fire service and police had been through it all—no one could say who'd caused that fire.

"Why not?" he said. "Thanks, Dylan."

While Danny poured their drinks and gave Scott his change, Scott talked about the time it took him to travel up from London to Dawson's Clough. He didn't say why he was so keen on visiting though.

"What sort of car do you drive, Danny?" he asked.

"I don't. I prefer two wheels to four." His bike, taxed, insured and legal in every way, was out the back if Scott chose to look.

"Really? In this weather?" Scott pulled a face. "You're a braver man than me, Danny Thompson. Give me four wheels—and a cover—any day. I've seen some great cars round town, have you? I saw a yellow Ferrari the other day."

"Does nothing for me."

"Perhaps there was a meeting of some sort on," Scott said, "because I saw half a dozen interesting cars. Did you see anything?"

"Nothing. Mind you, I don't take much interest in cars. Me and my mates, we like our bikes. We go all over on them. We've had some great days out in the Yorkshire Dales. A couple of dozen of us met up in Hebden Bridge the other Sunday. That was good."

The door banged open.

"Customers—welcome!" Danny greeted the four locals with a laugh. "What are you having, my friends?"

THIRTY-ONE

THE QUEUE FOR food and drinks was a long, slow-moving snake. Dylan scoffed at people who brought sandwiches and a flask of hot coffee to the football matches, but right now, he could see they had a point. It wasn't the same though. A pie and a pint was traditional half-time fare so, with Luke beside him, he joined the queue.

"What time are you going out tonight?" Luke asked.

Dylan groaned. "Seven for seven-thirty."

"What does that mean?"

"It means," Dylan said, "that you can arrive at seven if you must but under no circumstances must you arrive after seven-thirty because that's when things will be happening. Either drinks will be served at seven-thirty or dinner. It means that the evening will be hell. It also means your mum will be asking me what time we should set off every five minutes. She'll want to arrive on the dot of seven-fifteen."

Luke grinned at that. "Sounds like fun."

They shuffled forward a few inches. "Ha."

Terminal illness and dentists aside, Dylan hated dinner parties more than anything. He loathed them and could never understand how it could take several hours to eat a bit of food and listen to people boast about their kids.

If Maddie had extended the invite to him, he would have come up with an excuse as to why they couldn't attend. She hadn't, though. For some reason, she'd called Bev.

"What a lovely surprise, Dylan," Bev had said hours after accepting. "She said there would only be six of us there—her and her husband, me and you, and Tim's business partner—what was his name?"

"Eddie Bryson."

"That's it. Him and his girlfriend will be there. Won't that be nice? I thought it was really kind of her to invite us…"

Within an hour of accepting the invitation, Bev had started the usual panic about what she should wear. While he and Luke enjoyed the football, she was out shopping for a new outfit. She'd buy something and then, as soon as the next invitation came along, claim she had nothing to wear again. She had a wardrobe full of clothes she'd only worn once.

They moved forward and, a couple of minutes later, were at the front of the queue buying two hot meat pies and a pint for Dylan. As they stood to eat, they watched the TV screens for the half-time results from grounds around the country. Dylan gulped down his pint and they were back in their seats to cheer on the mighty Arsenal just as the whistle blew to start the second half.

The game was scrappy with passes from both sides going astray. It wasn't the poor football that robbed him of his concentration, though. Questions came and went. Sadly, no answers followed.

It was easy enough to know who'd killed Kevin

Mills. The same person who'd killed Prue. So who had killed Prue? The same person—possibly, presumably—who'd killed Jeremy Collins and tried to kill Jack McIntyre.

Suspects were plentiful enough.

In Dawson's Clough, there was wine bar owner and possible insurance fraudster, Danny Thompson. If Prue, during one of her drunken sessions, had mentioned her relationship with McIntyre, and boasted of having one of his miniatures hanging on her bedroom wall, Thompson could easily have decided to break in and—and what? That miniature had been there for all to see. Anyone could have found it easily enough and slipped it in a pocket. No. Whoever broke into Prue's home had been looking for something else.

Perhaps Prue, under the influence of Thompson's generous alcoholic beverages, had said she owned a McIntyre painting. McIntyre was famous for huge canvasses and only a knowledgeable few even knew he'd dabbled in miniatures. Perhaps Thompson had been looking for a full-size painting.

That didn't explain the attempt on McIntyre's life though. Thompson might be eager to get his hands on money, could even be a killer, but he hadn't met Prue when McIntyre was almost despatched to his watery grave. She'd had no previous links to Dawson's Clough and Thompson had lived in the town all his life.

Prue's landlord, Toby Windsor, was another that Dylan wouldn't trust as far as he could throw a sulking elephant. Again, though, he hadn't known Prue before she became a tenant of one of his properties. He could easily have known about her relationship with McIntyre, and about her owning a valuable painting, but he couldn't have made that attempt on McIntyre's life.

If, of course, there had been an attempt on McIntyre's life.

The story of the boating accident was McIntyre's. Dylan was expected to believe it, just as he was expected to believe that Prue left France because she didn't want to be involved with a womanising artist. Her reasons for moving to England and Dawson's Clough could have been completely different. Maybe she wanted to hide from someone and what better place than a sleepy northern town? Maybe McIntyre had threatened her. Maybe she knew something about him that would damage his marriage or his career. Maybe he'd needed to silence her.

According to McIntyre, Martin Collins was more interested in making money than his father's good health. Would he really kill his father? Dylan thought back to their meeting. Collins had come across as a man eager to expand his gallery, a man who'd said that his father was too set in his ways—but killing one's father would be a step too far for most people.

"Why do we always get crap referees?" Luke nudged Dylan's elbow.

"It's a sad fact of life, Luke."

Sod it. Dylan pushed it all from his mind and concentrated on the game on the pitch. Arsenal were in danger of losing if they didn't pull themselves together...

THIRTY-TWO

BEV HAD ONCE seen a TV documentary in which staff at Buckingham Palace had set out a long table for a banquet the queen was hosting. The painstaking procedure had involved white-gloved staff using rulers to check that glasses and cutlery were the exact distance apart. Bev wondered if Maddie Chandler had copied the idea.

She'd thought it wonderfully kind of Maddie to extend the invitation but had been living on her nerves ever since they'd arrived. She hardly dared to take a sip of wine in case she dropped the expensive crystal glass.

Her idea of a dinner party was having friends round for a meal. More often than not, those friends would congregate in the kitchen while she cooked. Or, more accurate, while she took something out of a packet and slammed it in the microwave. They helped themselves to drinks and used any odd glass they could find.

This was too formal for her liking. Everything—from the glasses to the exquisitely folded damask napkins—shouted money and class. As for employing caterers for six guests, Bev thought that was madness. She would have sliced up a melon for the starter and probably cobbled together a chilli or a curry for the main course. Dessert at Chez Scott was always fruit, ice cream or sorbet. She believed it was the company and the atmosphere that made for a good dinner party. Wine helped, too.

Still, the food had been eaten now and they were lingering over coffee served in fragile cups. A handmade chocolate was served with each cup. The chocolates probably cost more than Bev would spend on a week's food for a family of four.

Perhaps it had been kind of Maddie to invite them, but it didn't need Einstein present to figure out that Dylan was the one wanted at the table. Bev was simply an irritation.

Maddie was a good host. She was witty and charming, and her smile never slipped as she attended to everyone's needs, but Bev couldn't warm to her. Behind the smile was a coldness that was most evident when she spoke to her husband. Although she smiled at Tim when she spoke to him, Bev would bet they'd had a row before the guests arrived. She tried to picture Maddie and Dylan as a young couple but couldn't. She couldn't imagine that they'd ever been on the same wavelength.

Tim was the person Bev felt most at ease with. She liked him. He looked a little stressed, but at least he seemed genuine. He was a handsome man, the perfect foil for the beautiful Maddie.

The two other guests, Eddie and Shaz, were an oddity too. Shaz blundered on, talking about nothing in particular, and Eddie smiled indulgently. He looked tired of her company though. He seemed far more interested in Maddie than his girlfriend.

They'd been told that a few friends were calling in later and, just as Bev was finishing her coffee, four people turned up. Bev had forgotten their names within seconds of being introduced, but she was pleased to see them. The more the merrier. It took the pressure off the rest of them to make conversation.

They all moved from the dining room to a vast lounge. Some spilled into the conservatory. Maddie put some music on. Wine flowed freely.

Bev and Dylan wandered into the more informal conservatory and, just as Bev was about to suggest they leave as soon as possible, they were joined by Maddie and Tim.

"Beautiful plants," Bev said. "I feel as if I shouldn't come in here because I can kill plants with just one look."

"We don't have green fingers either," Tim said, "but these survive. If they're dead by morning though, we'll know who to blame."

"I noticed the paintings in the dining room," Dylan said. "They're good. Are they by anyone I might know?"

"Sadly not." Tim laughed. "The struggling artist in question is my nephew. He had an exhibition a couple of years ago to raise money for charity and we felt obliged to buy a couple."

"Ah. I just wondered. Well, with any luck, his paintings will be worth a fortune one day. Like Jack McIntyre's."

Bev had known he'd have to drag the conversation round to Prue. She'd tried to tell him that talking about dead sisters wasn't the done thing at dinner parties, but Dylan had always been a law unto himself.

"I wish," Tim said.

"I really can't believe you didn't know about Prue's relationship with Jack McIntyre," Dylan said, addressing them both.

"Not a clue," Maddie said. "I can't believe it either. I mean, what the devil would a talent like McIntyre see in someone like her? The idea's ridiculous."

According to Dylan, who admittedly had only met her briefly twenty years ago, Prue was a pretty, likeable girl with a lot of friends. Bev hated the way Maddie dismissed her sister.

"We didn't see a lot of her though," Tim said. "Our lives were so different, you see. She probably had a lot of boyfriends we never knew about."

Dylan nodded at that and Bev could see his mind working overtime.

"You saw her once when she lived in France, didn't you?" he said. "If I recall, you stayed with her for a weekend."

"That's right," Maddie said, "but she never mentioned any men in her life, did she, Tim?"

"Not to me."

"That night she got drunk and you sat up talking," she said. "She didn't mention anything then?"

"Not a thing."

"Someone must have known about it," Dylan said. "Someone must have known he was painting again too."

"Painting again? What makes you think that?" Tim asked. "I thought it was a well-known fact that he'd put down his brushes for good."

"Oh, he was definitely painting. And those paintings will be worth a fortune."

"Ah yes, you spoke to his housekeeper." Tim was dismissive. "She's probably mistaken. We can't be sure he was painting. Only McIntyre knew what he was doing and he's dead."

"Missing, presumed dead," Dylan corrected him.

Maddie's head flew up. "What do you mean? He's dead. Everyone knows that."

"Not necessarily." Dylan ran his finger across a plant's glossy leaf. "His body was never found, so he could still be alive."

Maddie laughed at that. "Of course no body was found. Good grief, lots of people are drowned and their bodies get eaten by whatever lives in the sea. He's dead, Dylan."

Eddie and Shaz wandered in. Shaz was laughing loudly at something Eddie had said. Her arm was hooked through his in a proprietorial manner.

"Who's dead?" Eddie asked.

"Jack McIntyre," Tim said. "We were just talking about Prue's relationship with the artist and Dylan was saying it's possible he's still alive. I suppose it is."

"Who knows?" Eddie didn't say "Who cares?" but it hung in the air between them.

"Of course he's dead," Maddie said.

"It would be interesting if he was alive though," Dylan said.

"Dylan." Maddie slipped her arm through his and, despite the smile, her voice was cool. "I'm paying you to look into Prue's death, not some drowning accident. Much more of this, and I'll have to put a stop to it all."

"I am concentrating on Prue," Dylan said, "but it's possible there's a connection."

"You're getting nowhere though," Maddie said.

Bev bristled on Dylan's behalf. She also bristled because Maddie had her hand planted firmly on Dylan's arm. "Dylan's never yet had a case he hasn't solved, Maddie. He will find out what happened to your sister. Trust me on that one."

Maddie smiled sweetly at Bev, those eyes like chips of ice. "We'll see."

"Let's hope so," Eddie said. "Maddie, we're running out of wine in there." He nodded toward the lounge.

Maddie let go of Dylan—reluctantly, Bev noticed—and went off to be the perfect hostess.

Talk turned to easier things, but still Bev was pleased when they were being driven home in the taxi.

"Maddie's still got the hots for you," she said.

Dylan smiled. "I know. She clearly doesn't know that I'm a—what am I?"

"Chauvinist? Misogynist? Pain in the butt?"

"Yeah. That'll be it."

"She's a strange one, isn't she?" Bev said. "I can't understand why she's bothering to employ you to look into Prue's death when she doesn't seem to care less about her. Unless it's just an excuse to get you in her bed, of course."

"That would be one expensive shag." He gave her a sideways glance. "Am I worth that much?"

"Never in a million years."

THIRTY-THREE

DYLAN WAS MEETING Jack McIntyre this evening—assuming the chap hadn't gone into hiding again—but first, he wanted a chat with Prue's parents. He'd spoken to them at Prue's funeral, and it had been clear they'd been at a loss to understand their daughter's death, but he wanted another meeting. He didn't want to intrude on their grief, but he did want to know all he could about their daughters.

He'd phoned last night, and Andrew Murphy had said they'd look forward to seeing him this morning.

Their home was beautiful. It was the family home—"too big for us now, really"—and had a cosy, welcoming feel to it. It was also worth a fortune. Presumably Maddie alone stood to inherit when the time came.

"It's good to see you again, Dylan," Ruth said. "Come into the kitchen, where it's warm. You don't mind dogs, do you?"

"I love dogs." He was greeted by an ageing dog of indeterminate breed who, before the grey had taken over, had been black.

"This is Sam," Andrew said. "He's fifteen now so he doesn't like to move too far from his bed."

"A bit like me," Ruth said with a smile.

Having welcomed Dylan, Sam retired to his basket in front of the warm Aga.

Without asking, Ruth made tea—using a teapot rather than tea bags—and poured for the four of them. Yes, four. The dog had its own pottery mug bearing its name.

"We know this isn't a social visit," Andrew said. "What is it you have to tell us, Dylan?"

"I wish I had something to tell you, but unfortunately, I'm not much further forward."

"But you don't agree with the police theory that Prue disturbed a burglar?"

"No, I don't. The painting, you see—" A brief frown crossed Ruth's face. "Maddie did tell you about the painting by Jack McIntyre, didn't she?"

"In passing," Ruth said.

In passing?

Needless to say, he didn't have to explain who Jack McIntyre was. Dylan really was the only bloke on the planet who'd never heard of the artist. "It seems that Prue knew McIntyre."

"Really? Well, it's possible, I suppose," Ruth said. "After all, she lived in France for a few years. He lived there too, didn't he? I think he died there. Wasn't there some sort of accident?"

"Yes. He and his agent were drowned," Dylan said.

"That's it," Ruth said. "And you think Prue knew him?"

"Yes. She didn't mention anything?"

"Nothing," Andrew said. "We'd remember something like that."

"Ah, well, it was just a long shot," Dylan said. "I thought I'd ask if she'd mentioned him or the painting at all."

Despite the welcoming home and the old family dog, the atmosphere in the room felt anything but relaxed. Ruth looked lost and desperately sad, but Andrew was so tense that Dylan expected him to snap in two at any moment. Maybe the strain of coping with his own grief as well as being strong for Ruth was proving too much for him.

The information Dylan really wanted was the sort that came out during a relaxed conversation. It didn't come from interrogation.

"Have you had Sam since he was a puppy?" He gave the dog a stroke and it promptly curled up and went to sleep with its head on his foot.

"Yes." Ruth smiled fondly at the dog. "When Maddie and then, later, Prue moved out, the house felt far too big. We'd always wanted a dog but Maddie was never keen. Prue longed for a dog and Maddie hated the very thought of it. Arguments raged so we did nothing. But when they both moved out, we moved Sam in. He's been such a good friend to us, hasn't he, Andy?"

"The best. He's a real character."

"He's obviously landed on his feet here. I don't know too many dogs who have tea with the family," Dylan said.

"He's spoiled," Andrew said, "but it does him no harm at his age. Prue was the worst. She'd bring him all sorts of things. It was nothing for her to turn up with a cake for him, and she always had a bag of treats in her pocket when she visited us."

"Really? Did she visit often?"

"Oh, yes," Ruth said.

"It's funny because Maddie said she didn't see much of her sister," Dylan said.

There was only a brief hesitation before Andrew spoke. "They weren't close because the age gap was too much. Maddie was five years older so it was difficult. When Prue was born, Maddie was starting school. When Prue was starting school, Maddie was off to the grammar school. When Prue was going there, Maddie was getting interested in boys. It's a big gap."

Dylan supposed it was. That gap was nothing compared to the one between Luke and Freya, but Luke already adored his sister. He happily played baby games with her and loved to make her laugh.

"Later, when they were grown-ups," Ruth said, "Maddie was always busy. A model's life is very demanding. And Maddie's had problems of her own. Well, you'll know that she suffers from depression. It's hard for everyone."

"Depression is a terrible thing," Dylan said.

"It is," Ruth said. "Everyone feels so helpless. It's terrible to watch your own daughter sink so low. She's seen good doctors, of course, and I suppose they do their best."

"I suppose that's another reason the sisters weren't close," Dylan said. "It must have been hard for Maddie to see Prue always looking so happy-go-lucky and carefree."

Ruth left the kitchen for a few moments and came back with a pack of photographs. "Have a look at these, Dylan. These were taken in much happier times."

Usually, Dylan would rather have his testicles removed without anaesthetic than look at pictures of other people's children, but these were fascinating. In every photo, Prue was smiling for the camera yet Maddie, who made her living in front of a camera, wasn't. Her expression was forced and any attempt at a smile failed miserably. In one picture, Prue was cuddling a cat and Maddie was looking at her sister as if she wanted to kill her.

As if she wanted to kill her—

"That was Smoke," Ruth said with a sigh. "Maddie had nagged and nagged for a cat so, one day, we bought her a kitten. Within a few hours, the kitten had fallen in love with Prue. No matter what Prue did, it wouldn't leave her side. It slept on her bed—really, it wouldn't leave her. Poor Maddie was so upset. We wanted to get her another kitten, but she wouldn't hear of it. She lost all interest in pets."

"The kitten died a few months later," Andrew said, "and that caused problems between them. Prue blamed Maddie because it happened when Prue was at school and—oh, let's just say that life was easier when we were pet-free."

"Mind you," Ruth said, a wistful expression on her face, "I'd give anything to hear the two of them fighting again. I miss Prue so much. Every time the phone rings, I expect it to be her. It's hard, Dylan."

Andrew gave his wife's hand a reassuring squeeze and Dylan wished he had words of comfort to offer.

"Maddie will still fight people every inch of the way," Ruth said, "but I'm determined to get through to her. I think she's lonely."

"She has Tim," Andrew said, still holding her hand. "He's a good man. Prue liked him, didn't she?"

Ruth smiled. "She believed he deserved a medal for putting up with Maddie." She was only half joking.

"Did you visit Prue when she lived in France?" Dylan asked.

"Quite often," Ruth said. "We worried she wasn't earning enough to feed herself properly so we liked to check up on her."

"She was fine," Andrew said. "She had a lot of friends. We had no need to worry about her."

"And she didn't mention any artistic friend or—?"

"No." Ruth was certain of that. "We met several of her friends, but they were neighbours or colleagues. None were artists."

The doorbell rang and Andrew jumped to his feet and strode out of the room.

"It was the postman." He returned with two brown envelopes and a package that was too big for the letter box. "More junk for the recycling bin and Sam's arthritis tablets. The vet sends his tablets out, Dylan. Can you believe that? This dog has better medical care than any of us."

Dylan smiled, as was expected, but Andrew's hearty, forced tone was as unnerving as his earlier edginess.

"More tea?" Andrew asked.

"No, thanks. It's time I was off."

Knowing he wasn't going to learn anything here, Dylan left them to their grief. It was time to head north and meet up with the celebrated artist.

THIRTY-FOUR

DYLAN ALMOST DIDN'T recognise Jack McIntyre. The world-famous artist was wearing a long waterproof coat with the high collar around his neck, and a wide-brimmed hat in the same green waxed material. As it had rained for days, his outfit didn't look out of place.

He was pleasantly surprised to see him waiting outside the church where they'd arranged to meet. It had been McIntyre's suggestion to meet in Dawson's Clough, one that had struck Dylan as odd, but he was pleased the artist hadn't done a runner.

"They've promised more April showers," McIntyre said, "so I suggest we find somewhere warm."

Dylan didn't need reminding that March had meandered into April. It would be four weeks tomorrow since Prue had been laid to rest in that cold, wet cemetery.

"I can recommend the Dog and Fox," he said.

"Sounds good to me."

They walked quickly until the smell of fish and chips slowed McIntyre. "I'm starving," he said. "Do you want any?"

"No, I've eaten."

Dylan waited in the cold while McIntyre went inside and bought a huge piece of cod and enough chips to feed the entire town. He soaked the lot in salt and vinegar, then emerged from the shop eating them from the paper.

"You can't beat fish and chips, can you?" McIntyre sounded wistful.

"No." The smell was making Dylan's mouth water and he wished now that he'd bought himself a small portion.

"So what's new?" McIntyre asked as they walked on to the Dog and Fox. "Have you discovered anything of interest?"

Dylan hated to admit it but— "No, not really. You?"

"I don't know." McIntyre concentrated on his fish and chips and was rolling the empty wrapping into a ball as they arrived at the front door to the Dog and Fox. He looked around for a litter bin, spotted one and tossed the paper in from three yards away. It landed inside and he smiled his satisfaction. "Right, let's get that drink."

Once they were inside and making the most of the pub's warmth, McIntyre removed his hat. His beard was as long and straggly as ever so it was unlikely anyone would recognise him.

They'd just sat with their drinks when a group of four people who'd been gathered round the log fire picked up their coats and left. Dylan and McIntyre leapt into those seats before anyone else could take them.

Before either of them could speak, Dylan's phone trilled out. Frank was calling and Dylan hoped it was good news.

"Sorry it's taken so long to get back to you, Dylan, but it's finally sorted. You can see CCTV at the art gallery tomorrow morning. Any good to you?"

"Perfect. Thanks, Frank. You coming along?"

"Count me in."

"I'll pick you up around eight-thirty then."

Dylan ended the call and hoped that, finally, he'd get a lead. It was a long shot, but he might get some clue as to what Prue had done on the final day of her life.

"So," Dylan said, turning his attention to McIntyre, "you sound as if you've heard something?"

McIntyre rubbed his beard. "I know a couple of dodgy dealers. They don't trust me and I don't trust them. They don't know who I am, of course. They believe I'm just some drunk who thinks he knows all there is to know about art. I was talking to them and asking them if they knew anything about what McIntyre was working on when he died. One reminded me that McIntyre had stopped painting. The other, older, wiser and far more shady, said someone else had been asking that same question, shortly after I—McIntyre lost his life. The chap in question was apparently quite sure he'd heard I was working on something new."

"Who was that? Could they give you a description? Anything?"

"No. They thought he was a dealer though and they described him as upmarket."

"And that's it?"

"I'm afraid so. It does make you wonder if someone knew I was painting again though."

"Think hard. Who did know?" Dylan asked.

McIntyre shrugged. "Only Coletta and Elliott Tolman, and I'd trust them with my life. And Prue, of course."

McIntyre might trust the Tolmans but they worked for him. It was natural that they would be subservient, and would pander to his needs and his ego. It would be easy enough for them to work out a plot to kill him. Coletta was in the house all the time and would know his movements. Tolman lived by the sea so was sure to know how to handle McIntyre's boat. They could easily have plotted McIntyre's demise.

"Did the Tolmans know you hid your paintings in the boathouse?" Dylan asked.

"They didn't know they were in the boathouse, but I told Coletta I was putting them out of sight and that she wasn't to mention them to Jeremy. Why do you ask?" Realisation dawned and, smiling, McIntyre shook his head. "As I said, I'd trust them with my life. Literally."

"They could have told someone," Dylan said. "Perhaps they enjoyed working for the local celebrity and being in his confidence. They might have boasted about just how far in your confidence they were. A word or two about your paintings would have impressed a lot of people."

"No." McIntyre refused to believe such a thing.

"That leaves Prue then." Dylan took a long swallow of beer. "If the Tolmans didn't tell people you were painting again, Prue must have."

"No." McIntyre certainly wouldn't believe that.

"Why not? She was young, she no doubt worshipped you and admired your work, and she must have thought her luck was in the day she hooked you."

"I was the lucky one, Dylan." McIntyre's voice had chilled several degrees.

"Her sister visited her in France a couple of months before you hit the water."

McIntyre frowned at him. "So?"

"So the sisters didn't get along," Dylan said. "So I'd stake my life on words being said. Maddie believed Prue was throwing her life away waiting on tables in France and would have wasted no time in telling her so. I'll bet she was embarrassed by Prue's situation. Perhaps Prue hurled a few words back. Maybe she told her sister that she was with a man who was richer than Maddie's wildest dreams."

"That's not like Prue."

"Maddie is a force to be reckoned with. Who knows how far she'd push someone?"

Dylan had expected a smile, or an agreement, but McIntyre merely fingered his shaggy beard.

"I remember the weekend they visited," he said. "It was out of the blue. Long overdue, but out of the blue. I suggested they stay at the cottage and we let them know we were a couple, but Prue wouldn't hear of it. She returned to her flat and pretended she was still living there."

"She didn't give up her flat when she moved in with you?"

"No. She was so anti our relationship that she was only ever staying for the weekend, then a week, then a fortnight. The only possessions she brought to the cottage were things she could pack in a rucksack and take with her. She went back to her flat and spent the weekend there with them."

"What did she say about the visit?" Dylan asked.

"Nothing really. She said it went okay and that was all. Thinking back though, she was quieter than usual afterwards. I asked if she was okay, if anything had happened, but she said she wanted to forget all about her sister. We never spoke of it again."

Dylan wondered if Prue had mentioned McIntyre to her sister, but it seemed unlikely. Maddie had heard of him—who hadn't?—but she'd struggled to believe that Prue had known him. Maddie had taken that miniature and thrown it in a bag with a load of rubbish. If she'd known Prue had been involved with McIntyre, she would have assumed it was indeed one of his paintings. She would have taken much better care of it.

Maybe the man sitting opposite him right now had been so determined to retain his anonymous lifestyle that he hadn't wanted anyone telling the world he was painting again. Perhaps, believing Prue would tell all and sundry, he'd decided to silence her.

Dylan hunted through his jacket pockets until he found the photograph he was looking for. He showed it to McIntyre. "Do you recognise this person?"

"Yes." McIntyre looked from the photo to Dylan and back again. "I don't remember his name—Mills, I think—but I know his body was found in a lake in Dawson's Clough. I've seen that photo in all the newspapers. What does he have to do with anything?"

"I believe he saw Prue's killer."

"What?" McIntyre visibly reeled at the knowledge. "You think that's why he was killed? You think Prue's killer—"

"I do." And it was quite possible that Dylan was

enjoying a drink in his favourite pub with that killer. "Have you seen any unusual cars around? Sporty, expensive, out of the ordinary in some way?"

"Only yours. Why?"

"It's possible that the killer was driving a car that caught Kevin Mills's attention. He was sixteen so I'm trying to think of the type of car that might interest him. I'm not sure my Morgan would. He'd think that too old, I imagine."

McIntyre considered that, a finger stroking his beard. "You're thinking along the lines of a top-of-the-range Ferrari, Lamborghini, Porsche perhaps? Then again, it could have been an old wreck that lacked a silencer and had go-faster stripes plastered all over it."

"I think it was unusual in some way, but yes, you could be right. A lot of kids have poor taste in cars."

"I'll get us another drink," McIntyre said and Dylan nodded his thanks.

It was motive that was bugging Dylan. Assuming McIntyre's story was true *(assume nothing),* it was safe to guess that his killer was driven by greed. He'd wanted to get his hands on McIntyre's paintings, or he had paintings to sell—either way, the motive was tied up with McIntyre's work.

The killer had needed to silence Kevin Mills. Again, the motive was fairly simple to see. Kevin had seen Prue's killer and that killer had to make sure he didn't tell the world.

But Prue? Only McIntyre, as far as he could tell, had a motive to kill her. If he'd believed she was on the brink of exposing him and his work, perhaps he'd decided to silence her for good. Maybe, despite his claims to the contrary, there had been plenty of contact between the two over the months.

Maddie kept popping into his head only to be dismissed. At the age of ten, eleven or twelve, she'd been photographed while looking as if she wanted to kill her sister. So what? Plenty of siblings struggled to get along. It meant nothing.

"Here we are." McIntyre put their drinks on the table and sat down.

"Thanks." Dylan took a swig of beer. They kept the best pint in the country in this pub, which made visits to the godforsaken north much easier. "What would have happened if Prue had left France, returned to England and told the world you were painting again?"

"She wouldn't do that."

"How do you know?"

McIntyre smiled at that. "I knew her. I trusted her."

"But if she had, what would have happened?"

"I'm not sure what you mean, Dylan. I suppose the media would have hounded me, wanting to see my new work. I would have shown them the Chaste Collection— the paintings of Prue."

"How would you have felt?"

McIntyre shrugged. "Betrayed, I suppose. But the Chaste Collection is my best work. Truly, I've never created anything like it. Probably never will again. I couldn't have kept quiet about it. As soon as they were finished to my satisfaction, I would have exhibited those paintings."

"Where are they now?"

"In a bank. They're quite safe."

Dylan was getting nowhere. His phone rang. He took it from his pocket, saw that Maddie was calling, and hit Answer.

"Hi, Maddie. What can I do for you?" He always felt the need to speak in a businesslike fashion to her. It helped keep images of blue bedrooms and smiley faces from his mind.

"Where are you?" she asked and he could hear a pout in her voice.

"In Dawson's Clough. I'll be here for the next couple of days. Why?"

There was a pause. "I need to come up there. I've booked myself in at the spa and—I'll drive up tomorrow. Shall we have lunch?"

He needed to talk to her. He had to know exactly what had happened during that weekend they spent with Prue in France.

"I can't do lunch," he said. "But how about dinner?"

"Even better. And then, after dinner, I'm sure we'll find some way to pass the time." Her voice was a purr.

"I'm sure we will, Maddie." Dylan ended the call and looked at McIntyre. "I appear to have a date with Maddie tomorrow."

McIntyre nodded, but didn't comment. Dylan wondered if McIntyre and Maddie knew each other. They both claimed ignorance of the other but it was an interesting theory.

THIRTY-FIVE

THE TWENTY-FIVE-MILE DRIVE into Manchester took just over an hour and they encountered rain, sunshine and snow. Bloody snow!

"I don't suppose spring bothers springing this far north," Dylan said, and Frank chuckled.

"Snow in April isn't unheard of. Maybe it's even snowing in London on you soft fucking southerners."

"No. The sun shines on the righteous, Frank."

The only parking option was the multi-storey car park. They left the car there and dodged the rain on the sprint to the art gallery.

Frank had the necessary paperwork—and the voice of authority—and they were soon sitting down to look through images recorded on the day Prue Murphy visited the art gallery.

Dylan had forgotten how much he hated looking at CCTV. The images were invariably crap and he often wondered if he'd recognise his own wife. The angle was always wrong, the lighting poor.

"It's a busy place," Frank said after a long hour had passed. "That's surprising for a weekday. At least, it surprises me."

"Me, too. You'd think people would have better ways to spend their time."

Another hour passed. And another.

"There!" Dylan paused the film. "That's definitely Prue."

She walked through the main doors and up to the desk. She was smiling. She had a bag slung over her shoulder and her hands were deep in the pockets of her jacket.

Three hours and they'd confirmed that Prue was indeed at the art gallery on the day in question. As they'd already known that, it could hardly be classed as progress. They continued to stare at footage.

"This," Dylan said, "has to be the most mind-numbingly awful job ever invented."

"Agreed."

Dylan was starving but they couldn't stop. He didn't want to have to come back tomorrow.

"Is that—?" Frank paused the film. "Could that be Maddie Chandler?"

"What?" Dylan peered more closely. "No. Of course not. It's nothing like her. And how would you know what she looks like? You've never met her, have you?"

"No, but I've done a bit of research on her. There are a lot of photos of her on the internet."

Of course there were. She was a model, or had been, and spent a lot of time in front of cameras.

"And," Frank said, "I can't believe she read an article that mentioned your name while she was up in Dawson's Clough."

Frank had mentioned that before. "Why not?"

"I checked with the paper," Frank said. "The last article that mentioned you was printed just before Christmas."

"So? It was probably an old paper she saw."

"Not in the sort of hotels she stays in," Frank said. "You might, at a push, find yesterday's edition but not copies from months ago."

"How else could she have found me? And why would she lie?" Dylan didn't have time for this.

"I don't know." Frank nodded at the screen. "Are you sure that's not her?"

"Yes." The woman in front of them was tall, slim, elegant and blonde. She was wearing a long leather coat and carrying a handbag. There were similarities, but it wasn't Maddie. Dylan was sure of it. "It was Maddie who told me Prue was here. She only knew that because she found a receipt in Prue's coat."

"Right."

Dylan didn't like Frank's tone, but he didn't have time to argue. Instead, they both continued to stare at images of people walking into the gallery on the day Prue was killed.

It was long, painstaking work.

"There she is." Dylan checked the note he'd made. "Prue spent a little over two hours in the gallery."

She'd walked in all smiles. She was hurrying out. It was impossible to see her expression because her back was to the camera. The bag was still slung over her shoulder. Her hands weren't in her pockets because she was striding past the camera and reaching for the door. There was no one with her.

"We're none the wiser," Dylan said. "She came, she

left. We knew that. She probably took the train home, watched TV, went to bed and disturbed a burglar."

But that didn't explain the attempt on McIntyre's life. If indeed, there was such a thing.

They looked through images from different cameras for the two hours of Prue's visit.

Just as Dylan was about to suggest they call it a day, he saw a man he thought he recognised. It was impossible to be sure, but the chap looked very familiar. He was wearing a white shirt, a dark tie and a short jacket.

"That looks like Eddie Bryson."

"Who? Oh, Chandler's partner? Are you sure?"

"No." Dylan tapped his pen against his chin as he first tried to see if it really was Bryson and second, tried to work out what it meant. "If it is Bryson, I'll bet Chandler isn't far away. Maddie thought her husband was having an affair with Prue. Maybe—just maybe—she's right."

Also, if it was Bryson, perhaps Maddie wasn't too far away.

"I'm having dinner with Maddie this evening," he said. "I'll see what I can find out."

"You do that. And find out where she read that article about you."

Dylan smiled at that. "Yes, boss."

THIRTY-SIX

WHEN DYLAN RETURNED to his hotel, the receptionist handed him a note. *I'm in Room 206. Ring me as soon as you arrive. Maddie xx.*

He'd assumed, wrongly, that she would have checked in to the more upmarket Carlton Hotel. He wished she had.

He took the lift to his room, showered and changed, and then lay back on his bed to stare at the ceiling. Maybe if he got up close and personal with her, she'd be more forthcoming with information. He wasn't going to leap into bed with her. Not that up close and personal. He did need her to open up though. She was the one paying him to look into her sister's death and yet he was coming to believe that she knew a lot more than she was saying.

Even supposing it was true, she was hardly likely to broadcast the fact that she was having an affair with her husband's business partner. Nor, having recently buried her sister, would she tell the world that she'd been unable to stand the sight of Prue.

He sat up, took his laptop from its bag and switched it on.

Information on her husband's company was sketchy. To the casual viewer, it looked to be a highly profitable affair. He and Bryson only dealt with properties that the very rich could afford. If you wanted a luxury home in Spain or the Algarve, Tim Chandler was the expert. Dylan would dig deeper and see what he unearthed.

At six-thirty, someone knocked on his door. He knew who it was before she spoke.

"I thought you were going to call me when you got in, Dylan."

He went to the door and held it open. She was wearing a short, figure-hugging black dress that showed off legs that went on forever. Clutched in her hand was a small black bag. Again, he was reminded of the girl he'd made love to in that blue bedroom all those years ago.

"Hi, Maddie. I was planning to call you but I had some work to do first. I'm all finished now though. Let's go and eat, shall we?"

She leaned past him and eyed his rumpled bed. "I can think of other ways to pass the time."

"So can I, but I need to talk to you about Prue."

She sighed at the mention of her sister's name. "Come on then. We'll have drinks in the bar first."

The bar was warm—and deserted. For the first time that Dylan could remember, no guests were sitting on stools and complaining to the barman about the weather.

Dylan ordered a pint of beer.

"Gin and tonic." Maddie gave the barman an irresistible smile but no "please."

As soon as their drinks were in front of them, Maddie decided they should sit on the sofa by a long, low table close to the fire. "We'll be private here." Her smile offered almost anything he wanted. All he wanted was the truth and he wasn't sure that was on offer.

"Good idea."

She sat close to him, much too close, with her arm through his so that he had to use his left arm to lift his pint.

"Right," he said, "I need to know what happened during the weekend you visited Prue in France."

"What?" The question took her by surprise and made her laugh. "What do you mean? Nothing happened."

"Tell me about it. Everything you can remember. What time you arrived, what you did, who you saw, when you left, what Prue did—everything."

"Okay, if it will make you happy. Let me think. We arrived early on the Friday evening. Maybe five or six o'clock. Prue had offered to meet us from the airport but that would have involved catching sixteen trains and four buses before we even glimpsed her flat so we hired a car and Tim drove us to her flat. She took us to a nearby pizza house for dinner. An awful place. Cheap and cheerful, Prue said. Cheap was the only accurate part of that." She took a sip of her drink. "Are you bored yet?"

"No. Carry on. How did Prue seem to you?"

"The same as Prue always seemed. Polite, smiling, ingratiating."

"Did anything happen during that meal?"

"Nothing. We talked about the flight, she kept saying how lovely it was to see us. Boring, boring, boring. Blah, blah, blah."

"Go on."

"After we'd endured our pizzas, we went back to her flat—poky doesn't even begin to describe that—and sat about talking for an hour or so. We had a couple of glasses of wine while we caught up on each other's news."

"What news did she have?"

"She talked mostly about the people who had flats in her building. I remember we had every resident's life story but I don't remember her talking about anything else. I'd guess we were in bed by eleven at the latest."

"Talk me through the following day," Dylan said.

"Okay, Saturday. We had breakfast at a nearby café—the weather was good, I remember that. We sat outside this little café eating croissants and drinking coffee. That wasn't too bad. Then we had a stroll round the shops in the vicinity."

"Did she see anyone? Talk to anyone?"

"No."

"Then what?" Dylan asked.

"We wasted the day as people do. In the evening, she said she was throwing a party for us. About a dozen of her friends turned up. All scruffy types and all carrying bottles of cheap plonk. Tim and I tried to be sociable but it was bloody difficult. As soon as the first guests left, I went to bed. I'd had the headache from hell all day. Tim sat up and got drunk with her."

"What did they talk about?"

"I don't know, Dylan." She sighed her irritation with the questions. "According to him, she said nothing that made any sense. You know the sort of rubbish people come out with when they're drunk. I gather it was that sort of evening." Her gaze was steely. "Whether they slept together, I have no idea. He says no, and I never asked her. I wouldn't be surprised though."

"And after that?"

"Is any of this important?"

"Yes."

"She was hungover the next morning, but we went to that café again for coffee and croissants. A couple of hours later, we set off for the airport. And that was that. Why is it important?"

"I believe she told someone about her affair with Mc-Intyre. I also think she told that person he was painting again. Now who would she tell? Her sister? The sister who tends to look down on her? The sister who thought she'd never make anything of herself? Don't you think she'd boast about being with a wealthy, successful man? I do."

"She didn't say a word about him."

He didn't know whether to believe her or not. Prue must have told her she was living with Jack McIntyre. Maybe Prue told Chandler. Either way, Maddie must have known about it.

"Why didn't you like Prue?" he asked. "And exactly how much did you *dis*like her?"

Maddie stared at him long and hard. "I loathed her."

He was surprised at such venom but didn't let it show. "I thought so. Why? What did she ever do to you?"

"What did she ever do to me?" She threw back her head and laughed. "She only ruined my life. I was happy until she came along. At five years of age, my life was over. You can hardly pack your bags and leave home at that age, can you? I was tempted, believe me. Everything revolved around her and she lapped it up."

"If you felt left out when Prue was born, surely that was your parents' fault? It wasn't hers, was it?"

Maddie shrugged and looked weary of the whole discussion.

"So why," he said, "if you hated Prue, did you ask me to look into her death?"

She smiled, a smile that was like the sun breaking through heavy cloud. "I needed an excuse to see you, Dylan."

A shudder ran down his spine. "How did you find me, Maddie?"

"I told you—"

"You lied. You said you saw my name in the local paper when you stayed up here following Prue's death. I checked with the paper's editor. My name hasn't appeared in the paper this year."

She slipped her arm through his. "I told a white lie. When Prue sent me a change of address card, I looked up Dawson's Clough on the internet and saw your name then."

"That was November. Why didn't you contact me then?"

"I didn't have a good enough excuse." She squeezed his arm. "It's wonderful to be together now, though, isn't it?"

He wasn't going to answer that. "Did you kill Prue?"

There was none of the shock or outrage he'd expected. "No."

"Where were you on the day she died?" he asked.

"At home. Alone. No alibi, I'm afraid, detective."

"You weren't with Eddie Bryson?"

That did surprise her. "Eddie? Why would I be with him?"

"I think he was in Manchester on the day she died."

"So? He and Tim are often in Manchester."

"I think he was at the same art gallery as Prue. Is he an art buff?"

"Not that I know of. Look, Dylan, I know you're getting nowhere with this, but it doesn't matter, truly. Let's have dinner. Let's enjoy the evening."

She was right about one thing. He was getting nowhere. But he would. He'd find Prue's killer if it took him to the end of his days.

"Dinner," she said. "Come on. Let's go to the dining room. And later—" She leaned close and whispered in his ear. "Later, we can refresh our memories…"

THIRTY-SEVEN

Dylan thought his own rented office was smart, but Tim Chandler's made it look like a cheap lock-up. The swanky address ensured that only the well-heeled would walk past and, hopefully, gaze in the window to see details of exclusive homes for sale beneath that hot foreign sun. If you were interested in buying a villa, all you had to do was chat to their friendly staff and arrange a free trip to Portugal or the Algarve. Dylan quite fancied the idea. He wouldn't want to live abroad but he wouldn't mind a sightseeing trip funded by Chandler.

What he wanted right now, however, was a good night's sleep. It had been late last night when he'd finally crawled into bed, having extricated himself from Maddie. He'd thought he was rebuking her advances on moral grounds, but his lack of interest had nothing to do with being a faithful married man. He hadn't spared Bev's feelings a thought. No, he'd stayed out of her bed because there was something about her he didn't trust. Twenty-year-old memories had tempted him, but the grown-up Maddie didn't.

He'd had little sleep though and, at first light, had driven to London and to Chandler's office.

He walked into the vast reception area where his feet sank into a cream deep-pile carpet. Sofas and easy chairs were provided for the comfort of would-be buyers as they perused the array of glossy colour brochures on show. On one wall, a screen showed mouthwatering properties in the sun.

He approached a curved reception desk behind which sat a young, slim and extremely attractive young girl with perfect hair, fingernails and teeth. Everything about her was perfect.

"Hi, I'm Dylan Scott. I have an appointment with Tim and Eddie."

She smiled a perfect smile and long slender fingers picked up a phone. She announced his presence to someone. "They won't keep you a moment," she said. "Would you care for a coffee while you wait?"

"No, thanks."

"Take a seat, Mr. Scott."

He didn't. He walked round the reception area, looking at huge villas that boasted swimming pools bigger than Dylan's home. Some had tennis courts. All were near a golf course. The time share properties were given a smaller space. They obviously weren't as lucrative. Gleaming boats in sun-kissed marinas had a section of wall to themselves. In a couple of photos, Bryson was standing on board an expensive boat smiling for the camera.

The receptionist's clone appeared.

"Mr. Scott? I'm Holly. Mr. Chandler is free now. If you'd like to follow me—"

Dylan followed her up a flight of steep stairs. Neither spoke.

"This way," she said.

Their feet sank into the thick carpet as they walked to the door at the end of the corridor. She tapped on the door before pushing it open. "Mr. Scott to see you, Tim."

Chandler rushed forward, hand outstretched. "Dylan, good to see you. Come in, come in."

Dylan shook his hand and walked into a vast office that was empty apart from a huge glass-and-chrome desk, high-backed chair and two or three armchairs set around a glass-and-chrome coffee table. Several large photographs of homes for millionaires adorned cream walls.

"I did say I wanted to see Eddie too," Dylan said.

"And so you shall. He's with our accountant at the moment, but he'll join us in a few minutes. He knows you're here. Can I get you a drink?"

"Thanks, but no."

On Chandler's desk was a silver framed photo of Maddie. She was smiling into the camera and it struck Dylan that her smile seemed genuine. It was the smile he remembered from twenty years ago. He hadn't seen anything of it recently.

"Take a seat, take a seat."

Jesus. Chandler was like a bloody parrot. Was he nervous? Dylan could think of no other reason for repeating every damn thing he said.

"Thanks." Dylan sat in an armchair by the coffee table.

"So how's it going, Dylan?" Chandler sat opposite him. "Have you made any progress? I'd love to be able to tell Maddie you were close to finding Prue's killer."

"Does she care?"

"Dylan!"

"Come off it, Tim. We both know that, for whatever reason, Maddie disliked Prue intensely. Loathed, I believe, was the term she used when telling me about it."

Chandler tugged at the knot of his tie. "They weren't close, but Maddie—well, she's difficult to fathom at times. She's really upset about Prue's death, more than she'll let on, and that's probably because they weren't close. I'm sure she has a lot of regrets. She's a tough little thing though. She won't let us know how much she's hurting."

"What happened to Prue and Maddie? Why were they so distant?"

"Nothing specific as far as I know," Chandler said. "I've always imagined the age gap was too great. Five years is quite a lot."

Again, Dylan thought of Freya and Luke and wondered if they'd ever be so distant. He didn't think so. "How many times has Maddie been treated for depression?"

Chandler got to his feet and paced the room to stand in front of the window and gaze out at the City. His back was to Dylan but, after a few moments, he turned round. He stayed where he was, his hip resting on the windowsill. "Half a dozen, but what does the state of Maddie's health have to do with Prue's murder?"

"Possibly nothing. When was the last time?"

"September. Why do you ask?"

"Before or after you visited Prue in Paris?"

"After." Chandler returned to his seat. "I'll ask again.

What does the state of Maddie's health have to do with Prue's murder?"

"I don't know yet."

"Are you any further forward?" Chandler's tone was mildly scoffing. "Are you sure you're not just giving Maddie false hope—and spending my money?"

"No, I'm not sure. I'm not sure that, even if I learn what happened to Prue that night, I'll ever be able to prove it."

"Sorry." Chandler patted Dylan's knee. "I didn't mean to sound ungrateful. I know you're doing the best you can."

Patronising shit.

"So Maddie returned to London after seeing her sister and sank into a depression," Dylan said.

"The two weren't connected, but for a timescale it's accurate, yes."

"Why weren't the two connected?"

"They weren't. Maddie was fine when we returned. Why shouldn't she be? She'd been working hard beforehand, which is one reason we thought we'd enjoy a weekend break. It was probably her workload that contributed to her depression."

"Did she go to a clinic? A hospital?"

"She spent six weeks at the Arnthorpe Clinic." Chandler was terse, and Dylan wasn't surprised. The Arnthorpe was used by the elite. Chandler's bank balance would still be recovering. She'd probably shared the sauna with royalty.

"She's fine now," Chandler went on. "She's on medication to keep her moods stable. It's just as well because she's had a lot to endure lately, what with Prue's death and the necessary work that goes with that."

The door opened and Eddie Bryson, smiling from ear to ear, strode inside. As the door closed behind him, Dylan wondered if he'd used his stapler to fix that smile in place.

"Hi, Eddie," Dylan said. "How are you?"

"Fine. What brings you here? Please tell me you'd like an eight-bedroom mansion in the sun." He laughed loudly.

"I wouldn't mind one," Dylan said, "but despite what Tim might think, I'm not earning enough."

Both men laughed. Dylan didn't.

"I'd really like to know where you both were on the tenth of February," he said.

"What?" Chandler looked as if Dylan had just asked him to run naked up the Mall.

"I need a few things clearing up," Dylan said. "So you were—where?"

"Me?" Chandler was either playing for time or was too surprised to think straight. "Well, I was in Portugal. I'd left the day before and returned on the Saturday evening. Why do you want to know that, for God's sake?"

"What about you, Eddie?"

"I can't remember offhand. I can check, of course, but you'll have to bear with me."

Of course he could remember. Everyone knew exactly where they were when news of someone's death broke. He might not have been close to Prue but he was close enough to Chandler for the death of his sister-in-law to register.

"That's okay," Dylan said, "I can refresh your memory. You were in Manchester."

Dylan watched him closely. Those CCTV images had been of such poor quality that he had no idea if Bryson was in Manchester or not but, when you tossed wild guesses in the air, you had to watch very carefully for any reaction.

"Was I?"

"Yes. You visited an art gallery."

"Well, well. If you say so. I remember being in Manchester around then, obviously, and I can remember escaping the rain and going inside a gallery to get a coffee, but I couldn't have told you when."

"So now you know. It's a coincidence, isn't it, that you were at the same art gallery at the exact same time as Prue?"

"Oh, my—" Bryson was either a good actor or as pure as the driven white stuff. Dylan would gamble on the former. "You mean I was at the same art gallery that poor Prue went to that day?"

"Yes."

"Oh, my." He shook his head, a sorrowful expression on his face. "I never met her so I wouldn't have recognised her, but even so. God, that's taking spooky a bit far, isn't it?"

"It certainly is."

"I remember now," Chandler said. "You called me from that gallery, Eddie. We'd had problems with the Lacy account and you phoned me to see what we could sort out. I remember you saying you had an hour to kill before meeting Dennis Pemberton, and because it was raining, you were passing it in a gallery's coffee shop."

"I remember, yes," Bryson said. "I still can't believe I was in the same building as Prue. It's a small world, isn't it?"

"Minuscule. Where was Maddie?" Dylan asked.

"Maddie?" Chandler thought for a moment. "At home. At least, I think so. She was certainly there when Prue phoned her that evening. She may have gone to the shops, I don't know. She was definitely in London though. Why all the questions, Dylan?"

"Oh, I'm just throwing out random questions to see where it takes me. What sort of car do you drive, Eddie?"

He'd already seen Chandler's car and there was nothing about it to raise a sixteen-year-old's attention. It was an expensive model, the latest Mercedes, but it wasn't out of the ordinary in a way that would have captured Kevin Mills's interest.

"Now this you don't have to take my word for. Here." Bryson was on his feet and gesturing for Dylan to join him at the window. "There's mine."

A lone VW Passat in dark green sat outside the building. It was disappointingly ordinary.

"What's all this about cars and galleries?" Chandler sounded tetchy.

"I'm just being thorough." Dylan gave him a confident smile. "Did you drive up to Manchester for your meeting, Eddie?"

There was the slightest hesitation. "No, I flew. It's

a damn sight easier and it means I can work on the plane. Why?"

"Just curious. What did you do? Get the train into Manchester? Hire a car? What?"

"I hired a car at the airport." He shook his head in amusement. "I'd love to know where you're going with this, Dylan."

So would Dylan.

"Prue and Jack McIntyre," he said. "What about that? Were either of you surprised to learn that she lived with him for a couple of months?"

"I was," Chandler said.

"I never knew her," Bryson said, "so I can't comment. I've seen photos of her though and no, I wasn't particularly surprised."

"He was painting again, you know." Dylan removed imaginary fluff from his jeans as he spoke. "If anyone could get their hands on those paintings, they'd never have to work again."

"How do you know that?" Bryson asked. "It can only be hearsay, surely. He's dead so he can't tell us."

"Oh, he was definitely painting again. I've managed to find the paintings. Six there are. Well, I found six. I suppose there could be more."

"My God." Bryson slapped his thigh. "Tell us more, Dylan. Where are they and how the hell did you find them?"

Dylan tapped the side of his nose. "You're better off not knowing, believe me. You wouldn't want to end up like Prue, would you?"

"You're not telling me Prue had them, are you?" Bryson said.

"I'm not telling you anything. Really, it's safer if you don't know where they are. They were at my house for twenty-four hours and I didn't relax for a second until they were out of there." Dylan rose to his feet. "Well, thanks for your help, gentlemen. Sorry I've taken up so much of your time."

He swept out of their office before they had the chance to say more.

THIRTY-EIGHT

THE RAIN WAS relentless. There was no escape. The sun had been shining when Dylan woke—in his own bed for a change—but it had lashed down for the journey from London to Dawson's Clough and it was still raining.

Dylan was attending his second funeral in thirty days, and this one promised to be even more depressing than Prue Murphy's, if that were possible.

The congregation packed the small church. As it was standing room only, Dylan had given up his seat and moved to the back of the church to stand with Dawson's Clough locals. At the front of the church, Kevin Mills's coffin was laden with flowers. The vicar stood guard as he tried to convince mourners that they shouldn't even try to understand God's will but should instead celebrate Kevin's short life, and take comfort from the knowledge that the Lord had chosen to take him to a better place.

What total bollocks.

The mourners stood to sing "Rock of Ages," which didn't seem particularly appropriate. Kevin's parents, standing to the left of the coffin, were rigid with shock, grief and tension. Kevin's mother was being supported by her husband, who was also hanging on to Kevin's weeping sister.

The hymn was sung with little enthusiasm. The vicar's voice was firm and strong but, other than that, no one could cope. Schoolchildren sobbed for the duration and family members couldn't find the strength for hymn singing.

When the final notes died away, Kevin's uncle, a big, broad man in an ill-fitting suit, stood behind the coffin to read from notes someone had written. He spoke of Kevin's love for planes, trains and cars, and he told mourners how Kevin had preferred football to schoolwork. Despite this, he said, Kevin had been a good pupil. His nephew had been a happy, friendly, helpful boy and a credit to his parents. His voice was unsteady as he spoke and he clutched a huge cotton handkerchief in his big hand.

Another hymn followed, more prayers, and then the coffin was being carried out of the church and into the windswept graveyard where the rain battered everything in its path. As he had at Prue's funeral, Dylan silently wished the coffin bearers well. The path was wet and slippery, but they would be used to such dangerous conditions.

Most of the mourners, Dylan included, unfurled large umbrellas. The undertakers made sure that Kevin's family was protected from the deluge. There was another short prayer in the rain before Kevin's coffin was finally lowered into the cold, wet earth.

A tortured gasp escaped Mrs. Mills's mouth and her husband had to increase his grip on her. Mother, father and sister each threw a red rose on the coffin.

Dylan had tried but he couldn't even begin to imagine what they were going through. Kevin was only a few years older than Luke, and the idea of losing Luke was unthinkable. Dylan had no idea how or if he would cope.

People offered their condolences to the family, and the family thanked the mourners for attending. All were invited back to the hall for sandwiches and tea or coffee.

Dylan headed back to his car. There was nothing he could say that would help the Mills family. Police had launched a massive investigation into Kevin's murder and, maybe, they'd be successful in finding his killer. Dylan thought it unlikely because he thought they were on the completely wrong track. Suggestions from a disgraced copper wouldn't be welcome though.

He started the Morgan and drove away from the church. The car was warm and his general dampness slowly disappeared, but the anger stayed with him. He'd love to get hold of the person responsible for ending Kevin Mills's life and for putting the Mills family through this ordeal. Their lives would never be the same again and Dylan was determined to make sure the killer's life was never the same.

He was turning right by the Nag's Head, onto the Clough's fiendish one-way road, when he saw two familiar faces. It was too late to stop. Once you were on this road, there was no escape for ten minutes. Normally, he'd break all traffic laws and reverse but he had a Tesco home delivery van glued to his back wheels. He drummed his fingers on the steering wheel as the traffic crawled along. Finally, he turned off the one-way system and drove back to the Nag's Head, but there was no sign of Danny Thompson or Toby Windsor, or of Windsor's white Mercedes. The two men had been standing in front of it, oblivious to the rain. Judging by the angry scowls and arm waving, their meeting hadn't been friendly.

So what had the town's favourite wine bar owner been discussing with Prue's landlord?

Dylan didn't trust either man. He'd bet neither would have any quibbles about making extra cash at someone else's expense.

He drove around the town centre but he didn't spot that white Mercedes, and Danny's Wine Bar was closed.

As he didn't have time to spare, he drove out of the town and to Frank's house. Pleased that Frank had the door open for him, he dashed from car to house without getting too wet.

"Bloody weather," he said. "Is it ever going to stop raining?"

"Of course. Lancashire's dry season lasts four days—the second week in June."

"Godforsaken place. Are you ready to go?"

"Two minutes." Frank went to the kitchen and switched off the radio. He came back to the hall, checked his pockets for his wallet, grabbed his keys from a round silver bowl and took a heavy jacket from a hook. "Let's go."

They sprinted to the car.

"I know you're not a fan of the force, and I can understand that, but I hope you're not withholding information," Frank said as they drove off.

"Nope. All I'm withholding is a hunch and they wouldn't thank me for that. I've learned nothing that they couldn't have found out a damn sight more easily."

Frank didn't look convinced. "So why are we going to the airport?"

"I told you. I want to know what sort of car Eddie Bryson hired." It had to be a wild-goose chase. Hire cars were all the same. They were a year or two years old at most, and they were small, medium or large saloons. "It's probably nothing but if I go on my own, they won't tell me anything. I need a bit of police authority with me."

"You'll get me into all sorts of trouble."

"So what will they do about it? You've retired, Frank. They can't fire you or lock you up in a cell, can they? In any case, they'd never admit that the revered DCI Willoughby had a blemish on his character."

"You're full of shit."

Dylan smiled at the insult. "I've found it helps."

"I've already got trouble." Frank wasn't smiling. "Someone's been asking questions about a certain file I let you borrow."

"You're kidding. Who? And what sort of questions?"

"The difficult sort. I don't know, but I have a suspicion that Carlton Amesbury is behind it."

"Amesbury? The constable who found Kevin Mills's body?"

"That's him. He's a good copper, or could be, but he's got an enormous chip on his shoulder. He likes to play the racist card at every turn."

"Ah. And we all know racism doesn't exist in the good old British police force."

Frank shrugged that off. "I think I've managed to put it all to bed by being a little economical with the truth, but I'm going to keep my eye on Amesbury. It sounds to me like he needs to be put straight about a few things."

Dylan didn't envy Amesbury. Frank might appear to be a nicely spoken, relaxed ex-copper, but it was never a wise move to get on his wrong side. If Amesbury had any sense, he'd give Frank a wide berth.

The rain eased a little as they neared the airport.

"As I was driving away from the funeral, I saw Danny Thompson in conversation with Toby Windsor. What do you make of that, Frank?"

"I'd say they were up to no good. Not that I know a lot about Windsor, and I can't say for certain that Thompson put a match to his premises. It's interesting though."

"It is. I don't know how they know each other, but they both knew Prue. Windsor had plenty of opportunities to look round her home, and there's no knowing what she told Thompson when she was drunk."

"Were either of them at the funeral?" Frank asked.

"No."

"How did it go?"

Dylan shuddered. "Nothing interesting or out of the ordinary happened but, Christ, it was a bloody depressing affair. I can't imagine what that family is going through. I can't imagine how they'll ever get over it either."

"They'll feel better when the perp is brought to justice."

"Will they?" Dylan wasn't so sure. "*We* might. I know I damn well will. But I'm not so sure they will. What will it matter if some stranger is banged up in

Strangeways for the next twenty years? It won't repair that family, will it? It won't bring a young boy home."

Dylan's phone rang and he checked the display. He was disappointed to see Maddie's name. He'd been hoping it was the lab calling to tell him that no way on this earth could Boris be his father. Christ, that was taking forever. Perhaps they hadn't been able to get DNA from the mug. Surely, they would have been in touch if that were the case.

He ignored Maddie's call.

There was a steady stream of traffic heading for Manchester Airport and Dylan wasn't surprised. Given the bloody awful weather in this part of the world, residents must be eager to jet off to sunnier climes.

He parked the Morgan as near to Terminal Three as he could and they walked into the building. He'd taken off his black tie, undone the top button of his shirt and replaced his suit jacket with his battered leather one, but he still felt dressed for a funeral.

"There are nine hire car companies," he told Frank, "so we may as well start at the first one we come to and go through them that way."

Over an hour later, they'd crossed off the first four companies on their list. No one named Bryson had booked a car through them. That didn't mean much if Bryson had travelled under a different name.

The woman at the fifth desk, however, was far more helpful.

"I'm sure it was booked through us. A friend of mine is called Bryson and I'm sure I've seen the name recently. Just a minute." She tapped through computer records. "Here we are. Oh, there are two records. It seems Mr. Bryson booked through us a second time and had the same car."

"What model of car was he given?" Dylan asked.

"A Chrysler. Would you like copies of the booking?"

"That would be very useful, Thanks."

A nearby printer churned out two sheets of paper and, smiling, she handed them over. "There you go. Anything else I can help you with?"

"No, that's it. Thanks for your help." Dylan checked the dates carefully and put the booking details in his pocket.

They walked out of the terminal building and back to the car.

"Now what?" Frank asked.

"God knows. I can't see that a mid-range Chrysler would be of any interest to Kevin Mills. They're common enough in the Clough. On the other hand, the dates fit. Eddie Bryson had that car when Prue was killed and he also had it when Kevin Mills was killed. Coincidence?"

"Probably." Frank thought for a moment. "Most of us use the same car hire company if we've had good service from them. We like to stick with the familiar. If you book a car that size and price, it's likely that you'll get the exact same car. If Bryson spends a lot of time in Manchester—"

"He does."

"Then, basically, you've got nothing whatsoever to go on."

Dylan's phone rang and again he hoped the lab

wanted to give him good news about those DNA samples. It was Maddie so he hit the Reject button.

"I wonder—" Dylan took the car rental paperwork from his pocket and studied it again. "I have a hunch, Frank."

"Yeah, but sadly, hunches don't put men behind bars."

"No, but they're a bloody good place to start…"

THIRTY-NINE

"WHAT TIME WILL Dad be home?"

"Luke, you've already asked me that. I don't know."
Bev slammed the fridge door shut. "He said he'd be
back in time for the match so any time now, I expect."

"He usually comes home on a Friday night." Luke
was determined to have a good grumble.

"But last night he had to stay over. It's no big deal.
He'll be here to take you to the game so stop looking
so gloomy. Your face will stick like that."

Luke let out a long sigh and took up his vigil at the
window to wait for the first glimpse of his dad's car
turning into the road.

Bev was furious with Dylan too. Okay, so she'd made
noises about hosting a return dinner party, but that was
just her manners showing. She'd had no intention of
actually going through with it. But now—Christ, she
couldn't believe she'd been talked into hosting a dinner
party for six guests. Six at the last count, at any rate.
Knowing Dylan, another half-dozen people could easily turn up. God, he had a bloody nerve. She wouldn't
have minded so much if she actually liked the guests
but the thought of competing with Maddie Chandler—

Not that she could compete. She wouldn't be employing caterers and the food would be basic. The plates

might match and glasses might be suitable, depending on what people wanted to drink, and that would be as good as it got.

With a sigh to match Luke's, she picked up the phone and hit the button for Dylan's number. When he answered, she wished she hadn't bothered. It was virtually impossible to hear anything over the noise of the car.

"Your son's about to hurl himself from a tall building and I'm thinking of following him," she said. "You will be home for the match, won't you?"

"Yes, we're about an hour away. Everything okay there?"

"No."

"Don't worry about it, Bev. And don't go to too much trouble, okay?"

"I'm not. It still takes hours to get everything ready though. The house needs cleaning from top to bottom—"

"Does it hell. I mean it, Bev, don't worry about it. Look, I'd better go. I'll see you in an hour."

The connection was cut. *I love you too, sweetheart.* She let out her breath. *Men!*

"Right, Luke, your dad will be home in an hour. Meanwhile, you can go and tidy your room, okay?"

"What? But I never tidy my room on match days."

"There's a first time for everything. Instead of looking like a wet weekend, you can do something useful. Go on."

Shaking his head and muttering to himself, he stormed out of the kitchen and thumped up the stairs.

She wasn't naive enough to believe he'd bother doing

anything as constructive as picking up his clothes or hunting out rotting apple cores and empty chocolate wrappers, but at least she wouldn't have to tolerate his grumbling and sighing while she panicked about the evening ahead.

She opened the fridge again, stared at the vast empty space and began writing her shopping list. So far, it consisted of booze, booze and more booze.

Thank God for her mother-in-law. Vicky had taken Freya out so she could get on, and she'd be taking the children back to her place to spend the night.

She wrote *Sherry* on her list. She wasn't sure if anyone drank it these days, but she ought to have some just in case. Half a bottle of the stuff she'd put in the Christmas trifle for the last couple of years was at the back of the cupboard, but it had probably gone off. It would be cheap stuff anyway and she could hardly serve that. Red wine, white wine, brandy, gin, mixers—

The first course would be melon. If people didn't like it, they'd have to sit and suffer. Besides, who didn't like melon. It was so tasteless there was nothing to like or dislike.

She'd then serve beef bourguignon and, again, people would have to like it. If they didn't— *Oh, shit. Damn and blast, Dylan.*

With such short notice, she'd hoped that no one would be able to make it. They'd all been delighted to attend though. Maddie had probably accepted because she had designs on Dylan. Husband Tim probably went where Maddie told him. Eddie Bryson and his girlfriend, Shaz, had also been pleased to accept.

What a nightmare. She couldn't imagine any of them in the kitchen mucking in.

She'd buy a pavlova or something for dessert. Oh, and she'd better get some decent coffee in. Chocolates, too.

She walked into the dining room and decided it didn't look too bad. It shouldn't because they rarely used it. Flowers—she must buy some fresh flowers to cheer it up.

After half an hour of banging around upstairs, Luke emerged, far more cheerful, and decided he'd go outside and mess around with his football. He was wearing his Arsenal shirt and was ready to go to the game.

"Is your room tidy?" she asked him.

"Yeah. It's okay."

It didn't matter. Guests wouldn't be going into his room. They'd only have cause to go into the bathroom and she'd already scrubbed that until it gleamed.

Dylan and Frank arrived within the hour and when Frank gave her a big hug, she felt her mood soften slightly. He was such a lovely man. He wasn't very successful at marriage, probably because, like Dylan, he put criminals first in his life, but he was honest, warm and genuine and one of those people who always put you at your ease.

"It's good to see you, lovely lady," he said. "How are things here?"

"They'll be a lot better when tonight's over." She glared at Dylan.

"But you're—" Frank broke off and gave Dylan a quizzical look.

"You're not staying, Bev," Dylan said. "Once they've all got here, you're going to be called away to a family emergency. You're staying the night with mum and the kids."

"What?" Bev couldn't take it in. "You are kidding."

"No. I thought I'd mentioned it, but no way are you staying here. Things could easily get nasty."

Bev wanted to kill him. After all the fuss, she wasn't even going to be enjoying the food and drink. What was the point though? She hadn't wanted to endure the evening so she supposed she should be pleased. She would have been a damn sight more pleased if Dylan had thought to mention this tiny detail.

"I'll help you get everything ready, Bev," Frank said. "I'm surprisingly domesticated."

"I would, too," Dylan put in, "but Luke would never forgive me if I didn't take him to the game."

"It's okay." Bev spoke grudgingly. "Your mum's taking charge of Freya for the day so I'll be able to get to the supermarket and shop unhindered. You could come with me, Frank, and be responsible for choosing the wine. I wouldn't know good from bad."

"You can count on me," Frank said. "It'll be fine."

Bev sincerely hoped so. But if she wasn't going to be there, it hardly mattered. She could blame Dylan if it all went wrong.

"We'd better get busy, Frank," Dylan said.

"What are you doing?" Bev asked as they began pok-

ing around in corners. "Don't you dare make a mess—
I've cleaned. What the hell's going on?"

"You're better off not knowing," Dylan said. "Trust
me, Bev."

FORTY

DYLAN THOUGHT THEIR meal had been surprisingly tasty considering he and Frank had taken orders from Bev on how and when to serve. The ordeal had been unbelievably drawn-out though. Dylan had thought they'd never make it to the coffee stage.

Maddie had flirted with him for the duration but her attentions had had zero effect. The fun-loving girl he'd known twenty years ago was long gone and the thought saddened him.

Tim Chandler and Eddie Bryson were polite and charming. Shaz, Eddie's bimbo of a girlfriend, talked crap. She was fascinated by celebrities and celebrity gossip. She spoke of famous actresses as if she was on intimate terms with them.

Frank, like Dylan, wanted to get down to business, but Frank was blessed with patience.

So far, no one had mentioned Prue.

"I'll get the coffee," Frank said.

Dylan supposed that living alone had taught Frank how to be such an attentive host. He'd taken instructions from Bev and seemed to know the kitchen better than Dylan.

When Frank returned, he had coffee and chocolates

that had been put in a sparkling silver bowl that Dylan had never seen before.

"It's such a shame Bev can't be here," Bryson said for about the tenth time. "I bet she was looking forward to having you to herself at last, Dylan, because you haven't been home a lot lately, have you?"

"No, but I've more or less finished now."

"Oh?" Maddie was instantly alert. "How do you mean? Are you giving up?"

"I mean that I'm confident I know what happened to Prue. Proving it could be tricky but—well, we'll have to wait and see."

Seeing Danny Thompson and Prue's landlord together had given him a sleepless night but, according to Thompson, they'd been having a dispute about one of Windsor's properties. Thompson had agreed to take on the lease, thinking it would be a cheaper option for his wine bar, and Windsor had allegedly increased the rent. According to Thompson, he'd been telling Windsor where he could shove his lease.

Dylan believed his story.

"Tell us more," Bryson said. "Of course, you mentioned those paintings of Jack McIntyre's. Where have you hidden those?"

"There's no need to worry about those," Dylan said. "They're safe enough."

"I for one will be happy if you've come to the end of your investigation," Chandler said. "I think it's high time Prue was laid to rest. It'll be far better for Maddie and her parents too. Perhaps they'll be able to move on."

"What about you, Frank?" Bryson was always keen

to bring Frank into the conversation. "Are you aware of the case Dylan has been investigating?"

Frank was nibbling on a chocolate. No one else had touched one as yet. "Oh, yes."

"Didn't I give Frank his full title?" Dylan asked. "Of course, he's off-duty right now but this is DCI Frank Willoughby. He's been a great help in Prue's case."

Chandler, Bryson and Maddie all stared at Frank as if he'd suddenly turned green and was wearing a baseball cap with an I'm From Mars slogan printed on the peak.

"Also," Dylan said, "it was getting to know you again, Maddie, that really helped me solve the riddle of Prue's murder. That and talking to Clare Finch."

"Who?" Maddie asked.

"Clare was Prue's best friend. It was Clare who nudged me in the right direction really. Oh, I had bits and pieces, a theory of sorts, but only when I spoke to her, and she said that you'd be the very last person Prue would call if she had a problem, was I able to piece them together. I know Prue called you that day, probably as soon as she arrived home from the art gallery, but she wasn't frightened, was she? If she'd been upset, frightened or worried about anything, she would have called her parents, a friend, maybe even Clare in Australia. No. She called you because you were connected with what was on her mind. She may have been confused. She may have been angry. But she wasn't frightened."

Maddie was scowling. "I thought she sounded frightened."

"No." Dylan picked up his coffee and took a long,

slow sip. He was enjoying keeping them dangling. "Let me tell you what I think happened."

"Please do," Bryson said with a laugh. "You're like a magician about to pull a rabbit from a hat, Dylan."

Dylan returned his smile. "When Prue was living in France, she had a weekend visit from her sister and brother-in-law and she got drunk. She was embarrassed the next day. She was also concerned that she'd said things she shouldn't have. She had every right to be concerned because I believe she told her brother-in-law, a man she liked and trusted, that not only was she having an affair with a famous artist but that said famous artist was painting again."

"Did she?" Maddie demanded of Tim.

"Good God, no, of course she didn't. I think I would have remembered her saying she knew Jack McIntyre, don't you?"

"Of course he would, Dylan." Maddie shook her head at Dylan. "Tim would have told me something like that. I might not have believed him but he would have told me. This is ridiculous."

Dylan was fairly convinced that Maddie knew nothing about it. Fairly.

"Hear me out. I believe," he said, "that Tim then told Eddie. So, we have two men with a struggling business—and yes, I've checked out your company—who happen to know where there are some extremely valuable paintings whose existence is fairly secret and where security is lacking. So Eddie decides to pay the artist's home a visit. Coincidentally, he chooses a day when Jack McIntyre's agent is also visiting. Nothing goes to plan though. When he's walking down the deserted lane to McIntyre's cottage, he meets Prue, who's walking back to the village."

"Me?" Bryson said. "You think I went to McIntyre's place? You think I met Prue? I've told you, I *never* met Prue. I wouldn't have known her from Adam."

"I know," Dylan said, "and she wouldn't have known you from Adam, so it would have been easy for you to pretend to be a tourist. So, you pretend to be lost and walk back to the village with her. When you've got rid of her, you return to the cottage. By now, though, McIntyre is entertaining his agent. While waiting and thinking what to do, you pay his boat a visit. It's less than a mile away so it passes time. When you're poking about on that, looking for anything of value, McIntyre and his agent turn up planning to put to sea for a couple of hours. I suppose you have no choice but to hide on board. But that's okay because you're pretty skilled with boats, aren't you? You used to have one, I gather. Also, I saw photos of you on board a jolly nice boat when I visited your office."

Bryson was on his feet. "I'm sorry, but this is libellous and I'm leaving."

"Sit down," Frank said with the hard voice of authority.

Bryson looked at Frank, looked at the wide-eyed guests at the table and sat down.

"Actually, it's slanderous," Dylan said, "but humour me, will you? So you hid on McIntyre's boat. You had plenty of time to think, didn't you? The paintings were valuable in their own right. They'd be difficult to sell but I'm sure you have contacts abroad. But then you thought how much more those paintings would be worth, and how much easier it would be to sell them, if McIntyre was dead. What could be better than a boating accident? So, when the time was right, you pounced. Your weapon was a fire extinguisher. You killed Jeremy Collins and then you went for Jack McIntyre and knocked him overboard."

"Dylan," Chandler said, aghast, "you can't possibly come out with stuff like this and accuse Eddie of such things. How can anyone know what happened on McIntyre's boat? It's preposterous."

"I know what happened because I have a witness. Believe it or not, someone was on the boat who saw the whole thing. I've invited him to join us for drinks and I'm surprised he isn't here yet. I'll send him a text."

"This is madness," Bryson said. "I've read up on McIntyre. There were only two people on the boat that night and they're both dead. There's no embarrassment in admitting you can't say who killed Prue, Dylan. I imagine the police are right and she disturbed a burglar. Why not let it rest at that?"

Dylan didn't waste his breath on answering. He was busy sending a text message.

Maddie was scowling at Dylan, presumably because she believed he'd wasted her money. Chandler looked furious, although it was impossible to tell who bore the brunt of his anger. Bryson, not surprisingly as he was the centre of attention, was blustering. He was blowing hot and cold, intrigued and angry, his face red one minute and a sickly white the next.

"I expect our guest of honour will be here in a minute," Dylan said. "Meanwhile, let me continue. To recap, Prue had said in her drunken state that Jack McIntyre was painting again and that those paintings were in his tiny cottage on the coast. Easy, yes? Except, having arranged a very convincing boating accident and then returning to the cottage, there was no sign of any paintings, was there?"

"I refuse to—"

The doorbell silenced Bryson. He alternated between fear and confidence.

"I'll go." Frank was already halfway out of the room.

"This will be my witness," Dylan said, smiling to the shocked gathering.

Dylan almost didn't recognise the man who followed Frank into the room. He was clean-shaven and wearing a dinner jacket and looked like the artist Dylan had seen smiling for cameras at exhibitions, rather than the scruffy bearded man Dylan had taken a liking to.

Bryson leapt to his feet so suddenly that his chair crashed back onto the floor. "I don't know what the hell you're playing at but I'm not staying. This—this charade has become too childish for words. Don't expect me to believe that this is really—I mean, any fool knows it's some two-bit actor you've hired for your little game. I'm not staying."

Frank was at the door, barring Bryson's exit. "Sit down."

"Who is this?" Chandler said, his face ashen.

"I'm Jack McIntyre." McIntyre gave the guests a

broad smile. "As you can see, news of my death has been greatly exaggerated."

"You expect us to believe that this is really McIntyre?" Bryson's tone was scoffing now. He'd finished his coffee and he reached for the wine bottle to refill his glass. "This is laughable. It's like one of those tedious mystery weekends people pay to go on. All second-rate actors and clichés."

"I agree that it's all a bit clichéd," Dylan said, "but let me continue. Having assumed that McIntyre and his agent were dead—lost at sea in a freak boating accident—you searched his cottage. You found nothing because, despite what Prue had said in her drunken state, there was nothing to find. You thought maybe Prue had the paintings, so one or both of you broke into her home and searched it. That's probably when you lost that button, Tim."

"Oh, no. You're not pinning anything on me." Chandler, usually so smooth and calm, was furious. "Okay, I'll admit that Prue told me about the paintings and I told Eddie. And that—you have my word on this—was the last I had to do with any of it."

"Shut up, Tim." Bryson's voice was becoming slurred. He'd clearly had more wine than Dylan had thought.

At least they knew that Prue had told Chandler.

"You went to Manchester and the art gallery," Dylan addressed Bryson, "probably to see if you could find out something about those paintings. Or perhaps, as you claim, it was a spur-of-the-moment thing. Either way, you saw Prue. Sadly, for her, she saw you. She recognised the man who'd pretended to be a tourist on the day she left France, the day that Jack was involved in that boating accident. You made a call to Tim from the cafeteria there. Perhaps she heard you and discovered who you were. Perhaps she was about to make herself known, to tell you that she was Tim's sister-in-law, when she realised you were the same man she'd met in France that day. I don't know. We'll probably never know. We do know, however, that she recognised you. You panicked and decided she had to be silenced. You broke into her home—again—and this time you killed her."

"No!" Bryson banged a furious fist on the table, making glasses jump.

"As you left her home, in your hire car, a young boy spotted you. He was more interested in your car's registration plate than he was in you. I couldn't understand that until I checked and double-checked the car you were given by the hire company. The car was ordinary enough. The registration plate, however, spelled his name. KEV."

"Jesus Christ," Chandler muttered.

"You had a witness," Dylan went on, "and so you went back to Dawson's Clough to look for him. Unfortunately for him, you found him. Just like Prue, Kevin Mills had to be silenced."

"I know nothing about any of this," Chandler said. "Nothing at all."

"Nor does he." Bryson was on his feet again. "It's a great theory, Dylan, but it's pure fiction. Even if it was true, you wouldn't have a hope in hell of proving any of it. Not a hope in hell. So if your little game is over, I for one am leaving. I won't say it's been a pleasure—"

"You're going nowhere," Frank told him. "There are a few detectives who want a nice long chat with you."

"You can't—"

"Ah, but we can," Dylan said. "You might be right in that I won't be able to prove any of this. However, while you've been eating and drinking and listening to my theory, police officers have been searching your homes—"

"Mine too?" Chandler was horrified.

Maddie's phone rang for the third time in five minutes. She ignored it.

"Yours too, Tim. And forensics officers are going through that hire car with their box of tricks. I wouldn't like to be in your shoes, Eddie, if they find anything that says Kevin Mills was in that car. It doesn't take much—a hair, a tiny drop of blood or saliva."

Bryson lunged at Frank in a bid for escape. Dylan had been ready for anything and he soon had Bryson pinned against the wall. He pushed the bloke's head against it and there was a satisfying bang.

"You're reasonably safe for the moment, Bryson." Dylan spoke in a whisper so that his words wouldn't be caught by the recording devices planted in the room. "But in the unlikely event of officers being unable to put you away for a very long time, I promise you this. I'll come after you and I will personally break every bone in your detestable body. And then I will kill you."

"You won't prove anything!" Bryson spat in his face.

"Maybe. Maybe not."

Maddie's phone rang yet again and Chandler rounded on her. "Is it so difficult to either answer it or turn the fucking thing off?"

Chandler's fury silenced the men. Only Maddie's voice broke the silence as she spoke to her caller.

"I think perhaps I should go," she said when the call ended. There was something odd about her voice. It was high-pitched and breathy, and it cracked. "I—that was my mother on the phone. My father—my father—he's dead."

A dozen questions kicked Dylan in the ribs. None would be asked, or answered, however, because Maddie collapsed to the floor.

FORTY-ONE

THE TAXI DRIVER taking Dylan and Maddie to her parents' home must have realised they weren't candidates for sparkling conversation. Dylan was keen to talk but Maddie was incapable. Staring ahead, her expression vacant and a little disturbing, she seemed suddenly frighteningly fragile. Her hands trembled in her lap.

Police officers had arrived as they'd been picking her up off the floor. Chandler should be sitting in this taxi holding his wife's hand and grieving for his father-in-law, but Maddie hadn't wanted him anywhere near her. Besides, he'd been arrested along with Bryson on suspicion of murder, attempted murder and a couple of dozen other charges.

Maddie hadn't said more than half a dozen words since she'd fainted, so Dylan had no idea if Andrew Murphy was dead courtesy of a heart attack, a car accident or a mugger.

"Which house number do you want, mate?"

Dylan looked at Maddie but she gave no indication of having heard the driver.

"It's at the far end," Dylan said. "That's it—next to those two tall trees."

The taxi stopped and Dylan handed over a note. "Keep the change."

"Yeah? Thanks, mate. Have a good evening."

There wasn't much hope of that. "Thanks. You too."

Maddie looked incapable of leaving the vehicle's warm interior so Dylan took her hand and gave her a gentle tug. Like an automaton, she got out and walked up the driveway to her parents' house.

"Maddie!" Ruth held the door open for them and reached for her daughter, but Maddie flinched from her touch and walked along the hall and into the sitting room.

She stood in the centre of that room. She was completely still and she seemed to be listening.

"Maddie," Ruth said again, but Maddie shook her head to ward off the distraction. Dylan was sure she was listening for something.

Then, just as she had back at Dylan's house, she fainted.

"We need to get her a doctor, Ruth." Dylan knelt beside Maddie. She was out cold. "No, we'll get an ambulance."

Ruth was already speaking to someone on the phone.

"Her own doctor will be here in a few minutes," she said. "This has happened before, Dylan. She'll be okay."

Dylan wasn't so sure. Ruth was beginning to unnerve him too. Her husband was dead and yet she looked icy calm.

Maddie's eyes fluttered a couple of times and then opened wide. Her gaze darted from Dylan to her mother. "Is he really dead?"

Dylan picked her up and carried her to the sofa. There was no weight to her.

"The doctor's on his way," he said. "Lie still and try to relax, Maddie. Okay? Do you want a glass of water? A brandy?"

"Is he really dead?" she asked again.

Ruth took her daughter's hand. "He's dead, Maddie. Trust me, he's dead."

Maddie was trembling. And shivering.

"I stayed in Cardiff overnight." Ruth might have been discussing the weather. "I found him when I got home. He took his own life."

"He committed suicide?" Dylan said, but no one answered him. No one seemed to even hear him.

"Let me get you a drink of water, darling." Ruth strode out of the room.

"Are you okay, Maddie?" Dylan could see she wasn't but he felt the need to say something. Anything.

She didn't answer.

Dylan paced the room. Had he got everything wrong? On the strength of a half-baked idea, a hazy image from CCTV and three letters, KEV, in a registration plate, he'd had two men arrested. What if he was way off?

Ruth fussed around her daughter, Maddie remained in a state of shock, and Dylan tried to figure out what the hell was going on and why in God's name Andrew Murphy had chosen today to end his own life.

Prue's parents had admitted visiting her in France. They went often, they'd said, because they worried about her. They'd denied knowing anything about Jack McIntyre, but so what? Prue could easily have told them. If Andrew Murphy had made the attempt on McIntyre's life, if Prue had found out—

He stopped his thoughts short. No way had Andrew Murphy killed his own daughter. Murphy hadn't been spotted on CCTV at the art gallery Prue had visited, he hadn't hired a car with an eye-catching registration plate. He'd taken his own life because he was a coward. He hadn't wanted to cope with the loss of his daughter and he hadn't thought twice about leaving his wife to pick up the pieces. That didn't sound like the Murphy he'd met, albeit briefly, either.

The doctor arrived wearing a smile and full evening dress. Maddie clearly didn't have to rely on tired and irritable out-of-hours NHS doctors.

While he and Ruth fussed around Maddie, Dylan kept out of the way. He wandered into the kitchen where Sam, the Murphys' aged dog, looked as bewildered as Dylan felt.

When the time was right, and God alone knew when that might be, he'd have to talk to Ruth and make sure that it really was suicide. If Murphy was mixed up in Prue's death, if Bryson was innocent—

He refused to believe it.

Yet Murphy's behaviour had struck him as odd from the first. The way he'd distanced himself from Maddie at Prue's funeral hadn't seemed natural. He'd clearly been on edge when Dylan had called at the house, too.

The minutes turned to an hour and then Maddie was being led out of the house and to a waiting private ambulance.

"I'm coming with you, darling," Ruth said.

"No. I want to be alone," Maddie said.

"But, darling—"

"No." Maddie looked like a zombie, one who would disintegrate before their eyes if they weren't careful, but her voice was firm.

Dylan and Ruth watched until the ambulance's red tail lights disappeared from view.

"Thanks for being here, Dylan," Ruth said. "Do you need to rush off or would you stay for a while? I'm having a drink."

He'd thought she was quite calm, but he could see now that he'd been wrong. She'd put a brave face on things, that was all.

"I can stay," he said and they walked back into the house and the warmth of the kitchen. "What happened, Ruth?"

"I stayed overnight with my sister." She went to a cupboard and found a bottle of brandy and two glasses. "Will you join me?"

"I will. Thank you."

"I got home around ten this morning."

That was more than twelve hours ago. Maddie's father had been dead for over twelve hours and she hadn't known.

Ruth put two glasses down on the table and poured generous measures of brandy into them. "Here."

"Thanks."

Her bottom lip trembled as she raised her glass to her lips and took a healing swallow. "All was quiet when I let myself in. There was no sign of anyone, not even Sam, so I went upstairs. Sam was lying outside the bathroom door." She took another gulp of brandy. "I went into the bathroom and found Andy. He'd taken a bath, swallowed a lot of pills, mostly my antidepressants, and slit his wrists."

Before Dylan could offer the usual condolences, she rushed on. "I called the police—I was so shocked I didn't know who to call. They came, we found a note he'd left, an ambulance came to take him away— As soon as I was alone, I called Maddie. It's not the sort of news to break over the phone but I knew she'd hang up on me if I asked her to come here or suggested I went there."

"She was at my place. It was—" He couldn't describe tonight's circus as a dinner party. "Tim and Eddie were there too. They've been arrested, Ruth."

Ruth had been about to lift her glass to her mouth but she stopped, her eyes wide. "Arrested? For what?"

"I believe Eddie Bryson is responsible for the attempted murder of Jack McIntyre, the murder of a sixteen-year-old, Kevin Mills and—" God, this wasn't easy. "And Prue."

"No!"

"I think so." At least, he had thought so. "They're being questioned by police. A car Eddie drove is being checked over by forensics experts."

"No," Ruth said again. "Not Eddie. And certainly not Tim. Surely, you can't believe Tim was involved, can you?"

"It's possible." Probable.

Ruth crossed the room, glass in hand. She bent to give Sam an absent pat on the head. "I'm sorry, Dylan, but I honestly don't think I can take much more."

Dylan didn't either. She seemed to be shrinking by the minute.

"You said Andrew left a note," he said.

"Yes. It said—oh, it said nothing really. Just that he was sorry."

"Have you any idea why he might have taken such drastic action? Why today? Has something happened?"

"I can't talk about it now." Ruth refilled their glasses despite the fact that Dylan had hardly touched his. "I can't even think about any of it right now. First Andy, now Tim—Sorry, but I can't deal with it."

"That's okay."

They sat in the kitchen, drinking brandy and then coffee, and talking about very little until the first hint of dawn arrived.

FORTY-TWO

"Isn't this fantastic, Dylan?" Bev grabbed a glass of champagne from a passing waiter. "Oh, my God! Look, there's that chap."

"Who?" The building was packed and Dylan had no idea who she was talking about.

"Him," she said. "With the long black hair. He's really famous. He was on that TV chat show a month or so ago. I'm sure it's him."

"He's so famous you don't know his name?"

"You must know who I mean."

Dylan still didn't have a clue who she was talking about and he wasn't interested in celebrity guests. He just wished McIntyre would put in an appearance so that they could applaud his talent and go home.

Bev sipped her champagne. "Isn't this fantastic?" she said again.

At last. A gaggle of press photographers walked into the room—backwards. Cameras flashed in a sudden frenzy of activity. The man those lenses were so determined to capture swept into the room as if he ruled the world. How Jack McIntyre had survived in that French backwater, Dylan would never know because he was lapping up the attention now. His smile broadened with every flashbulb that exploded in his face.

Dylan hated all this showbiz stuff. They'd come to see some paintings, that was all. There was no need for all the whistles and bells.

Some had come under duress. Well, one at least. Dylan wouldn't have hesitated in turning down the invitation but Bev had already accepted and spent a year's salary on a new dress.

According to McIntyre, this was to be a private viewing for a few select friends before the exhibition opened tomorrow. A private viewing for friends shouldn't need half the country's press in attendance. And not even McIntyre could boast so many friends. Or perhaps he could. Dylan had learned long ago that one's circle of friends increased with one's bank balance.

London was sweltering in a mini midsummer heat wave, but Collins's art gallery managed to stay refreshingly cool. That was the only plus point Dylan had found so far.

He'd been surprised that McIntyre had agreed to have his work shown here. Not so long ago, he'd suspected Martin Collins of killing his father and making an attempt to end his own life. Now, it seemed, everything was forgiven. Perhaps McIntyre felt a loyalty to his late friend, Jeremy. News of McIntyre's resurrection had rocked the art world—the media had talked of little else for the past couple of months—so he could have shown off his paintings anywhere.

"May I stand with you for the big unveiling?" Ruth Murphy came to stand between him and Bev. "I'm feeling quite nervous. Silly, isn't it?"

"Not at all," Bev said. "I'd feel exactly the same.

There are a lot of people here, aren't there? I was only expecting about twenty or thirty."

"So was I. As for all the cameras, I shall spend the rest of the day avoiding those."

More than two months had passed since Andrew Murphy had committed suicide and every time Dylan had seen Ruth since then, he'd been relieved to see that she looked to be coping. He wasn't sure she was doing much more than coping, but at least she was managing that. She was stronger than she looked. Having lost a daughter and then a husband in a short space of time, she needed to be. Added to that, she'd seen her daughter taken to a clinic and her son-in-law and his business partner arrested.

"How's Maddie?" Bev asked her.

"She's doing well. I don't want to tempt fate but I believe she may fully recover this time. I spent the morning with her and she was laughing, joking and looking very relaxed."

"That's excellent news. I'm so pleased for you, Ruth. Our children are a worry, aren't they?"

Ruth smiled. "Maddie will soon be forty and I don't suppose I'll ever stop worrying about her."

"Ladies and gentlemen, may I have your attention, please?" Martin Collins looked sickeningly pleased with himself as he called the vast room to order. Guests were eager to see the much-talked-about paintings so he didn't need to ask twice.

An expectant hush fell on the room.

"At last," Ruth said.

She'd echoed Dylan's relief but they were both to be

disappointed. There was a long and boring speech from Martin Collins that gave McIntyre's life story. Perhaps a guest had been stranded in darkest Peru for the past forty years and had missed a snippet. Just as Dylan congratulated himself on surviving that, McIntyre made a speech that was almost as long but, thankfully, slightly more amusing.

"And now," McIntyre said with a flourish, "I give you the Chaste Collection."

Dark blue curtains were pulled back from three walls and there, gazing down at them, was Prue.

"Oh, my," Ruth said just as the room erupted in a burst of delighted applause and cheering.

"They're amazing," Bev said.

Even Dylan, who hated art with a passion, had to admit that they were exceptionally good. They were bigger than he'd expected, but there was no mistaking the emotions on Prue's face in the paintings. Wait a minute. There were five paintings. McIntyre had told him there were six. What the hell had he said about them? Chaste—coy, happy, angry, sensual, timid and excited? Dylan couldn't remember but one was definitely missing. At a guess, he'd say happy was the absent painting.

Experts peered closely and Dylan overheard the ridiculous comments they were coming out with. He was reminded of connoisseurs who insisted on describing whisky as having a full-bodied smoky flavour with a hint of oak. Dylan wanted his whisky to taste of whisky not smoke, wood or any other damn thing.

He realised he was alone. Bev and Ruth had wandered off to inspect the paintings more closely.

Dylan could understand why McIntyre was so pleased with his work. It was as if the very essence of Prue had been captured. Every mood was reflected in her eyes.

"So, Dylan, what do you think?" McIntyre stood by his side, champagne glass in hand.

"They're not bad at all."

"Coming from you, I shall take that as an enormous compliment. Thank you."

"I thought this was to be a private viewing for a few friends," Dylan said.

"And so it is. The press are only here to raise some enthusiasm for the official opening tomorrow."

"The paintings aren't for sale, I gather."

McIntyre smiled. "Were you looking to buy?"

"What do you think?"

"I think not." McIntyre gazed up at his work, a smile of satisfaction on his face. "No, they're not for sale. I'm happy to share them with the world but, for the moment at least, they're mine."

"One's missing. I thought there were supposed to be six."

"Yes, I'm doing the unthinkable and splitting the collection."

"Happy is missing, right?"

"Very observant. I'm impressed." He took a long thoughtful sip of champagne and, off to his right, a flashbulb captured the moment. He didn't even blink. "That particular painting is to be a gift. I thought Ruth Murphy might like it as a reminder of her daughter in happy times. I haven't told her yet. I thought I'd see her alone later. It may be that she won't want it. We'll see."

"Really?" Dylan had liked McIntyre from the start. Well, he'd thought him capable of faking his own death and killing his onetime lover, but, apart from that, he'd liked him. "That's good of you. In fact, you've just restored my faith in human nature. I'm sure she'll appreciate it."

"I like to think so."

"Is it here? May I see it?"

"Yes. And yes." He gazed at the throng of guests. "Come with me."

Dylan followed him to the back of the room and through a door marked Private, No Entry. This led to a narrow hallway. At the end of that, they took a flight of steps down to the basement. Two men sat behind a long desk tapping information into computers.

"Could I borrow the key for a minute?" McIntyre asked.

"Yes. Of course." Realising the great artist was in their midst, one of the men jumped to his feet and, from somewhere beneath the desk, produced a key. He handed it to McIntyre. "Do you want to sign for it?"

"No need. We'll only be a minute. Thanks."

The door was directly opposite the desk. McIntyre opened it and a light came on automatically. The room was dingy and cluttered, a storeroom.

"Over here." McIntyre strode to the back where several paintings stood. He pulled back a big white sheet to reveal his work of art. "This is Prue. The beautiful young woman I fell in love with. The woman who should be here today."

The painting was amazing. In Dylan's view, it was the best of the collection. Prue's head was thrown back and she was laughing as she danced through the surf in bare feet. She was wearing a simple white dress that swirled around her legs. It was the body of a young woman with the face of a five-year-old at Christmas.

"It's good," Dylan said. "Really good. It's also a very generous gift."

McIntyre shrugged that off. "A painting is only worth what someone is willing to pay for it, Dylan."

True, but a lot of people would pay a disgusting amount of money to own it.

"Does Ruth even know it exists?" Dylan asked.

"Not yet. I've simply told her I'd like a word with her this afternoon." He took a step back to admire his work. "I hope she'll approve."

"I'm sure she will."

McIntyre dangled the key from his fingers. "I'd better get back before they send out a search party."

"Yes. I'll be leaving in a couple of minutes, things to do, but I'm glad I came." Surprisingly, it was true.

"So am I, Dylan. Don't be a stranger, will you?"

"I won't. It's your turn to buy the drinks, I believe."

McIntyre smiled. "I believe it is."

They returned the key to the desk and went back to the party. The editor of some glossy magazine or other soon grabbed McIntyre for an interview. An interview he seemed delighted to give.

Dylan's phone, switched to Silent for the afternoon,

vibrated in his pocket. He looked at the display and hit the button to answer it.

"Mr. Scott, I'm so sorry it's taken so long to get back to you." Ms. Johnson from the lab sounded bright and chirpy.

"That's okay." It wasn't okay. Their inefficiency had cost him several sleepless nights. He couldn't believe that, when he'd chased them up about the test he'd booked, they'd had to admit to losing the results. He'd wanted to kill each and every person responsible. "Have you managed to do another test?"

"There's no need," she said. "We found the original test results. For some reason, they'd been cross-filed."

What the hell did "cross-filed" mean? He didn't know and he didn't really care. All he wanted was the verdict. He swallowed hard. He wasn't even sure he wanted that. In fact, at the moment, he was damn sure he didn't want it.

"Our tests were thorough and complete," she said. "We can tell you that there is no genetic relationship between the two samples you provided."

No genetic relationship. No genetic relationship—

"You're sure?" he said. "There's no doubt?"

"None at all, Mr. Scott."

"Thank you." The relief was immense. Not that he'd been really worried that Boris was his father. He'd known from the start that Bev was talking nonsense.

"You're welcome," she said. "We'll be mailing our report to you later today."

"Thank you," he said again. He ended the call and

stood for a few moments to let the good news sink in. Boris was not his father. Thank God for that.

This called for a celebration. He went in search of Bev and found her busy gossiping to Ruth.

"I'm nipping out for a bit," he said. "I may pop back later but you can get a cab home, can't you?"

Bev rolled her eyes at him. "Typical. On the rare occasions you actually take me anywhere, you abandon me to find my own way home."

"*You* brought *me*," he reminded her.

"So where are you going?"

"I need to see someone."

"Okay. I'll stay on here with Ruth."

Dylan gave her a quick kiss, said his goodbyes to Ruth and headed toward the exit. On a small table in the corner of the room were a couple of unopened bottles of champagne. Deciding McIntyre could afford it, he grabbed one. McIntyre had said it was his turn to fund the drinks anyway.

Finding a couple of glasses was much easier and, with those pocketed, he left the building.

FORTY-THREE

"SHE'S DOWN BY the lake, Mr. Scott," the receptionist said. "Would you like me to send someone to find her?"

"No need, thanks. I'll wander down there."

The receptionist nodded and smiled at the bottle and glasses in his hands. "Are you celebrating?"

"I certainly am. And the sun's shining. That's a good enough reason."

"Yes, it makes a pleasant change, doesn't it? Let me know if you can't find her."

"Will do."

Dylan stepped out of the cool building, walked across lawns so immaculate they could have been trimmed with nail scissors, and on to the lake. It was deserted except for a duck and half a dozen ducklings and, there, sitting on a wooden bench taking advantage of the shade from a willow, Maddie.

"Hey!" She put down the book she'd been reading. "What are you doing here? I thought you were mixing with the great and the good of the art world."

"I escaped." He sat beside her. "I bring gifts—so long as you're not averse to warm champagne."

"And glasses too. You think of everything."

"I try. Can I tempt madam with a glass?"

"You certainly can."

The cork flew out with a satisfying pop and he managed to fill two glasses without spilling too much. He handed her a glass and chinked his against it.

"To your good health," he said, and she smiled.

"Thank you." She was wearing a simple white dress, very much like the one worn by Prue in McIntyre's paintings.

Dylan took off his jacket and tossed it over the back of the bench. His tie went in his pocket.

"How did it go?" she asked.

"Pretty well, I suppose. There were a couple of hundred people there though so it was a bit of a crush. The press were there too so it wasn't the quiet affair I was expecting. I think your mother was pretty shocked too."

"She was here this morning."

"So she said."

"We had a long chat about—stuff."

"Good." He leaned back against the bench, stretched his legs out in front of him and closed his eyes. A welcome breeze cooled his skin a little. This was far preferable to being cooped up in an art gallery. "I thought she was looking pretty good today."

"So did I."

"And she said the same about you. She thinks you're doing well."

"I am."

He smiled at the spirit in her voice.

"I feel as if a huge black cloud has gone from my life," she said. "I feel lighter. Less weighed down. Does that sound crazy?"

"No."

"Mum doesn't talk about him much," she said. "In fact, she hardly mentions him at all. I think his name slips out when she forgets. That suits me. If I hear his name mentioned once before I die it'll be once too often."

"Why didn't you tell me, Maddie?"

"Tell you what?" she asked.

"You know what."

Dylan had spent hours drinking brandy and then coffee with Ruth on the day Andrew Murphy slit his wrists, and he'd called in the following morning just to make sure she was okay. It was then that she'd told him the full story. Along with a note saying he was sorry and asking for forgiveness, Murphy had left a couple of dozen letters that Maddie had written over the years. In them, Maddie had taunted him for sexually abusing her as a child. She'd sent newspaper clippings detailing cases where men had been sent to prison for several years. She'd reminded him he should be facing the same future. Three letters had been sent since Prue's death and a fourth had arrived on the morning Murphy ended his life. He hadn't opened it. He'd simply put it with the others, and left them on the kitchen table with a note saying he was sorry.

Once Ruth had started talking, she hadn't been able to stop. She'd told him how ten-year-old Maddie had tried to tell her what was happening and how Ruth, unable and unwilling to believe such things of her husband, had slapped her daughter hard and made her promise never to utter such vile lies again.

Maddie hadn't. She'd been abused for years and she

hadn't told a soul. Instead, she'd poured her hatred and anger into those letters to her father.

"And say what?" she asked. "Oh, by the way, my sister's dead and my father sexually abused me." She shuddered. "It was over. It was best forgotten."

Except she hadn't been able to forget. She certainly hadn't been able to forgive. Few women would.

"I didn't mean then," he said. "I meant twenty years ago. Why didn't you tell me then?"

"What?" She laughed at that. "When we were in bed? As in 'By the way, Dylan, you're far better than my father'?" She knocked back her champagne. "What difference would it have made?"

"A lot."

"You think so?"

He was certain of it. He wasn't sure exactly what he would have done but it would have included smashing Andrew Murphy to a pulp.

"We could have talked about it," he said. "We could have sorted something out."

"No." She slipped off her sandals and stretched her feet in the grass. "We were little more than kids then. We didn't have time for talking. In any case, I wasn't so bad then. In those days, I believed I could cope with it. I'd left home so I knew he'd never touch me again. I thought I was over it all. I can't explain the reasoning behind it, but I felt worse about it as I got older."

Dylan could understand that. Some scars refused to heal. They remained painful.

"There was no real need to tell you back then," she said. "And if I had, you would have made a sharp exit and ended up in someone else's bed, someone who didn't come with a mountain of baggage, someone who wasn't totally screwed up."

"Rubbish."

"Besides, I often thought it was my fault," she said. "I hated Prue from the moment she was born. I suppose I'd been spoilt and didn't like someone else stealing my thunder. So when he came to me and told me I was special—that's how it started. He'd creep into my bed, tell me I was his special daughter—" She shuddered. "As much as I hated him, I did feel as if I was superior to Prue. It didn't last. I soon realised that I wasn't special at all."

"He never touched Prue?"

"God, no. She was far too precious for his disgusting perversions. The more he came to me, the more I hated her. She was the special one. She was the one he couldn't bring himself to violate." She gave him a wobbly smile and sipped her champagne. "Let's forget him. None of it matters now."

It did. It probably always would.

Ruth had told no one else about the letters and, after a great deal of thought, she'd burned them on the Aga in her kitchen. They'd given an old dog a little extra warmth.

"Mum and I talked about the miniature, too," she said. "After a lot of thought, we've decided to auction it and donate the proceeds to charity. All we have to do now is agree on which charity will benefit."

"Really? That's good."

"Yeah. Mum said I should keep it but I don't want it.

I don't want the money either. I mean, the money would come in very useful, but I want a fresh start. We decided that some good may as well come from it. Hark at me. I'll be turning into Mother Teresa next."

Dylan smiled at the thought. "There's not much chance of that."

"True. So what were the paintings like?" she asked. "Did McIntyre do my sister justice?"

"He did. I was very impressed." He reached for the bottle and refilled their glasses. "Prue was very beautiful in her own way. Yes, he did her justice. I'll take you to see them when the fuss has died down."

"I'd like that. Not," she rushed on, "that I need taking anywhere. I'm not an invalid, you know."

He smiled. "I know."

"It's funny, but I miss Prue. Crazy, isn't it? I didn't see her from one Christmas to the next, and now I miss her."

"That's understandable."

"I only had to look at Prue to know how bad I was being. She was so bloody nice. Really, she never said a bad word about anyone, she'd do anything without a word of complaint—she was unbearably bloody *nice*."

Before he could agree with that, she said, "What do you *really* think will happen? To Tim, I mean."

"I don't know." Chandler was currently on bail and, even after the trial, Dylan suspected he'd be a free man. It was impossible to prove that he'd been involved in any of it. Gut instinct said he had. Evidence was less sure. "They're trying to tempt Eddie with promises of a reduced sentence if he dishes the dirt on Tim. Even if he does, though, they'll still need hard evidence. He'll probably be a free man."

"What about Eddie?"

"Eddie's future features a cramped cell with little or no daylight. He'll be behind bars for years."

Officers were gathering evidence on an almost daily basis to make sure the jury found Bryson guilty of all charges. Forensics officers had found hair and fibres that put Kevin Mills in the car Bryson had hired. CCTV put Bryson at the art gallery on the day Prue was murdered and that car in Dawson's Clough at appropriate times. They could prove he'd been in France when the attempt on McIntyre's life was made. They were working closely with French officers at the moment.

Frank phoned Dylan every couple of days with updates. There was no way Bryson would walk out of this one.

Frank hadn't needed a word with Amesbury because the young constable had gone to Frank to apologise. Whether it had been a genuine apology, or whether finding out that he was in line for promotion had persuaded Amesbury not to make enemies, they didn't know. It didn't matter. All questions about borrowed files had been forgotten and Frank was once again privy to useful information.

"Is that definite?" she asked. "He won't get away with it, will he?"

"Never in a million years. Trust me."

Dylan hoped Bryson never tasted freedom again. Nothing would bring Prue or young Kevin Mills back, and their families would have to learn to live with the loss, but Dylan would feel better knowing that Bryson was paying with his freedom.

"What about you and Tim?" he asked.

"I've instructed my solicitor to start divorce proceedings." She spoke calmly. "I'm leaving here next week—"

"Really?"

"There's no need to sound so surprised. Yes, I'm out of here next Friday. I'm only here now because I'm enjoying being waited on hand and foot. I considered staying with my mother but—" she pulled a face "—I can't stand being in that house."

"That's understandable."

"So my mother and I, get this, are having a fortnight's holiday in Cornwall. I'm going to buy a house down there. Somewhere quiet. By the sea."

"Good grief." He examined the label on the champagne bottle. "Is this stuff going to your head?"

Smiling, she slipped her arm through his and rested her head on his shoulder.

"I need to look at finances," she said, "and God knows what state they'll be in by the time Tim's court case is over, but that's what I plan to do. My mother will give me a loan to buy my place by the sea, if necessary. I may have to pay money to my agent because I've cancelled my contract with her. The work I've been getting lately isn't worth the bother. Besides, I'm sick of modelling. And I'm way too old for it."

"And what do you plan to do in your little house by the sea?"

"I'm not sure. I love fashion and I'd really like to

send my own designs into the world. But that's the future. Short-term, I'm going to cook." Laughing, she lifted her face to look at him. "I adore Italian food so I'm going to learn to cook it. And I'm going to relax for a year or so. Just chill out." She shrugged. "Basically, I'm going to enjoy living on my own. I intend to chill out and get fat."

"Sounds like a plan to me."

"Yeah." She drank her champagne. "Will you come and visit me in my home by the sea?"

"I might."

"Might isn't good enough, Detective. Will you come and visit? Yes or no?"

"It depends on how well you learn to cook Italian food."

She laughed. "The food will be superb."

"In that case, how can I refuse?" He refilled her glass and felt obliged to make another toast. "To your home by the sea, Maddie. May your future be a lot happier than your past…"

* * * * *

Reader Service.com

Manage your account online!

- Review your order history
- Manage your payments
- Update your address

*We've designed
the Harlequin® Reader Service
website just for you.*

Enjoy all the features!

- Reader excerpts from any series
- Respond to mailings and special monthly offers
- Discover new series available to you
- Browse the Bonus Bucks catalog
- Share your feedback

Visit us at:

ReaderService.com

RS13